Phantom in the Pond

Dorothy Bodoin

A Wings ePress, Inc
Cozy Mystery Novel

Wings ePress, Inc.

Edited by: Jeanne Smith
Copy Edited by: Joan Powell
Executive Editor: Jeanne Smith
Cover Artist: Trisha FitzGerald-Jung

All rights reserved

Wings ePress Books
www.wingsepress.com

Published In the United States Of America

Wings ePress Inc.
3000 N. Rock Road
Newton, KS 67114

Dedication

To Mike Nickele, Layla's good friend and mine.

* * *

One

Red candles in ornate brass holders cast a glow on the tablecloths, deepening the forest green and scarlet colors of the plaid. The centerpieces were baskets filled with gilded pinecones and decorations that resembled leaping flames. The effect was festive—Christmas-in-July festive—or would be until one noticed the Gothic-lettered sign: *Welcome to Hell.*

"Oh, my! It's all so beautiful." Lucy Hazen reached out to touch one of the burning pinecones, and the gold Zodiac charms on her bracelet jangled in alarm.

"Careful," Brent Fowler said. "That's real fire."

Quickly she withdrew her hand.

"Not really, Lucy," he added with a devilish wink. "It just looks real."

"Everything is perfect," she murmured.

"Anything for our famous horror writer. I even ordered a thunderstorm for the evening." A roll of thunder underscored his words as rain pounded on the windows.

We had gathered at the Hunt Club Inn to celebrate the premier of the movie based on Lucy's young adult horror novel, *Devilwish.*

Filmed in Foxglove Corners, it featured familiar places and locals in walk-on parts. The event, movie and celebration, was the highlight of my summer, made more special because my husband, Deputy Sheriff Crane Ferguson, was able to accompany me.

I freed my hand from his warm grasp and patted raindrops from my hair. A little rain couldn't spoil our evening. On the contrary, it added to the ambience.

Camille, my neighbor on Jonquil Lane and aunt by marriage, started as thunder crashed over the inn.

"Everybody, let's sit," Brent said. "Lucy at the head of the table. Annica, you're with me."

My sometime partner-in-detection positively glowed to be thus favored. We women had agreed to wear red or black in honor of Lucy's movie. Annica had chosen a shimmery dress of crimson and garnet chandelier earrings to complement her red-gold hair, while I wore my favorite black dress with crystal jewelry.

Brent indicated a space in the middle of the table, in front of the largest basket. "Helena, you're right here."

A stunning beauty with auburn hair, warm brown eyes, and a rare peaches and cream complexion, Helena smiled and lowered herself gracefully into the chair.

Helena Millay was not one of Lucy's intimates, which prompted Brent to make her feel especially welcome. She had joined our group in a move to placate the Fates. I smiled as I recalled Lucy's apprehension when she learned that our party would number thirteen.

"Thirteen is an unlucky number," Lucy had declared. "We can't afford to jinx *Devilwish* now that it's been safely released." She referred to the series of setbacks and tragic happenings that had accompanied the making of the movie.

Brent was unimpressed. "Superstitious claptrap."

"I'm serious, Brent."

Mentally I reviewed the guest list. Relatives, friends, and fellow members of the Lakeville Collie Rescue League. Yes, with Crane and me, we were thirteen.

"It wouldn't hurt to invite a fourteenth guest," I said.

"Okay, but who?"

"There must be someone who'd love a nice prime rib dinner, good wine, and devil's food cake."

Reciting the Inn's renowned menu, I could hardly wait to eat.

"Mmm. Who?" Brent stared into space as if to find the answer there. Finally he said, "I have it! Helena Millay. She boards her horse at my barn. Helena just moved to Foxglove Corners and probably doesn't know many people yet."

"That's perfect," Lucy said. "Please invite her."

That was how Helena, a virtual stranger, came to join our group. Crane pulled out the chair next to her for me, and I slipped into it, wondering how fake fire could look so realistic.

"This is an elegant place," Helena murmured. "Let's see. You're Jennet."

"And this is my husband, Crane."

No need to add his title as he was off duty.

Crane reached over me to shake her hand. "Welcome to Foxglove Corners, Helena."

A somber young waiter moved silently around the table serving garden salads. Another followed his steps, pouring the wine.

"A toast," Brent announced. "To Lucy Hazen, our one and only celebrity."

A faint blush stained Lucy's cheeks. "And to good friends. I couldn't have done it without you."

That was Lucy, retiring and ever-gracious.

I took a sip of wine and turned to Helena. "Have you read *Devilwish*?"

"Not yet, but I loved the movie. That Mr. Horn was so sinister, and those poor kids...They fell so easily into his trap."

"Lucy writes for young readers, but people of any age can enjoy her books," I pointed out.

One subject down. I floundered, wondering what to say next. *How do you like living in the country? Have you ever gone fox hunting?* No, not that. The sport, long established in Foxglove Corners, was too controversial. Brent was a fox hunter. I and most of my friends championed the fox.

Horses? Helena boarded her horse at Brent's stable.

"I take it you like riding," I said. "Sue Appleton has horses."

Sue was seated at the far end of the table with her young summer helpers, Diane and Kristie, and Ronda Leigh, a fellow member of the Lakeville Collie Rescue League of which Sue was president. If Sue were seated closer to us, we could discuss horses.

Helena's face lit up. "I just bought my mare, Bonny, and in a few days, I'm going to have a dog."

"What breed?" I asked.

"A rough collie."

Ah, I thought, thinking of my own seven collies. The magic word.

When collie lovers meet, they form an instant bond. Was Helena buying a puppy? Who was the breeder? What color was the dog? What was his or her name? I didn't know which question to ask first.

"Arden is a retired show dog out of a Wisconsin kennel," Helena said. "She's a tricolor. I almost bought a puppy, then I heard she was available. I had to have her."

"Are you having Arden flown to Michigan?" I asked.

"I'd be afraid to do that. No, I found a pet land transport company on the Net. It's called Sea-to-Sea. It's more expensive, but Arden will be safer."

"You'll have to come visit my collies," I said. "Halley came from a breeder, but the rest are rescues. I have one of each color," I added. "Even a bi-black."

Brent's booming voice drowned out our conversation. "Here come the prime ribs—and the whitefish for you vegetarians. Both of you."

I pushed my salad to the side. I'd only eaten a bit of it, a tomato slice and an olive. Now that the prime rib had arrived, salad was a lost cause.

~ * ~

The rain continued throughout dinner, enhancing the atmosphere with rumbles of thunder and lightning flashes. In keeping with the mood, orange frosting flames decorated the two devil's food sheet cakes with their simple message: *Congratulations, Lucy.*

Annica volunteered to cut the cake, dividing it into several large slices and a few slivers for those who'd eaten their fill of prime rib. As she passed the plates around, Helena asked Lucy a question often posted to writers.

"Where did you get the idea for *Devilwish*, Lucy?"

"I borrowed it. The plight of the individual who makes a bargain with the devil occurs throughout literature."

The Tragical History of Doctor Faustus, I thought. More recently, *The Devil and Daniel Webster*. Stephen Vincent Benet's classic short story was part of the American Literature curriculum at Marston High School. As a teacher in the English department, I had taught it almost every year.

"I just transferred the story to a modern school. The devil appears as Mr. Horn, a charismatic college professor who tempts students by offering them their hearts' desire. Beauty, popularity, a dream career, their true love."

"For a while I was afraid the students would lose their souls," Helena said.

"I write horror, but I also write happy endings."

"How wonderful to have your heart's desire," Annica said.

Crane laid his hand on mine and whispered, "I do."

"Not when it came time to give the devil his due," Lucy pointed out.

"Hell," Brent said. "If you want my opinion—"

Before he could complete his statement, the power went out, leaving only the red candles for illumination.

Two

The noise level rose perceptibly. A modicum of brightness returned as the wait staff scurried to the tables with extra candles. From the main dining room came a faint cry followed by a petulant complaint: "How am I going to see to eat?" A child wailed. Who kept a child up so late?

"Oh, no!" Leonora, my fellow English teacher at Marston High School, turned to her husband, Jake, as if he had all the answers. "What do we do now?"

"We power on," he said.

"Don't worry," I told her. "The Inn has a generator."

Which was more than we did at home. I thought of my seven collies alone in a dark house. They didn't even have moonlight for illumination. We had left lights on for them, anticipating that they'd stay on. As a general rule they weren't afraid in storms, except for the timid blue merle, Sky. She would be in her safe place, under the dining room table, and I imagined one of the other collies would keep her company there. Probably Misty.

"Does this happen often in Foxglove Corners?" Helena asked.

"Fairly often," I said. "We prepare for it with extra flashlights and batteries, blankets in the winter, and we have a wood burning stove."

"I hope we didn't lose power at home," Leonora said.

Jake shrugged. "It could be worse. It's eighty degrees out."

"But we have so much food in the freezer."

"It'll keep. For a while."

Our waiter materialized in the shadows with a coffee pot in each hand. "More coffee while it's hot?"

I held out my cup. The cake had made me thirsty, and in spite of the burning candles, I felt a slight chill. It must be the sound of all the rain pouring down on the earth.

"Did you order the power outage, too, Brent?" Lucy asked.

"Sure did, and timed it for the end of dinner."

"Well, I love it," she said. "I can't think of a better way to wind up our evening."

Neither could I. With dancing shadows and firelight and haunting darkness, to say nothing of the incessant pounding on the windows that held their own in the onslaught, it was a tiny preview of hell.

Sue Appleton stopped to thank Brent for his hospitality. "We'll be on our way," she said. "The girls are spending the night with me. Come over and see my horses, Helena," she added, obviously having talked to Helena previously. "We're the only horse ranch on Squill Lane. Practically the only house."

Helena happily agreed to do so.

Brent disappeared and came back with an armload of black umbrellas. "For those who don't want to get wet," he said.

"Thanks," Sue said. "We'll share it."

I gazed at the emptying tables. The power failure had brought a definite end to the party. People stirred, said their goodbyes, and taking umbrellas, moved toward the exit. Sue, Diane, and Kristie had already left. Before long only Lucy remained at the table, supervising the transfer of leftover cake to boxes.

"I hate to see the evening end," I said.

"We can continue celebrating tomorrow," Brent pointed out. "Dinner at your house. I'll bring the wine."

"Don't forget to bring Lucy," Crane reminded him.

"Lucy—sure. And Annica."

Dinner for three guests. My mind leaped ahead to menu planning. Did I have enough on hand to cook a meal for five or would I have to go to the store?

"See you tomorrow, then, Fowler," Crane said.

He took my hand and ushered me toward the door and the darkness where the candlelight didn't reach. "Be careful, honey," he added, and we went outside, fairly blown to the Jeep by the high wind that had accompanied the storm.

~ * ~

Jonquil Lane was always dark at night, never more so than in a power failure. A tiny light flickered in the window of the yellow Victorian across the lane from our house, indicating that Camille and Gilbert were already home. They'd brought out the candles.

The rain had lessened to a disheartening drizzle, but the ground was saturated. I cringed at the prospect of muddy paws. But the night was warm, and the humidity had returned.

Our green Victorian farmhouse burst into view in the Jeep's headlights, and seven collies filled the night silence with indignant barking.

Why did you leave us alone in a dark house?

Crane parked behind my Ford Focus and, hand in hand, we made our way up the walkway to the side door. No stranger to power failures, we kept flashlights in a kitchen drawer, along with candles and matches. It was too late to light candles, though.

Crane opened the door, and the dogs converged on us with hot breath, soft fur, and plaintive yips. The humans were home. All was well in their world.

Crane lost no time in turning on the flashlights. He set one in the window and slipped another in his belt. Candy nudged his leg and bolted through the door, closely followed by Misty, the white collie. Halley, my first collie, and Gemmy, brushed against me for homecoming pats, while Star and Sky lagged behind. Last came Raven, our rare bi-black collie, who had slowed down somewhat after healing from a broken leg.

"I'll take the dogs out," Crane said. "You get ready for bed."

I would, as soon as I poured fresh water and set out biscuits for the dogs' late night snack. Then I remembered to switch on the kitchen light and a lamp in the living room. Of course no light issued forth, but when the power came back on—if it did during the night—we'd know.

On the other hand, Brent had invited himself to dinner tomorrow, and I could hardly serve cold cuts. Crane could barbecue chickens or...I wondered if my favorite little restaurant, Clovers, had power. If so, I could buy take out dinners. Lucy would likely bring leftover cake for dessert.

You'll think of something.

When you live alone, a power failure is a mere annoyance. However, when you're married to a handsome deputy sheriff, the finest in the land, it adds an extra layer of ambience to romance. With that cheering thought, I carried two of the lantern flashlights upstairs and waited for Crane to come inside with the dogs.

~ * ~

We woke the next morning to the bedside lamps throwing their soft light over our faces. Great! We had power. I could fix Crane a pancake breakfast and cook a proper dinner for tonight's guests.

He bounded out of bed, full of energy as usual, while I wished the night had lasted a little longer. Halley and Misty, who slept in the doorway presumably to stop nighttime intruders in their tracks, came over to my side of the bed for their traditional wake-up petting.

With all the activity around me, I might as well get up.

In the kitchen, I stirred eggs into pancake batter and surveyed the waterlogged vista through the window. The woods across Jonquil Lane had withstood the storm, although fallen branches littered the ground. The yellow Victorian had a fresh-washed gleam, but the flowers in Camille's spectacular gardens struggled to raise their heads.

The earth would soon revive, though, and our summer heat wave showed signs of continuing. It was already hot in the house.

Crane opened the door and our collies bounded into the kitchen. Candy gravitated toward the stove where the pancakes were turning golden brown. Crane sat at the table, the dogs milled around, and I realized I was ravenous.

What a perfect way to start the day! All of us together and the power back on.

~ * ~

That evening Brent took a long sip of his coffee and fell upon his second piece of devil's food cake.

"I have an announcement to make," he said.

A sunbeam landed on his dark red hair. It was the color of a certain kind of maple leaf in autumn, a shade any woman would kill for. His eyes radiated with excitement. Misty sat at his side like a stone statue, her eyes fixed on the cake which, being chocolate, was forbidden to her.

Annica tapped her pink seashell earring, and it made a soft clinking sound. "Don't keep us waiting."

"I didn't want to intrude on Lucy's night, so I thought I'd wait till we were all together. I bought another house. You're going to like it, Jennet. It's one of your favorite things. An old Victorian on an acre of land."

"Is it haunted?" I asked.

"Could be. I don't think so. It's pretty run down. The house has been on the market for years. There was talk of demolishing it to build three new houses on the property, but I couldn't let that happen. They accepted my offer yesterday. I left the developer in the dust."

"I hate developers," I said. "They chew up every spare inch of land."

"And we sure don't need all those fancy big houses they build," Annica added. "Who's going to buy them?"

"Young people with families," Lucy said. "As for myself, I'd rather have the land."

I agreed. Further up Jonquil Lane, an unfinished development of French Chateau style houses had been abandoned when the developer went out of business and left the state. In his wake, the houses slowly deteriorated as nature stepped in to reclaim her own. The place was dark and forbidding—and dangerous. It drew ne'er-do-wells and had set the stage for more than one confrontation with evil.

"Are you going to open another restaurant like the Spirit Lamp Inn?" Lucy asked.

"I sold the inn."

"Will you renovate the house and move into it then?"

"I'm staying in my house till they carry me out," he said. "The new place is going to be for the dogs."

Three

"That requires an explanation," Lucy said.

"Which dogs?" Annica asked. "All of them?"

"Not my own dogs." He ate his last piece of cake and set the dessert plate on the coffee table. Misty eyed the crumbs longingly but didn't move.

Brent had a massive guard dog of indeterminate pedigree, fittingly named Napoleon, along with a collie, Chance, and his rescues.

"I got to thinking," he continued. "Lila and Letty over at the shelter have a dog who's been with them for years. He has a few medical problems, and his age is against him."

"Don't forget our Rescue League's new program," I reminded him.

Matching geriatric collies who have little chance of finding a forever home with senior citizens had been my idea, and so far it had been successful. My Star was one of those hard-to-place collies, traded in by her owners for a new puppy.

Brent nodded. "It isn't enough. I talked it over with Sue last night. There aren't enough senior owners to go around. Not everyone has a fenced-in yard, and most people want a young dog or a puppy."

"Are you talking about a retirement home for collies?" Lucy asked. "If so, I think it's a good idea."

"When the new place is renovated, they can have the run of the house and an acre of land to play in. Or sleep. Whatever they want to do."

"Who'll take care of them?" Annica asked.

"That's the next step. I'm going to hire a caretaker to live in the house. He'll be responsible for the dogs, and who knows? Some of them may find homes of their own."

"It's a generous idea, Fowler," Crane said.

Brent had the funds to make his dream a reality. We could continue our 'Seniors for Seniors' program. We'd just go to Brent's house to find the dogs, and Sue could concentrate on placing younger collies.

"Where is your house located?" Lucy asked.

"In Foxglove Corners on Loosestrife Lane. Do you know the street?"

None of us did.

"There's a weeping willow on the property," Brent said. "It must be a century old. At least."

"I'd love to see the house before you start tearing it apart," I said.

"Me too." Perhaps Annica sensed a waiting mystery. In any event, she didn't like to be left out of what she called my adventures.

"You can do that," Brent said. "I'm having the kitchen remodeled in a week or so. That'll give you time to look around. I already have a waiting list for the dogs," he added.

"I'm so proud of you, Brent," Lucy said. "It's the rare man who uses his wealth to benefit helpless animals."

He bent down to ruffle Misty's fur. She usually sat in his lap when he visited us. This evening, with the proximity of the chocolate cake, he had had kept her on the floor.

"How will we get in?" I asked.

"I had the locks changed." He pulled a key out of his pocket and set it on the coffee table beside the plate.

"Can we go tomorrow?" Annica asked. "I have a day off and don't have a class."

She attended Oakland University in Rochester and worked as a waitress at Clovers to pay for her tuition and books. I often wondered how she had time to share my so-called adventures, but desire finds a way.

"I'm free," I said, "and it should be a nice day."

"It's a date then. What's the address?"

"Hold on." He pulled an index card out of his wallet. "It's the largest and oldest house on Loosestrife Lane. You can't miss it. Hey, Jennet, is there any more cake?"

"A whole half. Anyone else?"

"I never turn down chocolate cake," Crane said.

Annica jumped up. "I'll make more coffee."

In the kitchen, while I cut the rest of the cake into generous slices, Annica said, "Just think, Jennet. We have another empty house to explore. Maybe it's haunted. Brent didn't say it wasn't."

I had to smile at her exuberance. "Don't count on it. Not every old house is haunted."

"There must be a reason it stayed on the market for so long."

"Probably it needs too much work for the average buyer," I said. "Brent can afford to turn it into his dream house. Canine dream house," I amended. "Maybe his new house had a story associated with it. And maybe a ghost.

~ * ~

The next day Annica's fellow waitress, Marcy, called in sick.

"I have to work," she said. "Mary Jeanne doesn't have anyone else."

I assured her we'd go another day, but as I ended the call, I realized there was no reason I couldn't visit Brent's new house on my own. I found Loosestrife Lane on a map of Foxglove Corners. I could easily walk there; it was only a little farther than I usually took the dogs, only in a different direction. I was going to take the collies for a walk anyway.

I studied the map. I'd follow Squill Lane to its end, turn left, then right at a crossroad. I'd pass a bridge, then look for a massive weeping willow tree.

After lunch, I leashed Halley, Sky, and Misty, pocketed Brent's key, and set out.

The sun was warm, but brisk winds cooled the air, and wildflowers gleamed in the light, their many colored petals shining like jewels. The rain had breathed new life into the flora of Foxglove Corners. All but a few puddles had dried.

The dogs were ecstatic with the new route, excited by all the marvelous scents it offered. I came to a bridge spanning a restless creek and in the distance saw the weeping willow Brent had described. It was ancient, full and graceful, trailing long fronds to the ground.

"We're here," I said and walked a little faster. Tall spires bearing dark pink flowers lined the way. The plants were loosestrife, rarely seen as they had fallen out of favor as an invasive species. But they were gorgeous, lending bright color to the vista in its many shades of green.

The house sat far back from Loosestrife Lane, enclosed by a white picket fence. It was a magnificent if threadbare relic of Victorian times with high turrets and generous gingerbread trim in every possible place.

Among its many amenities were two porches. One of them wrapped around the west half of the house, stopping beyond the front door. The other, on the east side, was a small semi-circle held up by three white pillars. It couldn't be accessed as a porch because it lacked a door leading from the house. Like a heavily ornamented crown, a graceful cupola sat on top of it.

The gate was locked, but near the willow, four pickets had fallen back into the yard, leaving a gap wide enough for anyone to walk through. It was as if a vehicle had plowed into the fence. Besides repair, the pickets needed a coat of paint. One more item on Brent's restoration list.

When I reached the willow, I brought the dogs to a halt. Beyond the fence I beheld a massive fishpond encircled by large rocks, some of which were dislodged or missing. Behind it rose a rock garden whose plants were choked with weeds. To one side, a pair of lawn ornaments, pale pink flamingoes, lay on their side, their paint peeling.

Stagnant rainwater and a prodigious amount of algae filled the pond. Twigs and leaves, remnants of past autumns, lay lightly on its surface, and willow strands dripped down into the water. Was that a Hershey wrapper? Yes, doubtless blown from some distant point.

The abandoned pond was the most forlorn sight I'd ever seen, once-elegant, now languishing in an abandoned yard. But how beautiful it would be if it were cleaned and filled with pure Michigan water, with goldfish swimming in its depths. The ornamental flamingoes could be repainted and placed around it to look as if they were drinking, and missing rocks could be replaced. With the weeping willow shading the whole, the pond would become the focal point of the grounds.

Add a few lawn chairs, and you'd have a place to dream away the summer hours.

A memory stirred. We'd had a fishpond in our yard when I was a child, smaller than this one but every bit as wonderful.

Regretfully, I tore myself away from the pond and led the dogs through high grasses toward the house, which was, after all, my main reason for visiting Brent's property. A feeling of sadness went with me.

Four

I inserted the key in the lock, and the door opened onto a stuffy, chilly expanse of bare hardwood floors and walls covered with faded paper. A long hall flowed into a large room, no doubt the living room, judging by the fireplace. Windows coated with seasons of grime offered a distorted view of the grounds.

Misty yanked on her leash, communicating her desire to explore. She fixed her eyes on the staircase that rose upward into darkness.

"Slow down," I told her.

The echo of my words sounded eerie in the silence. Sky whimpered. She was used to furniture and warmth. In other words, the familiar. But Halley took any new experience in her stride. As long as I was at the other end of the leash, she was happy.

The floor plan was simple. A dining room opposite the living room, both the same size. At the back of the house, a kitchen showing its age with fifties' décor and a black phone attached to the wall. Ruffle-edged curtains had faded to a dull yellow. I recalled that a kitchen renovation was at the top of Brent's list.

Nothing of the former inhabitants remained in these rooms. Nothing tangible, that is, but there was something.

Didn't something always stay behind in an empty house? Misty sensed it. I did as well.

Her impatient yip drew me back to the present. She wanted to go back to the stairs to see what surprises the second floor held. Sky sneezed and scratched at the linoleum.

Halley and Sky weren't interested in exploring, but I wasn't about to leave them alone on the first floor, although I'd locked the front door behind us. We'd check out the upstairs then, even if all we saw was more of the same.

I grasped the cold, dusty railing. To my dismay, it wobbled. Darn. Brent should have warned me it was unstable.

This house is dangerous.

From what far, mist-enshrouded place had that thought come?

Keeping my hand well away from the railing, I led the collies upstairs to another hall. All of the doors on this level were open. Room after room swam in sunlight that revealed cobwebs dangling from the ceiling and draped in corners. Floors bare of rugs, faded wallpaper, chairs, and tables—everything that made a house livable had been whisked away.

Except... One room was different. It held a bed, a nightstand, a dresser, and a tall chest in an outmoded Mediterranean style, all crammed into a small space. A gray king-sized sheet covered a twin bed. Dust layered the tops of the furniture. Unable to resist, I opened a dresser drawer. Lined with brittle, yellowing paper, it was bare of possessions.

What had I expected?

I wondered why Brent hadn't mentioned the furnished bedroom. Had he even viewed the entire house? What about the attic? The basement?

Maybe there was more Brent hadn't told me.

Feeling uneasy, even with three large dogs for company, I decided I'd seen enough. The dim rooms and musty air resented our presence. If that were possible.

The dogs were getting restless. Sky pressed close to my body and Misty pulled on her leash again.

"Come, girls," I said and led them down the stairs to the first floor and outside, making certain the door was locked behind us.

It was a pleasure to take deep breaths of fresh air. The earth smelled oddly of freshly mowed grass, although I walked through long blades and weeds heavy with dew. Shades of green assailed my eyes, and pink spires of loosestrife swayed in the wind.

I turned toward the fishpond. Misty gave a whimper and pulled hard on her leash as if she were responding to a strange lure. We had plenty of ponds in the woods of Foxglove Corners, but they were natural, part of the environment. Someone had built this one, poured cement, placed rocks around its circumference, and planted the rock garden.

I hoped Brent wouldn't take the pond apart as he redesigned the grounds. He might fear one of the dogs would drink from it or swallow the goldfish.

No, a feral cat might do that. Or any other predator. This was a complication I hadn't considered.

But please. Let him keep the pond. Forget about the goldfish.

He should have the pond drained. Standing water bred mosquitoes, although I hadn't suffered a single bite in spite of being surrounded by dampness.

Misty came to an abrupt halt at the pond's edge and peered down into the water. I looked down with her, expecting to see our reflections mirrored in its depths.

There was a reflection, but it wasn't Misty's. Another collie met my gaze. This dog had a mahogany sable coat. One ear was tipped, one pricked. It couldn't look less like my white, tricolor headed Misty.

An impossible reflection. I should see Misty and myself and the other collies.

I did; I saw all four of us. Now. But a moment ago, in our place I had seen the stranger dog.

I knelt on the damp grass that grew at the pond's side and ran my fingers through the water. It felt slimy, not at all like the pure cool water I'd envisioned. Disintegrating leaves, broken bits of wood, and the incongruous candy wrapper I longed to remove lay on its surface. If only that wrapper hadn't been lodged in the pond's center.

There was no dog's image.

Once again, what did I expect?

Imitating my action, Misty dipped one white paw into the water and hastily drew it out. She sniffed at the stones and gave a puzzled whine.

Where's the other dog?

I pulled her close to my side. The house might not be haunted, but the pond was.

I didn't doubt what I had seen. True, I had a lively imagination that often ran away with my common sense, but I knew I hadn't conjured a collie's reflection out of stagnant water and nature's debris. Foxglove Corners was known—at least to me—for its psychic activity. In the surface of the abandoned fishpond, I had seen a fleeting, unnatural reflection.

Why not call it by its proper name? Phantom.

~ * ~

I couldn't wait to tell someone about the collie in the pond, but Crane was still patrolling the roads and byroads of Foxglove Corners, and Brent, who had to be informed about the phenomenon, didn't answer his phone. I left him a cryptic message, wanting to wait to give him the news about his house in person.

That done, I drove to Clovers. If Annica hadn't had to work today, she'd have been with me. As it was, she'd have to hear about my experience after the fact.

I opened the door to the faint tingling of green clover chimes and beheld a happy sight: Annica filling the dessert carousel with cherry tarts. "'Made with fresh Michigan cherries," proclaimed a hand-lettered sign on one of the tiers. Her pink dress and garnet earrings complemented the color of the fruit.

"Back so soon?" she asked.

"I went early," I said. "Wait till I tell you what I saw."

Her eyes lit up. "I know. A ghost."

"Not exactly. Close."

"Grab a booth," she said. "I'll be right back and we'll sample the tarts. They're still warm."

Clovers' owner, Mary Jeanne, insisted that her waitresses know what each item on the menu tasted like so they could describe it to their customers. Lucky ladies.

It was too early for the lunch crowd, and all of Annica's tables appeared to be served. She brought two pots of tea and two tarts to my favorite booth that had the best view of the woods across from the restaurant.

"What did I miss?" she asked.

"There's a fishpond on Brent's property. I saw a reflection that couldn't be in its surface."

"I don't understand."

I told her about Misty looking down into the pond and a strange collie looking back at her. "It only lasted a second," I said.

She grinned. "Isn't it funny that most of your ghosts are collies?"

"There was the ghost in the library and the Spirit Lamp Inn," I said. "The ice skater—"

"And dogs, dogs, dogs. I said most, not all. Do you suppose the collie drowned in the pond?"

The idea hadn't occurred to me. Collies in my experience fell into two categories: Those who avoided the water like Sky, and dogs who loved to swim.

"The pond isn't that deep," I said, imagining Misty leaping in and out of it.

"How do you explain the reflection then?"

"I don't know enough about the house yet to form an opinion," I said.

"Speaking of which, what's it like?"

"Run down and badly in need of painting, but it'll be lovely when Brent renovates it. He's already looking for old time pictures of children and dogs. There's one oddity, though. One of the bedrooms has furniture left in it."

"He can keep it for the caretaker."

"Yes, after a thorough cleaning." That would be one item Brent could cross off his list.

"We only have a couple of weeks before the place is overrun with contractors."

Noise, country music on a radio with the volume turned high. The smell of paint. I shuddered at the thought of the upheaval. Any one of those could send a respectable ghost fleeing.

"Let's make the most of them then," she said. "I want to see that marvelous fishpond that doesn't reflect reality."

I wanted to see it again, too. Even more, I wanted to know its secret.

Five

The clover chimes jingled and in walked Brent clad in denim and a forest green shirt, bringing the vitality of the outdoors with him. He spied us and strode toward our booth, booming out a hearty hello. A few diners turned to stare at him.

Instantly Annica brightened. Her cherry tart forgotten, she switched with ease to waitress mode.

"What can I get for you?" she asked.

"Black coffee, a ham sandwich, and whatever you're having." He glanced at her half empty plate. "That looks kind of small."

"We have a whole cherry pie in the kitchen."

"Good. I'll have a piece. Make it a large one."

As she hastened to fill his order, he said, "I couldn't make head or tails out of your message, Jennet."

That, of course, was my intent. My aim was to build suspense and give him my news in person.

"I walked over to your house this morning," I said. "Guess what? It *is* haunted."

"By what?"

I described the face of the collie in the pond. "It came and went in a heartbeat, but I know what I saw."

"Are you sure you didn't see a man-made image? Like a deflated balloon floating on top of the water?"

To be fair, I gave this momentary consideration. But the collie in the pond had been a genuine reflection, not a spent balloon.

"Then where did it go?" I asked.

"Easy. To the bottom of the pond."

"What sank it?"

Annica came back bringing the coffeepot and Brent's special mug with his name engraved on its side.

"When I look in a pond or lake, all I expect to see is water," Brent said. "If I want to see my reflection, I look in a mirror."

"Your pond has unusual properties. Why won't you just believe I saw a ghost?"

He grinned. "I like to play... What's that game? Devil's helper?

"Devil's advocate," Annica said. She poured Brent's coffee and he took a mighty gulp.

"Is anyone making my sandwich?" Brent asked.

"Yes. Mary Jeanne herself." She sat and resumed eating her tart.

"What did *you* see, Annica?"

"Nothing. I couldn't go with Jennet."

"Then you and I will check it out together. Tomorrow?"

"After my Chaucer class," she said.

I intended to return to the pond as well. Brent's reluctance to embrace my evidence caused me to second guess it. Could my mind have created a collie's face out of brown leaves and twigs? I didn't think so. In the meantime, would the ghostly image appear in the isolated garden even if no one was there?

"I'm going to fix those pickets," Brent added. "I can't have kids tramping through the yard. They'll have to stay away when the dogs come. Someone might get hurt, and I'd be liable."

"I didn't see any kids in the neighborhood," I said.

No curious children. No hungry animals. No birds. Nothing.

Only the phantom in the pond.

~ * ~

Later that day with meatloaf dinners from Clovers ready to serve, I took Halley, Gemmy, and Star to visit Sue and her collies at the horse ranch.

Star, the oldest of my pack, seemed to have more stamina these days. With better food, the companionship of her collie sisters, and, most important of all, the knowledge that she was loved and wanted, she'd blossomed into a confident and happy dog.

Moving with the wind, we crunched down the gravel on the lane, all of us invigorated by the fresh smell in the air. We passed the unfinished development with its deteriorating structures steeped in silence and shadow. And onto Squill Lane and the ranch.

Sue and her collies were outside enjoying the sunshine. The dogs played with branches and their Frisbees while Sue tried to take their pictures. Meanwhile, her horses grazed, ignoring the canine antics. The free-running collies converged on my trio and renewed their acquaintance while we settled ourselves on the porch in a patch of sunshine.

"Our website needs updating," Sue said. "We have three new collies. One's a senior."

"Where are they?" I asked.

"Emma and Ronda are fostering them. Two are litter sisters. We're hoping to place them in the same home." Without a proper segue, she added, "Helena Millay is getting pretty worried these days."

"Helena from Lucy's party?"

"The same. She was expecting her new collie, Arden, from Wisconsin, but the dog didn't arrive when they said she would."

"That's a long way to come," I said.

"Arden should have been in Foxglove Corners on Tuesday morning. This is Thursday, and Helena hasn't even had a message."

"What's the holdup?" I asked.

"Helena doesn't know. That's the trouble. She can't contact the transport people."

I could see why she was growing anxious. Anything could have happened between Wisconsin and Michigan. But why wouldn't the transport company keep her informed?

"Didn't she find the company online?"

"Yes, but now the web page has been taken down," Sue said.

"She must have their information. Can't she call them?"

"She tried. The number isn't in service."

"Uh oh."

"Exactly."

"Did she pay them?" I asked.

"She sent them a check for four hundred dollars, but that isn't the point. Where's Arden?"

"Do you remember the name of the company?"

"It's Sea-to-Sea. Helena said they have several glowing reviews. Had, I should say. The website is gone."

"Let's backtrack," I said. "I assume Helena called Arden's kennel?"

"She did. The owner verified that Sea-to-Sea picked up the dog. The men were friendly. Arden went with them happily enough, and they drove away."

Sue let her voice trail off.

I added, "Into the vast unknown."

"Very poetic, Jennet. They took Helena's money, then Arden disappeared in transit. The company looked so reliable on paper. I should say, on the screen."

I shuddered at the possible scenarios that formed in my mind. Helena was the victim of a scam, one that preyed on a person's desire for a dog and on a helpless collie.

"What is Helena going to do?" I asked.

"Right now, she isn't sure. She's waiting, still hoping there's some explanation."

Misty shoved her nose into my lap. I stroked her head, thinking. Crane and I had a stable home. I couldn't imagine a circumstance in which we'd have to move one of our dogs to another place. I'd heard horror stories about dogs traveling by plane but never one in which a transporter failed to deliver a dog to its destination. The only way to ensure a pet's safety is to enlist the aid of a trusted friend.

I could imagine one of those glowing Internet reviews:

John and Jane will provide your dog with all the comforts of home. A heated van, fresh bedding, the dog's own dish and food, along with his favorite toys. We'll treat him as if he were our own pet.

Honeyed words to beguile the unsuspecting, to convince them that their best friend would be safe in their care. The owner would never see the dog again.

"How can I get in touch with Helena?" I asked.

"I have her number. Why?"

"Someone has to help her. Arden is a collie in distress. We're the Collie Rescue League."

"Maybe there's just been a delay," Sue said. "Something the transport people couldn't help. Like an accident or car trouble."

"Then why wouldn't they find a way to notify Helena?"

"You're right."

I knew I shouldn't rush my judgment, but every instinct told me that Sea-to-Sea was a scam. That without our intervention, Helena would lose Arden before she ever saw her. Arden might suffer an unspeakable fate.

"What can we do?" Sue asked.

"First, find out everything there is to know about Sea-to-Sea."

"And if they're not a legitimate service?"

"Then we hold them accountable," I said. "And hope it isn't too late for Arden."

Six

On Friday Sue and I visited Helena in Lakeville. She lived on a quiet, shaded street that dead ended in a rustic park. Her small blue-sided house and fenced yard would be ideal for a retired show dog.

"All her home needs is a collie," Sue said.

"Agreed. We have to find the collie."

Helena opened the door, and an aroma of coffee drifted out into the humid air. She was waiting for us, her peaches-and-cream complexion pale and drawn, her auburn hair held back with a black band.

"It's good of you to concern yourselves with my Arden," she said. "I don't know where to turn."

"We'll try to help," I assured her.

We will help.

A graceful arch divided the tiny hall from a large living room. It was practically two rooms in one but minimally furnished with a sofa, two chairs, all three in dark green velvet, and a pair of matching end tables. And an empty crate lined with colorful throws. Its door was open.

Helena took a silver framed picture of a stunning tricolor collie from an end table. Posed against high drifts of snow, Arden was magnificent, black and tan and white, with a heavy coat and sweet expression.

"This is Arden," she said. "The breeder sent it to me. She said Arden was a loving collie, very intelligent, and so far as she knew, in good health."

"Why did she give her up?" Sue asked.

"The usual reason. To make room for the younger ones. But she wanted the right home for Arden. I assured her I could provide that."

I set the picture back on the table. "I have two tricolors, Halley and Candy."

If I'd lost them... Well, I didn't want to think about that. I *had* lost Halley once, and indirectly that was how Candy had come into my life, brought to me by a young man who wanted the reward for finding Halley.

"Jennet and I have taken on tough situations before," Sue said. "We've always won. We will this time."

"I hope so."

We accepted the coffee she offered and sat quietly for a moment. When the silence grew noticeable, Helena said, "I never dreamed something like this would happen. I read all the company's reviews. It seemed like the perfect solution."

Sue nodded. "Too good to be true."

"I should know by now not to believe everything I read online. I'm beginning to think Sea-to-Sea doesn't exist."

"Oh, it exists all right," I said. "As a scam."

"I've spent hours on the computer trying to find them."

That was what I'd planned to do. I'd still do it, hoping to discover a small detail Helena might have missed. Then I'd think of another approach. More than one. No doubt Sea-to-Sea prided itself on being elusive, but they must have left their footprints somewhere.

"Arden is still young, and she's a beauty," Helena said. "She hasn't been spayed. I'm afraid she'll end up in a puppy mill having litter after litter."

That was a possibility, along with plenty of ghastly alternatives.

"We'll have to work fast," I said. "She's been missing... What? Three days now?"

"Since Tuesday."

Time enough for her to have been transported to the West Coast or the Gulf Coast. Or anywhere.

"What can we do?" Helena asked.

I wished I had an easy answer. "Let's brainstorm. What can you tell me about Sea-to- Sea?"

"Just what I remember from the website. They were two young men, former vet techs who became friends and went into business together. Their names were Roger and Jack, probably aliases. They promised to make transporting a dog to a new home a happy experience for both pet and owner."

"Did they say where Sea-to-Sea was based?"

She frowned. "No, I don't think so."

"How did you pay them?"

"They wanted a check made out to Cash. I gave them one. The man, Roger, gave me a receipt. His signature is practically illegible."

Darn. That would have tipped me off. If only the charge were on Helena's credit card.

"I feel like such a fool," she said. "I was just so anxious to have Arden and I didn't want to have her shipped."

Helena had made a mistake. She was too trusting, but she wasn't the only one to be taken in by clever scammers.

Sue touched her arm lightly. "If we have anything to say about it, you'll have Arden. Give us some time to come up with...er...something."

I glanced at Sue, hoping to communicate that time was a commodity we couldn't afford.

"We'll try our best," I said.

~ * ~

After an intensive Google search, I found several land transport services. One of them, the Flying Carpet, was located in Lansing, the state's capitol. It had a modest number of five star reviews, and the site included a form a prospective customer could fill out to estimate the cost. I submitted a request for the price of driving a dog from Wisconsin to Michigan and was instructed to wait for an e-mail.

This wasn't going to be easy.

The Sea-to-Sea van had left Wisconsin with Arden aboard, destination unknown. How could we ever hope to find them? Were we already too late to free Arden from the trap Helena had unknowingly placed her in?

No, I told myself. *Don't give up before you start.*

I shut the computer down and rested my eyes. A dark road took shape in my mind. An unfamiliar landscape. A van. On both sides, a picture of a dog lying beside a fireplace, a cozy depiction designed to inspire confidence.

When a situation looked hopeless, I turned to Lucy Hazen who was sometimes able to see events before they happened. Not always, and they weren't always faithfully represented. But possibly she would know where that van was headed. The name of a state, even a city, would help. If Arden had already arrived at her destination, Lucy might know that, too.

Sue and I needed help. It only made sense to add Lucy to our team.

~ * ~

A small forest of conifers hid Lucy's home, whimsically named Dark Gables, from Spruce Road. I drove down a heavily shaded driveway, considering the drawbacks of the isolated location. But Lucy lived with a dog, her collie, Sky, and felt that most people wouldn't know a house stood beyond the fir trees.

From inside, Lucy's collie barked a welcome. Like many dogs, she was somehow able to match the sound of the car to the driver. Lucy came to the door, dressed in her signature black, brightened with several gold chains.

"What a lovely surprise," she said as Sky dashed out to the porch and danced around my legs.

I hadn't thought to call, but Lucy welcomed company. It must be lonely creating worlds in which zombies and werewolves roamed free, but that was the world in which Lucy chose to dwell.

"Come in," she said. "We'll have tea."

"I was hoping you'd say that."

I was happy to escape the sultry July heat. Inside the house, ceiling fans kept the air in motion, and curtains held the bright sunlight at bay, except in the sunroom. Here in the light, Lucy wrote her books and read tea leaves for her friends. With luck she would see that long dark road or maybe the Sea-to-Sea van in my cup.

Sky trotted along ahead of us, knowing that tea meant cookie.

"I have another collie in distress," I said. "Do you remember Helena Millay?"

"Our fourteenth guest? I do. She's a lovely woman."

"She hired a land transport service to bring her new collie, Arden, to Foxglove Corners, but it looks as if she's been scammed."

I gave her the details, admitting that I didn't know how to begin tracing them.

"That's terrible," she said. "But I don't know how I can help."

"I was hoping you'd have one of your premonitions."

As soon as I uttered the words, I realized how naïve they sounded. Lucy's premonitions didn't appear on demand and usually concerned her friends.

She said, "Perhaps if I could talk to Helena... If I saw Arden's picture..."

"We can certainly visit her. Sue and I offered our help, but we may be asking the impossible of ourselves."

Lucy busied herself with tea making and searching for a tin of shortbread cookies. "I can imagine how Helena must feel. She intended to give Arden a good home and instead may have delivered her into the clutches of Evil."

"We can't let Evil win."

"Let's see if the leaves can direct us," Lucy said.

At one time I had looked on tea leaf reading as an amusing parlor game. Make a wish and see if it comes true. Learn about the presence of an enemy before she appears. Forewarned is forearmed. At some point, although I had begun to believe, although Lucy still insisted that I take her predictions with the proverbial grain of salt.

If Sue and I were going to return Arden to Helena, we needed every weapon in the arsenal.

I drank my tea, nibbled on shortbread cookies, and prepared my cup for a reading. And waited while Lucy studied the formations created by the leaves.

At last Lucy said, "I see something, but I don't think it has anything to do with a stolen collie. It looks like a pool or pond, and a heavy cloud hangs low over it."

Seven

Lucy's white teacups had no extraneous blossoms or scrolls to interfere with the patterns formed by the leaves. She pointed to two minuscule circular shapes near the top of the cup.

"This is the pond," she said, "And here's the cloud, directly above it."

In my opinion, the formations didn't resemble a pond and a cloud, but then I wasn't a gifted reader of tea leaves with one foot in the world beyond.

"Brent has a fishpond on his new property," I said. "I don't know about low-hanging clouds, but I saw something odd in it or rather on it. The pond may be haunted."

Lucy listened to my tale of the unknown collie who had displaced Misty's reflection in the pond. "Fascinating. I know you're going to solve the mystery. Now that I *can* help you with."

"But Helena needs us to find Arden."

"That's a whole other problem, Jennet. You and Sue can pursue it. This one requires my expertise. Has anyone else seen the reflection?" she asked.

"Brent and Annica were going to check it out. I don't think they saw anything, or I'd have heard about it."

"I must see the pond," she said. "Can we go together?"

"Sure. I have Brent's key if we want to take our investigation inside, but I already did that. The house is empty except for some furniture in one of the rooms."

"Whatever is going on with the pond may have its origin in the house," Lucy pointed out.

"I *did* sense an unwelcoming atmosphere," I said, knowing Lucy would understand what I meant.

"Does Brent know the house's history?" she asked.

"Only that it's been on the market for years. No one mows the grass or cuts the weeds regularly. It's a virtual wilderness."

"That," Lucy said, "is a breeding ground for supernatural manifestations."

"And mosquitoes."

I thought about the reflection of the unknown collie in the pond, wondering again if it appeared when no one was there to see it. An idea slipped into my mind.

"Maybe it needs Misty's presence to appear."

As she looked confused, I elaborated. "I saw the phantom collie when Misty was looking into the water. It reacted to one of its kind."

"I have to see this pond," Lucy repeated. "My writer's imagination is awake and clamoring for more."

"We should go soon before the renovators take over."

Lucy nodded. "We can't let anything stand in the way of Brent's home for geriatric collies. If you think it'll make a difference, let's take Misty with us."

I called Misty my psychic collie. She had shared some of my out-of-this-world experiences and on one occasion had seen a spirit that more or less hid itself from me. Ironically, it was another ghost dog.

"I agree, and we'll take lots of pictures. We may have a photogenic ghost."

"Even if we don't, Brent should have some before and after pictures to hang on the wall," I said.

~ * ~

It rained the next day, a steady downpour that turned Jonquil Lane into a quagmire. The dogs adjusted to the inclement weather, either sleeping or sitting at the window, staring glumly outside.

Meanwhile, in another part of Foxglove Corners, fresh rainwater was falling on the pond, bringing its level higher. The leaves and twigs would move in the watery onslaught and form themselves into a canine face for no one to see.

Or the phantom collie would emerge from its depths, gaze at the willow strands that dipped down to the surface—and try to escape.

Mmm. Why *couldn't* he escape? All he had to do was climb out of the pond. Unless some unknown force kept him there, a prisoner.

Not caring for the scenarios my mind was dredging up, I sent my thoughts in another direction—to the house where the manifestation might have its beginning. My initial exploration had been cursory, affected by the musty atmosphere.

Brent hadn't been particularly curious about the furniture left behind by some past tenant. I didn't suppose it had any connection to the mystery in the pond. But one never knows.

I looked forward to going through the empty rooms again, this time with Lucy. I might well have overlooked something crucial to our understanding of the pond mystery. Misty, Lucy, and I—I fancied us an unbeatable team.

But we needed the rain to stop, and that wouldn't happen today.

In mid-afternoon, noticing the skies had grown perceptibly darker, I turned on the television to see a 'Severe Weather' alert in effect. At least no tornado warnings or watches threatened my home. I was about to turn it off when a few sentences caught my attention.

There's a new breed of dognapper in town. Watch Kate in Your Corner tonight at five to learn about this new scam and how to avoid it.

The picture of a van with a map of the United States on its side filled the screen. The name on the van was Sea-to-Sea.

I promptly called Helena to tell her to watch the five o'clock news.

"So someone else fell for their lies," she said.

"Maybe more people. Kate Brennan will keep us updated. Keep hoping, Helena."

I then alerted Sue to the program, and at five o'clock, I turned on the TV again and watched a half hour of local news before *Kate in Your Corner* came on.

I'd watched Kate Brennan on previous newscasts, following her as she targeted unscrupulous vendors. The bridal shop that suddenly closed its doors. leaving brides without their wedding gowns. A jeweler who accepted rings for cleaning and substituted paste stones for diamonds. A contractor who'd botched a remodeling job and left town.

Kate was the kind of reporter you'd want as your advocate when your case seemed hopeless. Friendly and compassionate with a sharp no-nonsense edge, she inspired confidence as she worked hard to secure justice for everybody.

Tonight dressed in a long beige raincoat, she stood in a robust wind that blew her long blonde hair into her face. She was interviewing a couple in front of their house. They both spoke with soft southern accents, but the wife, Marguerite Tyrill, was doing most of the talking while her husband stood at her side glowering into the camera.

"We wanted to make our move to Michigan as smooth as possible for the dogs," Marguerite was saying. "Especially for Lady. She gets carsick."

Marguerite dabbed at her eyes with a tissue and leaned against the side of the blue Camry in the driveway.

"So we set off without them and never dreamed they wouldn't end up in our new home."

Kate gave her a sympathetic smile. "How did you learn about Sea-to-Sea?"

"Lyle here did a Google search. We were impressed by all the good reviews they had, so we hired them."

Lyle said, "They took our check and picked up our dogs and that's the last we saw of them."

"This happened two weeks ago," Marguerite said. "Can you help us? It isn't just about the money."

Lyle shoved his hands in his pocket. His glower grew more menacing, and it didn't take much imagination to know that he carried a gun. "We want our dogs back. And when I track those guys down they'll wish they hadn't messed with me."

Kate made an attempt to defuse his rage, but Marguerite interrupted her. "It's like they drove right off the map," she said.

Off the face of the planet, she must mean. Immediately I thought of Brandemere Road. It had a chilling reputation for leading unwary passersby to a place where they dropped off the earth and vanished forever. It was a vastly exaggerated but often repeated tale. No one disputed the fact that several unexplained disappearances had occurred on that road.

Be that as it may, that couldn't have happened to the Sea-to-Sea van, but it might as well have.

Kate explained that she had made several inquiries but hadn't been successful in finding the people behind the company—yet. Undaunted, she promised to return next week with an update and ended her segment with pictures of two of the lost dogs, a sheltie and a sleek black lab.

"Remember," she said in parting, "Kate is in your corner. She'll get results."

Eight

A warm wind blew over the pond, stirring the water into motion. Lucy and I stood at its edge waiting to see a collie face materialize on the surface. Misty had dipped one white paw in the stagnant water and promptly withdrew it, as she had before. Now she lay at our feet, apparently having lost interest in whatever phenomenon called the pond home.

So much for my psychic collie.

Lucy slapped at her wrist. "Darned mosquito."

They were out in full force. Fortunately my white blouse had long sleeves, but I wished I had worn boots. My shoes were already damp.

"It's a mess, but it'll be charming when Brent has it cleaned," Lucy said.

"I wonder if the phantom dog will show itself then." I gazed at the algae and the leaves and other debris that swam in the pond. The candy wrapper was still there. "Or maybe I imagined it," I said.

"Is that what you really think?"

"Well, no."

"Good, we still have a mystery."

I glanced at the castaway lawn ornaments lying on their sides in the rock garden. "Pink flamingoes are the ultimate cliché, but they're right for the pond."

"They were made to last," Lucy said. "With a little paint they'll be as good as new."

Not bright pink paint but a subdued mixture of pale pink and peach with black brushstrokes to indicate wings. Custom flamingoes.

"Can you sense the melancholy that hangs over the pond?" I asked.

"I can. It's like a dark low-hanging cloud. Something happened here once. It wasn't good."

"It may have involved the collie," I said.

"Probably."

Misty flopped over on her side and closed her eyes. I tugged gently on her leash. "Time to move," I said.

As we waded through grasses and weeds still wet with dew, I could only hope the pond's story didn't involve a collie who had died in the swirling water.

As we approached the house, Misty tugged on the leash, coming to a stop in front of the semi-circular porch with the cupola on top. She fixed her gaze on the ground, currently overgrown with clover and dandelions.

"This way, Misty," I said, tugging back.

On the wraparound porch, I turned Brent's key in the lock and held the door for Lucy to enter the house. Freed from her leash, Misty pranced inside ahead of her. I wondered if something called out to her with a voice only she could hear.

"It's musty in here," Lucy said as I closed the door. "It needs airing and cleaning."

The echo bounced back to us. *Airing... Cleaning...* Misty sniffed the bare floor and sneezed.

"It needs a lot of work," I said. "But when it's ready, Brent's geriatric collies will have a good home of their own and all this land to explore."

"Whoever Brent hires as a caretaker will have a dream job."

I led the way to the kitchen, suddenly aware of a faint pleasant aroma. "Renovating the kitchen is at the top of Brent's list."

A shiny new coffeemaker sat on the counter, along with a tin of Maxwell House and an unopened package of maple frosted doughnuts. Misty placed her paws on the counter and sniffed the doughnuts. I pushed them out of her reach.

"Brent must have brought them," I said. "He must have been here recently."

But Lucy didn't appear to be listening to me; nor was she looking at the counter. She stood at the sink, staring through a window with a hairline crack zigzagging from top to bottom.

"Do you see something?" I asked.

"Nothing untoward, but the window will have to be replaced," she said.

"Brent plans to have new windows installed throughout the house."

"That won't change anything," she said. "Someone experienced panic in this house, and its imprint never left."

Ah! She could sense something, first at the pond, now inside the house. I was right to bring her.

"Something happened, and the very walls absorbed the emotion," she said. "I can almost feel it, a mindless debilitating terror."

"What happened?"

"I don't know." She touched the counter and closed her eyes. "But the fear is so intense, it's almost my own."

I let my eyes sweep the room, every corner, trying to see beyond dated avocado appliances. Had it ever been a cozy place with a vase of flowers on a round table and perhaps a crystal stand holding a cake? If the kitchen had a story to tell, it was keeping its secrets from me and even from Lucy, who felt the panic but didn't know what had caused it.

Of course Brent's newly-purchased house had been a home at one time, perhaps to more than one family over the years. A line from a poem I'd memorized in school came to me. *All houses wherein men have lived and died are haunted houses.*

I was eager to move on, anxious to know what Lucy would sense in the other rooms.

"Where's that pestiferous pup?" I asked.

She'd left the kitchen while Lucy and I had been distracted.

"She's conducting her own exploration," Lucy said. "Don't worry. She can't get out."

"And she can't get into anything," I added. "Let's go upstairs. Don't touch the banister. It's unstable."

We paused on a small landing to admire the one bright touch in the abandoned house, a small pane of stained glass with sunlight streaming through its rainbow colors.

"Most geriatric dogs won't be able to go up and down stairs," Lucy pointed out.

"That's okay. The second floor will be strictly for the caretaker. Misty!"

As I reached the top of the staircase, she came bounding toward me. A cobweb dangled from her collar. Ugh. I brushed it off with my hand. "Where were you, girl?"

I turned to Lucy, but she hadn't followed me, having come to a standstill on the landing. She was looking through the stained glass window, an unmoving figure in black that contrasted sharply with the rainbow tints.

"Lucy? What is it?"

"The fear is on the landing, too," she said. "It's not quite so strong, but strong enough. I can feel what she felt. Her emotions stayed behind."

"She?"

"It was a terrified woman. She felt trapped on this landing."

"But you were aware of her fear in the kitchen. Do you think someone was murdered in this house?"

"There's no way of knowing without researching the house's past."

"Misty doesn't seemed concerned," I said. Then I looked for her. She'd wandered away again, moving as quietly as a spirit.

She was restless, I realized. Searching. Perhaps sensing a little of what Lucy did. Looking for something.

"Let's see if there's anything to be found in the rooms," I said. "We'll start with the furnished bedroom."

Misty had found it already and leaped up onto the mattress where she had an excellent view of green maple leaves on a tree that grew too close to the house.

"Get down from there," I told her.

She leaped onto the floor with a little growly protest.

"Brent will probably throw out the mattress," Lucy said. "Look. One of the spokes broke through. The bed's headboard is gorgeous though."

I had to agree. All scrolls on dark wood with an intricate pattern on the posts, the bed was an elegant example of Mediterranean style. So what if it had long gone out of style? All it needed was dusting and polishing and a colorful comforter with fluffy pillows.

"This was her room," Lucy said. "I feel her fear here, but it's faint. It's like she was just becoming aware that something was wrong."

I crossed to the window, but all I could see were leaves shaking fitfully in the wind. "Brent should have that tree cut down."

"It looks like he bought a haunted house," Lucy said. "We'll have to tell him."

I could feel something myself. Not quite fear, but... What? Anxiety? That wasn't it either. Somehow I'd have to learn the history of the house. Otherwise, I'd continue to wonder about it.

Nine

The next day at Clovers, Annica joined me for a lime cooler. With a touch of cooling mint and the air conditioning, one could almost forget the temperature in Foxglove Corners had stalled at ninety degrees.

"I didn't see a collie in the pond," Annica said. "But all that algae—yuk. That's super scary. Isn't algae alive?"

"It's an organism. So, yes, in a way. But it isn't an animal."

She glanced at her cooler. "Now that I'm thinking about algae, mint doesn't look so appealing."

"Mint is a plant," I said. "An herb. Think peppermint patties and mint chocolate chip ice cream."

"Crème de Menthe," she said, getting into the spirit of the discussion.

"Think about how beautiful the pond will be when it's cleaned and filled with pure fresh water," I said.

"Brent is letting me paint the flamingoes. One will have its head toward the water like it's drinking. The other will be looking at the house." Then in a dizzying subject change, she added, "Does Lucy really think the house is haunted?"

"She said a woman who once lived there had been so terrified by something that her emotions seeped into the very walls."

"Terrified by what, I wonder?" Annica asked.

"Lucy couldn't tell."

"Let's see if we can figure it out. Maybe she was trapped in an abusive relationship. Or she was in the house alone when someone broke in. Or she had an attack or seizure and couldn't get to a phone."

"Any or all of those...possibly," I said. "We're just guessing."

"Then there's no actual ghost," she said.

"There's the collie in the pond."

"That might have been an illusion. You said it was there and gone." She snapped her fingers. "Like that."

"I didn't imagine it." I was certain about that now.

"What we're left with is a low-level haunting," Annica said. "What was a dog doing in a pond, anyway?"

"Trying to cool off? Dogs love water. Our collies can't get enough of running through the sprinkler."

I suspected it wasn't that simple, though. The explanation for the phenomenon eluded me, but I suspected it must have been a serious one, perhaps sinister. A sinister reflection. A ghost.

"On a day like today, I'd like to run through a sprinkler myself," Annica said, taking a sip of her drink. "This is *so* good."

I followed her example, trying to isolate the ingredients in the lime cooler which Annica refused to divulge, even to me. I tasted lime, of course, and vanilla and mint and... Vernors ginger ale? I had a Drinkmaster at home. One day soon I resolved to duplicate this satisfying summer drink.

"Just don't think about algae anymore," I said.

"Or grasshoppers," she added.

"Ugh."

Annica drank more of the cooler, then more. Soon it was gone. My advice had worked.

"If the house is haunted, I want to help you catch the ghost," Annica said. "Even if it's just the dog in a pond."

"I have a feeling the two may be connected," I said. "But I have to know a lot more about the situation. What frightened the woman? Did the dog belong to her? They may have been separated by decades. Or not. We're starting with very little. Lucy sensing a woman's fear and my brief glimpse of a dog in the water. And a line of poetry," I added. *"All houses wherein men have lived and died are haunted houses."*

"Longfellow, right?"

I nodded.

"It's enough to make a decent mystery," Annica said.

~ * ~

That evening Brent showed up at our doorstep with a Farmer's Market bouquet for the house and liver tarts from Pluto's Gourmet Pet shop for the dogs. Seven collies who wanted us to think they were starved gathered around him, smelling the treats which I thought had a disgusting aroma. But then I wasn't a dog.

"I've come to ask you for a favor, Jennet," Brent said as he handed the flowers to me and the Pluto's shopping bag to Crane. He flopped into everybody's favorite chair, the rose velvet rocker. "It's about the house."

I waited for him to invite Misty onto his lap where she knew she was always welcome. Sky lay at his feet, content with the second best place in the house. When everyone was comfortable, he said, "I think you'll want to do this."

"Don't keep us in suspense. Do what?"

"A little research on the house. Lucy tells me there's a bad vibe associated with it. I want everything perfect before I move my geriatric collies in. Chances are they've had enough trauma in their lives."

"Did Lucy say 'bad vibe'?" I asked.

"Not exactly. That's my take on the situation."

"Why can't you do your own research, Fowler?" Crane asked.

"That's not my thing. Jennet is the ghost expert."

"Thank you. I think."

"You're the intellectual one. I'm a man of action."

I couldn't argue with that.

"When I heard about the developers' plan to demolish the house, I rushed in to outbid them. I didn't ask questions. After you told me about the pond and I talked to Lucy, I had a little meeting with the realtor. He admitted there'd been rumors about a haunting way back in the seventies."

"Wasn't he supposed to tell you about it before you signed any papers?" Crane asked.

"According to law, yes, but he was desperate to unload the property, and I wanted it. So the subject didn't come up."

"That's why the house stayed on the market so long," I said.

"That and its condition, which got worse every year. Will you do it, Jennet? Go on a ghost hunt?

"With pleasure." I glanced at Crane.

"It seems safe enough," he said. "Unlike that search for the land transport company."

I hadn't forgotten about my prior commitment to Helena Millay, but my efforts in that direction were stalled like the temperature in this current hot spell.

"In the meantime, I'm moving the pond to the top of the list," Brent said. "I hired a gardener to replant the rock garden and take care of the grounds. The place looks like a jungle now."

"Are you going to stock the pond with gold fish?" I asked.

"Eventually."

"That'll be a great finishing touch."

But restoring the pond was mere window dressing. Readying the house for occupancy had to come first.

"Have you found a caretaker for the dogs yet?" Crane asked.

"I'm interviewing a couple tomorrow. They sound good on paper. I have three senior collies who need a home. One was surrendered to a high kill shelter."

I cringed at the idea, at the circumstances that had brought the collie to a place of death at what should have been a happy time in his life. Well, he was going to be one of the lucky ones.

"Where is he now?" I asked.

"At my barn. That's going to be my holding place."

On the surface, everything was falling into place. Of course, all the restoration in the world wouldn't banish the remnants of a past trauma so strong it had imprinted itself on the structure's walls.

If only I could find out what had happened to the house on Loosestrife Lane.

Don't forget the pond. Something had occurred there, too.

"Now for the important stuff," Brent said. "What are we having for dinner?"

~ * ~

These days I always watched the five o'clock newscast, not wanting to miss *Kate in Your Corner* and her promised update on Sea-to-Sea. She was also investigating other matters. Like a horror story of a pet parlor that somehow lost three dogs and a family dealing with an unfinished second story and a vanished contractor.

"I'm going to turn the TV on for just a while," I said, as we sat in the living room over banana cream pie and coffee.

"Don't mind me," Brent said. "It's time for *Kate in Your Corner*. I follow her, too."

Today Kate was on the trail of Sea-to-Sea. They had contracted with a Maple Creek man, Harold Camden, to deliver a pair of Labrador retriever puppies to his farm. Horace's story was similar to Helena's: A hefty amount paid by check, two dogs transported to an unknown destination."

"That's close by," Crane said.

"It's the third case in this part of Michigan that we know of," I added. "We should get together with that couple from Tennessee and compare notes. Maybe Kate missed something."

"She's pretty thorough," Brent pointed out. "But she doesn't always get her man. Or woman."

I turned back to the television. Kate considered the possibility that Sea-to-Sea was operating under another name. I gleaned an important piece of information from her report. All failed transports had taken place in the same week, none recently. Or perhaps there were victims out there who didn't realize they weren't alone. In which case would others hear of Kate's broadcast and come forward with their stories?

There was strength in numbers. A meeting was a good idea if all concerned parties would agree to it.

Ten

That night I dreamed about the pond. Not the one on Brent's property but the half-remembered pond of my childhood home. We had a pair of flamingoes, too, graceful birds painted light pink. One appeared to drink from the pond; the other seemed to be watching our house.

What had become of them? I couldn't remember—if I'd ever known.

In the dream I was small again, perhaps eight or nine, and fascinated by this wondrous corner of the yard. Misty, who wouldn't be born for several years, slipped by me, a silent white shape, scrambled over the rocks, and sank in the water.

I tried to call her back but couldn't make a sound, which happens so often in dreams.

I was going to lose her. But no...Moments later she emerged from the water, her coat dripping with algae. Her snow white fur had turned a sickening shade of green. Dog-like, she began to shake, and immediately the befouled water soaked my dress through. And I was cold. So cold.

Algae, I thought on waking. *Nasty stuff.*

Fully awake, I oriented myself.

I was in our bedroom, safe under the covers. Light was cautiously breaking through the dark of night. Crane lay beside me, a solid, comforting presence. Misty slept at the side of the bed, my side. I leaned over to stroke her head. She didn't stir, and I closed my eyes, letting the odd dream drift away.

For a moment before sleep claimed me completely, I heard a sound of water.

~ * ~

Sue and I made a plan. She would contact Harold Camden, explain our interest in Sea-to-Sea Transport, and ask him to come to a meeting at the horse farm while I notified the Tennessee couple, Lyle and Marguerite, of Helena's dilemma and our determination to find the stolen dogs.

Lyle, the gun carrier, answered the phone. I listened to a ten-minute rant directed toward the fraudulent transport company before I was able to deliver my message. He agreed to attend our meeting and once again threatened violence to the men who had taken his money and kept his dogs.

Kate's segment didn't air on the news that evening. I was disappointed but knew that investigations take time. She might not have any leads yet. Wouldn't it be satisfying if Sue and I tracked down Sea-to-Sea before Kate did?

But it wasn't a race. Money aside, five dogs were at risk, two of them puppies. I could only hope we would find them in time.

The meeting was set for the coming Friday. As the next day was free and Annica didn't have to work, we agreed to pay another visit to Brent's property. After a light lunch at Clovers, we set out for Loosestrife Lane, both of us hoping to feel what Lucy had felt or to see a collie reflected in the pond.

To that end I took Misty. As I attached her leash to her collar, fragments of last night's dream came back to me. What did it mean? If a dream can have a significant meaning, that is. Surely I wasn't going to lose my dog in the murky water.

Don't worry. Just don't let her run free.

I didn't intend to do that anyway.

Luckily the house was within walking distance—well, a long walk—and a steady breeze cooled the hot air. Summer had a firm grip on Foxglove Corners, and I realized I'd rather be on my way to investigate a haunted house than on any exotic vacation. In any event, with our seven collies, vacations weren't on our agenda.

"I'm going to make curtains for the kitchen," Annica announced as the massive weeping willow came into view. "What do you think of blue gingham? Or should they be sheer?"

"I love gingham," I said. "But since when do you sew?"

"I don't," she admitted. "My mother is going to make them for me, but Brent doesn't have to know that."

"He wouldn't care," I said. "In my opinion, Brent is sufficiently impressed with you. You don't have to pretend to be what you aren't."

"I'll help her, so it'll be sort of the truth." We came to a brief standstill as Misty sniffed at a purple weed. "Do you really think so?" she added.

"That Brent is impressed with you? It's obvious."

"I think so, too."

Ah! To be in love and not quite sure if your feelings are returned. I'd been in Annica's place once. It had been an exhilarating time but a stressful one.

"I wonder why Brent hasn't fixed the fence yet," Annica said as we went through the opening left by the fallen pickets.

"He didn't drain the pond either."

The state of the water repelled me. Once again a memory of my dream returned. While Annica strolled over to the flamingoes, I held tightly to Misty's leash and stared down at the mess of water, yard debris, and algae.

And the face of a dark sable collie appeared on the surface where Misty's reflection should be. Light wreathed his body, blocking the scummy water in that one section of the pond only. One ear was nicely tipped, the other was pricked.

Misty lunged forward and placed both paws in the water, giving a pathetic little whimper.

I pulled back on the leash. "Annica! Come here."

But she was too slow. In the blink of an eye, the apparition changed. Misty's face took its place, along with my own reflection holding on to her leash, both of us wearing puzzled expressions.

"Did you see the phantom dog?" Annica asked.

"Yes, but only for a moment."

She trailed her hand in the murky water. "There's nothing here now. Where did it go?"

"Where all ghosts go, I guess."

"Wouldn't you know it? I was right here." She pulled a tissue out of her pocket and dried her hands. "The next ghost is mine."

Misty hovered over the pond like a lawn statue, undoubtedly wondering, as we did, where the phantom dog was now.

"I don't think it'll reappear today," I said. "Shall we see if we can find one in the house?"

Annica nodded. "Maybe it's inside. Or at the bottom of the pond."

Neither theory was likely. The dog could be buried nearby, however.

I glanced at the house. In that moment, I didn't see how Brent could ever transform it into a happy home for geriatric collies, no matter how much fresh paint covered the walls or how many pairs of curtains graced new windows. It looked gloomy and forbidding, steeped in a melancholy that was almost palpable. It reminded me of the kind of house you'd find on the cover of a traditional Gothic novel from which the heroine, clad in a long white gown, flees in terror.

But this was real life, not fiction, and Annica and I were going toward the house, not running away from it. Curiosity can't be denied. But I remembered that it killed the cat.

~ * ~

The key stuck. I tried to turn it, but it didn't move. It was as if it had encountered a tiny barrier within the mechanism.

I pulled it out and tried again—and again.

Meanwhile, Misty was watching some invisible activity at the base of the cupola porch. Perhaps a dandelion moving in the breeze.

Annica said, "What's that you used to say? The house doesn't want us here?"

Trust Annica to remember everything I said if it related to a ghostly endeavor.

"There! I have it!"

"That was strange," she said. "You expect things to be off kilter in an old house, but Brent had the locks changed."

I shrugged. "I must have had the key in the wrong way."

We were inside, breathing stale air. I tried to open one of the front windows but they didn't budge, obviously having been painted over too many times. I reminded myself that Brent would have new windows installed.

Annica sneezed. "Darned dust motes."

I had let go of Misty's leash, but she was dragging it behind her and would be easy to catch if she elected to go on an adventure.

"This is the most unfriendly house I've ever been in," Annica said.

"You'll feel different when it's furnished."

"Where did Lucy sense the fear?" she asked.

"In the kitchen and on the landing."

The aroma of coffee drifted out of the kitchen, blended with a faint scent of cinnamon. Misty was already there, barking at something. I followed the sound and saw what had excited her. Someone had opened the package of doughnuts and eaten half of them, scattering crumbs on the counter.

"Brent must have been here," Annica said.

"Brent or someone."

Brent wasn't one to leave a mess for somebody else to clean, especially when that somebody else didn't exist yet. Which led to a troubling thought. The house issued a silent invitation to a vagrant. But if I had trouble gaining entrance with a key, how was a home invasion possible? Just in case, we'd better make sure no windows had been broken.

Annica ran her hand over the walls. "Lucy says the terror was absorbed into the walls? I don't feel anything. They're just walls. Cold and dusty."

"We don't have Lucy's talents," I pointed out.

"I wish I knew what happened."

"I'm going to the library tomorrow and check out Miss Eidt's vertical file," I said. "The *Banner* used to run true ghost stories every Halloween. Some had local settings. Maybe I can learn something about this house."

"I hope so, but like I said before, this is a low-level haunting. A face in the pool, a feeling of terror. All I feel is desolation, but when we have canisters of dog food on the counter and soup simmering on the stove..."

"Soup?"

"Made with marrow bones. For the dogs," she added.

I frowned, becoming aware of a far-away scratching sound, the kind my collies make as they rake their nails over a rug in hope of turning it into a nest.

There shouldn't be any sound at all in the house. Unless Misty...

"Did you hear that?" I asked.

"Hear what?"

"That scratching."

"Yikes. Rats?"

"Don't jump to conclusions. Do you hear anything at all?"

"Not even Misty. Where did she go?"

I had my answer. The haunting was playing for me alone.

Eleven

How could Annica *not* hear the scratching sound? It might have been in the next room or upstairs—or in another dimension, as we were in a haunted house.

From the second floor, Misty gave a high-pitched collie yelp. *Come see what I found!*

"Upstairs," I said and hurried to the staircase, not waiting to see if Annica was following me.

Misty's yelp turned into a fury of frustrated barking. She met me at the top of the stairs, tail sweeping back and forth, eyes bright with some secret discovery.

The scratching had ceased. Had it been Misty after all?

She ran to the furnished room and stopped at the doorway, looking over her shoulder as if to make certain I'd deciphered her message. Which I hadn't.

Annica caught up to me. "What's all the commotion about?"

"Misty knows," I said. "She sensed something."

"Well, Misty. What's wrong, pup?"

Annica's question elicited another yelp as Misty padded into the room. I didn't know what I expected to find, but Annica, Misty, and I were the only ones inside. The scratching began again, but out in the hall or in another room. If it had more than one source, that wasn't good.

"Do you think you heard a rat?" Annica asked.

"I hope not. No, I think it's our ghost trying to cross over onto our plane."

"What?"

"The ghost dog, not the frightened woman. The phantom from the pond."

"I told you so," Annica said. "The collie moved to the house. But where did he go?"

I watched Misty leap up onto the mattress as if were her property. Instead of lying down, she stood a bit unsteadily, sniffing at it and running her nails along the sagging top.

"That isn't the sound I heard," I said.

"Well, no, you heard a ghost sound." Annica strolled over to the dresser and opened drawers, one by one. "Nothing." She turned to the nightstand. "This is empty, too. The ghost wasn't considerate enough to leave us any clues."

I opened the closet door. All that remained inside, besides about a dozen hangers, all pushed together, was a shelf lined with brittle old paper. Whoever left the furniture in the house had moved everything out first. Every little trace of her existence. Yes, her.

I imagined the frightened woman had slept in this room. Again, one of the house's minor mysteries tugged at me. Why was this bedroom suite left behind when the other rooms had been stripped of their furnishings? If no one wanted it, it could have been sold or donated to a charity.

"I'm not exactly sensing fear or evil," Annica said, "but this bedroom gives me the creeps. Let's move on."

"Yes, there's nothing here."

I called Misty, who took her time about jumping off the mattress. As I reached for her leash, something dropped down from my shoulder and fell on the floor to lie glistening on the bare hardwood.

Dropped down from where? And when had I acquired it?

"What's that?" Annica asked.

I picked it up. It was a tiny gold sticker, the kind once used to attach photographs to album pages. It would have been one of four. They been called—what? Reinforcements? Where was the picture?

"Where did that come from?" Annica asked.

"Your guess is as good as mine. It may have fallen from the shelf when I was looking in the closet." I slipped it into my pocket. "This may be the only thing we find today."

Out in the hall, the sound of scratching insinuated itself into the heavy stillness again. It seemed to originate downstairs. Or maybe in the attic. I couldn't tell. Misty tilted her head and growled. She, too, was confused.

"Do you hear it now?" I asked.

"Hear what? Misty growling?"

"That scratching noise."

"Now you're reminding me of that Poe story where they buried a woman alive and she scratched her way out of her coffin."

Madeline in *The Fall of the House of Usher*. Good grief. I wished Annica hadn't remembered that story. Not here. Not now. Well, it was better than imagining rats.

"To answer your question, I don't hear anything," she said. "I wish I did. Let's check out the other rooms."

By then the noise had died away. Silence wrapped its arms tightly around me. I breathed deeply and tried to form my flyaway feelings into coherent thoughts. The air in the room was toxic, giving rise to unhealthy fancies. Like a person being walled in alive.

That couldn't happen in this day and age.

No doubt about it, Brent had purchased a strange house, but negative feelings aside, it was an evocative place, one with an irresistible pull.

All the other rooms on that floor proved to be vast empty spaces, coated in the ever-present dust and festooned with cobwebs. The windows were intact and impossible to move as were the ones on the ground floor. No one could have broken into the house through a window.

It appeared that the little gold reinforcement was going to be our only find of the day. For all the good it would do.

"Let's finish our tour," Annica said, apparently unaffected by the house's miasma.

~ * ~

"What on earth?"

I stared at the kitchen counter, not ready to believe what I was seeing. Only two doughnuts remained in the package, whereas there had been four when we'd left the kitchen.

"It looks like we have a hungry ghost," Annica said. "Or a hungry collie."

Misty placed her paws on the counter, nudged the box, and licked her chops.

"Not Misty," I said. "She left the kitchen before we did and was with us every minute."

"Who then?"

Who indeed?

I shrugged.

"Oh, well, since everybody's doing it..." Annica broke a doughnut in two and ate it. "It's fresh," she added. "Is that a clue?"

"It didn't come from the Hometown Bakery. I don't recognize the brand."

"I know," she said. "Brent came by when we were upstairs. He didn't know we were here. He ate a couple of doughnuts and left."

I shook my head. "Misty would have let us know."

"Then we're back to our ghost," she said. "Either the phantom in the pond or the frightened woman. Do you want the last doughnut?"

"You have it."

Quickly she scooped it up. "We'll give Brent something to wonder about. Who ate his doughnuts?"

Noticing Misty's hopeful stare, Annica broke off a small piece for her. "Your psychic collie isn't very helpful today."

"I wouldn't say that. She reacted to the scratching sound."

"By barking and growling? What does that tell us?"

"That we're not alone in the house," I said.

"I never thought we were."

Ghostly noises forgotten, Misty yanked the empty package down to the floor and began to lick the crumbs left inside. Whatever powers she possessed, when food was concerned, she was like any other dog.

~ * ~

Outside the house, the air had a lightly spiced floral scent. Carnations, I thought, mixed with the smell of freshly mowed grass, although no one had come near the lawn with a mower and the only flowers I saw were the pink loosestrife. They were beautiful but not fragrant.

We made our way to the pond and the wide gap where the pickets had broken away. I tapped the 'camera' icon on my phone. "Before we leave, I want to take some pictures of the pond."

"Why? It's seen better days."

She gazed into its depths, at the crumpled leaf bits and twig pieces and the incongruous candy wrapper. "If I look long enough, I may see the dog," she said.

Misty must have had the same idea. She stepped over the rock border and lowered her head to the surface.

To drink? Quickly I tugged her back to my side. Some dogs lack even a shred of common sense. But she must be thirsty. I knew I was.

Annica couldn't seem to tear her eyes away from the water.

"Do you see anything?" I asked.

"Just an unsightly mess." She paused, finding her phone and taking a picture of her own. "I can see how the wind could rearrange the debris into a picture that resembled a dog's face."

"That isn't what happened," I said and took another picture, coming as close to the edge of the pond as I dared.

For just a moment, a wave of vertigo distorted my vision. Was it possible for a person, a child, perhaps, to fall into the pond and drown? Or to be blown off his feet by a high wind?

Unlikely. The pond water wasn't that deep. Anyone with legs and arms could easily climb out of it.

So forget that grim theory.

Unless the person hit his head and lost consciousness.

"I'm going to make a copy of these for Brent's before and after file," I said, not adding what I was thinking.

Maybe my clever little phone had captured the face of the phantom collie.

But when I clicked on 'Photo,' all I saw was an expanse of befouled water.

Twelve

Six of the noisiest children in creation were playing on slides in the rustic park across from the Foxglove Corners Public Library. Their happy squeals and screeches competed with the barking of the two small brown dogs that circled the swings. Oh, to have such energy in this beastly heat.

I walked up to the porch of the library, tossing a greeting to Blackberry, Miss Eidt's cat who lay on a wicker chair regarding me with cold jewel-bright eyes and no welcome whatsoever in her aspect.

The old white Victorian had once been the Eidt family home. Years ago, before I came to Foxglove Corners, Miss Elizabeth Eidt had donated it to the town to use as a library. She had also donated many of her own books and stayed on as the town's only librarian, living in a compact and picturesque ranch house not far from the Corners.

Miss Eidt was a bona fide institution in our town, a kind and generous person I counted among my close friends. Even on hot, humid summer days, she presented a crisp, professional appearance to her patrons, wearing stylish pastel suits and a pearl necklace or sometimes a colorful silk scarf.

As I set a box of pastries from the Hometown Bakery on her desk, she looked up from the book she was reading with a bright, albeit slightly distracted, smile.

"I have assorted Danish," I said. "A couple of them are your favorite, apricot. I hope you're hungry."

"As it happens, I skipped breakfast. So yes, I'm ravenous. What brings you to the library on this scorching day?"

"I'd like to look through your Supernatural file," I said.

One of the charms of our hometown library was the smooth blend of old time features and modern conveniences like computers and WiFi. I often wondered if we had the only vertical file left in the state.

"This can only mean you have a new mystery," Miss Eidt said.

"I do. It's a haunted house, courtesy of Brent Fowler."

"How exciting! Tell me about it."

I described the house on Loosestrife Lane and its peculiarities, then told her about the fishpond.

As I showed her the pictures I'd taken, she murmured, "How lovely. That's a magnificent willow."

I wished I'd been able to capture the phantom collie with my camera.

"The pond is part of the haunting. I saw a collie's face reflected in the water when Misty was looking in the pond." As she looked puzzled, I added, "It was a sable and white collie, not Misty's reflection."

"Only that?"

I guess I hadn't adequately conveyed the mystifying feeling I associated with seeing the phantom in the pond.

She scrolled through the camera roll again. "Is the collie still there?"

"I only saw it for a few seconds when it vanished."

Mmm. A swim-by ghost dog. How odd." She handed my phone back to me. "Is Brent moving into the new place?"

"No, he intends to open it up to geriatric collies who have little chance of finding forever homes. He's looking for a caretaker or maybe two."

"Imagine thinking of that," she said. "Brent is one man in a billion."

"You won't get any argument from me."

Miss Eidt placed a bookmark in her book and rose to open the door to her homey office. "I'll put the kettle on. You know your way around the vertical file, and you might want to check the Supernatural section. We have a new book titled *Haunted Northland*. It has a lot of material on Michigan ghosts and even a chapter on Foxglove Corners."

There could be a whole book on our ghosts. I often thought that Foxglove Corners was a hotbed of psychic activity. In truth, it was.

She brewed tea, opened the bakery box, and left me alone to conduct my research. I found what I was looking for immediately, a thick manila folder titled 'Haunted Places in Foxglove Corners,' and spilled the contents on the table.

I separated the *Banner's* Halloween features from the other material, mostly articles about inexplicable events and troubled spirits. Before long, I was reading stories that caught my interest even though they weren't remotely connected to haunted houses. Like an illustrated account of the *Eloise* insane asylum by a ghost hunter who had toured the facility before it was redeveloped. How I would have loved to have been one of that company.

Two major stories were missing from the files, but only I or perhaps Brent or Annica could remedy that. First were the oddities of Huron Court, the time twisting road. I could attest to the fact that a traveler, whether on foot or behind the wheel of a car, could find himself transported without warning to another season in another time.

Then, there was the wildflower garden that Brent and Annica had planted on the ground where a magnificent pink Victorian had once stood. Also on Huron Court. Violet-like flowers that nobody had planted had sprung up from the soil, along with blossoming plants that grew taller and healthier than their relatives and seemed to have a life of their own, trapping people who stepped inside their territory with tenacious vines.

These true stories were missing because only a few people were aware of them. By mutual agreement, we rarely discussed Huron Court or the time we'd fallen victim to its spell.

"How are you doing, Jennet? Are you ready for more tea?"

My heart skipped a beat as Miss Eidt opened the door. I'd been so lost in my research that I was unaware of other people in the library. I glanced at my cup—half full and certainly cooling.

"And you didn't eat a Danish. How unlike you."

I smiled, knowing she hadn't intended to comment adversely on my passion for all things sweet.

"I'd better check out the new book," I said. "Later, when I find it, you and Debbie can join me."

Debbie was Miss Eidt's young assistant who aspired to be a librarian when she graduated from the university.

"Debbie's on a camping trip with her family," Miss Eidt said.

"It'll be just us two then," I said.

And a dozen Danish.

"Later, then," Miss Eidt said and stepped back into the library proper, leaving me to replace the material I'd scattered on the table.

~ * ~

The library was one of the quietest places in Foxglove Corners. People moved soundlessly up and down aisles like ghosts. They sat at long tables reading or lounging in comfortable chairs with books or magazines. An occasional whisper or footfall broke the silence, but nothing else dared defy Miss Eidt's unwritten rules of library conduct.

It was amusing to see how she controlled her teenaged visitors during the school year. She should have been a teacher.

I strolled past the Gothic Nook set aside for Gothic fiction, old and new. Miss Eidt had worked hard to find atmospheric furniture for this part of the library: Tiffany style lamps, antique tables, and even a silver tea service that served as a decoration only. A reader could sink into one of the velvet chairs and travel back in time with a thrilling tale of damsels in distress and tall, dark, handsome heroes.

I rarely left the library without at least one Gothic novel. Today, however, I was on the trail of another book.

Haunted Northland appeared to live up to Miss Eidt's enthusiastic endorsement. It was a thick, handsome volume with photographs and artistic renderings of the hauntings described therein. At least a quarter of the book dealt with Michigan hauntings. I noted that I would be the first to borrow the book.

A swishing and an inconsiderate tapping of heels alerted me to the presence of someone else in the section. A woman in a long black vintage skirt with a cream colored blouse rounded the aisle. Her single ornament was a curious necklace that seemed to be made of black lace and silver.

Edwina Endicott, self-proclaimed ghost hunter who was probably the most annoying woman in Foxglove Corners. Was it possible that she wouldn't recognize me?"

"Jennet Greenway!" she exclaimed in a loud voice that Miss Eidt would decry. "I was just thinking about you."

Oh? I doubted that.

"It's Jennet *Ferguson*," I reminded her.

"Oh yes. You took that dashing deputy sheriff out of circulation."

"I guess I did."

And remember that, I thought.

"I knew I'd find you back here with the ghost books."

We had met before in front of this same shelf. Edwina and I shared an eerie connection, both having seen the ghost of a girl, Violet Randall, strolling down Huron Court with her dog.

"What did you find?" she asked, reaching for *Haunted Northland.* "A new edition?"

I held on to the book. Knowing Edwina, I suspected she might try to take it from me. "Miss Eidt told me about it," I said.

"You're checking it out, I guess?"

"Yes."

"Well, I want to read it when you're finished. What are you looking for? A ghost or a haunted house?"

I sighed. It made no sense to allow this woman and her aggravating nature and loud voice to cut me off from any information she might have. After all, it seemed that she spent her life chasing ghosts. Or at least reading about them.

"It's a house," I said, but I didn't mention the pond. I wasn't sure why.

"Where is it?" she asked.

"Here in Foxglove Corners on Loosestrife Lane. I understand the place has been vacant for years. My friend plans to renovate it."

"Wow!" she said. "Your friend must have money. Loosestrife House is the biggest wreck in town."

Thirteen

"You're aware of it then?" I asked.

"Oh, my, yes. It's fascinated me since I was a little girl. I used to walk over to the house and dream I lived there. I'd pretend the flamingoes could talk and fairies danced around that old weeping willow tree."

"You must have been very young," I said.

"Around seven or eight."

And a solitary child, but I didn't say that. "Was the house vacant at the time?"

"I'm not sure," she said. "Nobody ever chased me away. But I remember there were goldfish in the pond. Who but the homeowners would supply a pond with fish?"

"You called the house a wreck," I reminded her.

"Well, it needs painting. Who knows what the house is like on the inside?"

"Shhhh!" An older woman with a cloud of pure white curls and sunglasses pushed up into her hair appeared in the aisle, glowering at us.

"We can hear you all the way over there." She gestured vaguely at one of the shelves. "This is a library, I'll have you know. Some of us are trying to read."

"Sorry," I murmured.

Edwina said, "You look like my first grade teacher, Miss Blanche. Did you teach at Foxglove Corners Elementary?"

The woman ignored Edwina's question and, with an indignant sniff, stalked away.

Edwina pulled her black lace necklace away from her throat. She frowned; it might have been choking her or felt rough against her skin.

I lowered my voice. A little. "Did you ever hear any rumors about the house? That it was haunted?"

"Not exactly, but there was a mystery associated with it."

"Could it have been a murder?" I asked.

"More of a disappearance. A woman went missing. As I recall, they never found her body, so she could have met with foul play."

"Do you remember her name?

"Heavens, no. It's not like I ever knew her."

"Was she the owner?"

"I suppose she must have been or she lived there."

I wished Edwina's memory were sharper, but she'd been a child when fantasizing about talking flamingoes and fairies. Maybe the disappearance had happened during that time. Although Miss Eidt had a folder for Local Disappearances, without a name I would be floundering. At any rate, I'd already stayed at the library longer than planned. I had dogs to take care of and dinner to cook.

"Will your friend post 'No Trespassing' signs on the grounds?" Edwina asked.

"I think he will, and he plans to fix the fence. Anyone can just walk right in now."

A home invader could also jump over the fence at any time, if he were young and agile.

"Before he does that, I think I'll pay a visit to the house for old times' sake," Edwina said. "I despise change. Don't you?"

"This will be a good one," I assured her.

I could have told her that soon several elegant collies would be running on the grounds of Loosestrife House, but for some reason I didn't. Eventually she would find out the house's new purpose. Which reminded me. Before Brent brought in his carpenters and caretaker, I had to rid the house of its negative energy and the fear that had been embedded in the walls.

I thanked Edwina for the information and promised to return *Haunted Northland* as soon as possible. Once again I walked passed the Gothic Nook, promising myself to come back to browse and continue my research soon. After all, I had all summer.

"Shall we have our tea now?" Miss Eidt asked as I checked out my book.

"I should be on my way. Maybe you can share the pastries with your Summer Reading Club. Kids are always hungry."

She nodded. "For ice cream and candy. Danish are too sophisticated for them, but they won't go uneaten, I promise."

"I'm afraid Edwina and I annoyed one of your readers."

"Mrs. Frost. She told me. Don't worry about it. That was her complaint of the day."

I wasn't worried, but I didn't like to antagonize people. More to the point, I hoped the Frost woman hadn't been eavesdropping on our conversation. My interest in Loosestrife House was my own business.

~ * ~

Heat slammed into me as I closed the library door, leaving the deliciously cool air inside. One short walk to the parking lot, and I would have access to air conditioning again.

The noisy children and their dogs had left the park, and a mesmerizing haze settled over the Corners. The Ice Cream Parlor looked as if it were closed. Nothing moved, and the silence was absolute. Even the dogs in the animal shelter were quiet.

As I drove away from the library, a shrill ping drew my attention, but I elected to wait to see who was sending me a message. Crane's views on distracted driving were well known and unshakable.

It was just as well I waited until I was home and parked in my own driveway to open the cryptic message from Brent: *Donut stuff tonite.* He hated texting and used as few words as possible and bizarre spelling. What on earth did this one mean?

Could he have eaten the doughnuts and managed to do so without alerting Misty to his presence? Or... I couldn't think of an alternative that didn't have its roots in the Twilight Zone.

Wait and see.

In the house I gave the collies fresh water and biscuits but couldn't interest any of them in a walk. Well, it was too hot. Too hot to create a dinner. Too hot to bake. In the end I decided on steaks to grill—Crane could do it—and set out to put together a magnificent salad. We'd have ice cream cake roll for dessert.

~ * ~

Brent was adamant. "I bought the doughnuts for you and Annica. I wasn't at the house yesterday or the day before."

"Then who ate them?" Crane asked.

"Misty. Who else?"

"I don't know when she could have eaten them," I said. "She was with us when they disappeared. I mean when they were eaten."

"Are you sure she wasn't out of sight for even a minute?" Brent asked. "That's all it would have taken." He turned Misty's head and stared into her eyes. "Did you eat the missing doughnuts, girl?"

She wagged her tail, not being one to incriminate herself.

"That's the best explanation," Crane said.

"The easy one," I countered. "But now that I think of it, Misty was out of our sight and for longer than a few minutes. We were upstairs. She was trying out the bed in the furnished room and we were wondering about the source of the scratching sound."

"About that scratching sound." Brent frowned. "I was hoping you'd solve the existing mysteries, not come up with new ones."

I was about to throw yet another one his way.

"I ran into Edwina Endicott at the library today," I said. "She considers herself an expert in the supernatural. She told me about a mystery connected to the house. A woman disappeared."

My statement set off a barrage of questions.

"Who disappeared?" Brent wanted to know. "How long ago did this happen?"

"Did they ever find her?" Crane asked.

"Why didn't the realtor tell me about that?" Brent added.

"That's all Edwina knew."

"It isn't enough," Brent said. "Not even you can solve a mystery with so little information."

I looked at him, then turned to Brent. "Would you care to make a small wager?" I asked.

Crane laughed. "Not when I see that look in your eyes."

"What look?"

"Confidence," he said. "You love a challenge."

"I don't deny it."

Challenge was apparently the new watchword. Every time I turned around, I seemed to run into another one. Waiting for my attention was the situation with Sea-to-Sea Transport and the stolen dogs.

"But I may not wrap the mystery at Loosestrife House up before your deadline," I said. "Oh, yes, your new house has a name."

Fourteen

I stirred uneasily in my chair in Sue Appleton's family room, wishing I hadn't come to this evening's get-together. Could I suddenly remember a burgeoning emergency at home?

Probably not and still hold on to my credibility and Sue's goodwill.

The meeting was different from our typical Rescue League gathering. The trappings were similar: Coffee, tea, and cookies, with Sue's collies on their best behavior. But the ambience was wrong. The collective angst of the guests was practically another presence in the room. It left no room for congeniality and barely tolerated civility.

Harold Camden, a burly man with a reddish beard, wore a shirt emblazoned with an ominous message: *Guns Forever*. A thin veneer of gentility—easy to see through—didn't mask the anger in his dark eyes.

He addressed Lyle and Marguerite. "I saw you guys on TV. Same thing happened to me. I was supposed to have a pair of labs. Why aren't we going after those grifters?"

"Because we don't know where they are," Sue pointed out.

She looked uncomfortable, squeezing her mug of tea as if she thought she could break it, and that would be a good thing. I was reasonably certain Harold was carrying a gun. Who would bring a weapon to a private home for a meeting intended to benefit everyone present? An easy question to answer. Harold and Lyle, the man from Tennessee. I wasn't sure about Lyle's wife, Marguerite. In place of a purse she carried a tote embroidered with kittens and daisies and large enough for a half dozen guns.

"They may be operating under another name," I said.

Harold snapped his cookie in half, then fed pieces to Scarlet without asking Sue's permission. "Then Sea-to-Sea Transport doesn't exist? I thought that *Kate in Your Corner* woman was going to help us," he added.

"I'm sure she's doing all she can," Helena said.

"Well, I'm not." Harold reached for another cookie. "Got any beer, Suze?"

Sue frowned. "Sorry. Just coffee, tea, and cookies—or water. And it's Sue."

"Guess I'll make do with coffee."

He rose and filled an empty mug to the brim. A bit of dark liquid splashed on Sue's paper table runner. He ignored it.

What a clumsy lout!

"Kate isn't doing enough," Lyle said.

"Does everyone have enough to eat and drink? Just let me know." Sue sent a beseeching glance at me. As if I could defuse the rapidly deteriorating situation.

I tried. "I made a list of other transport services. Two of them appear to be legitimate. Three haven't responded yet. Two others are suspicious. As you may know, the Sea-to-Sea website has been taken down." I read the names aloud. "As I see it, we have five possibilities to investigate."

"Who are they?" Lyle demanded.

Quickly I read the names I'd jotted down earlier. "I suggest we get in touch with each of them. Say we have a dog to transport from Point A to Point B."

As Harold looked puzzled, I clarified. "Each one of us should contact each service."

"Then what?" Helena asked.

"We create a fictitious dog we need to transport. No dogs will be harmed in making this plan."

"Rover," Harold announced with a straight face. "I like it.

Polite laughter greeted his comment. Good. A touch of levity might alter the tone of the meeting. Sue sent me a grateful look.

"Rover," I said. "Okay. He's a three-year-old show collie being shipped to a new kennel in...let's see. Kentucky. He's been known to start fights with other dogs. He has to be handled with care."

"Will we all have the same dog?" Helena asked.

"You all can make up your own dogs," I said. "It's not like you're going to have to produce them."

"I repeat. Then what?" Helena asked.

"I say, Sue," Harold said. "Got any more of these oatmeal cookies?"

She sprang up, obviously glad to have a tiny respite, leaving me to address Helena's concerns.

"We bombard them with questions. How long have they been in business? Can they give us the names of satisfied customers? Has anyone ever lodged a complaint against them? What provisions will be made for the dogs' comfort on the ride? Most of all, you need a believable reason for shipping your collie to Point B. For example, the kennel in Kentucky wants to invest in a new stud dog."

"Won't work," Lyle snapped.

I could picture him answering the door with a shotgun in his hand or threatening a transporter with violence.

I dabbed at my throat with a tissue. Unfortunately, Sue's air conditioning had malfunctioned, but she had all the windows open and the fans stirring hot air around. Still it was warm and close in the family room. Heat and discomfort were guaranteed to raise tempers to a boiling point.

"Why won't it work?" I asked.

"Like they're gonna tell you who they cheated," Lyle said.

Helena spoke up. "At this point, wouldn't we need to have an actual dog? The dog we plan to transport?"

"An actual dog. Sure. We can come up with one."

"But don't let them take her," Marguerite said.

"Of course not."

Superimposed over the image of a gun-toting Lyle I saw our good friend, Lieutenant Mac Dalby of the Foxglove Corners Police Department. He'd arrest the bad guys and carry them off to jail. The stolen dogs would be restored to their owners.

Dream on.

"Why don't we let Kate do her job?" asked Helena.

"Bad idea," Lyle said. "At the rate she's going, we'll never get our dogs back."

Sue came back in, escorted by Bluebell and Icy. She carried a tray with another dozen oatmeal cookies. She hovered over Harold. For a moment I thought she was going to drop them in his lap.

"Bad idea," she echoed.

Choosing to interpret her comment as a criticism of my 'catch the villain' trap, I said, "Can you think of a better one?"

"Not at the moment," Sue said. "I'll get in touch with Kate Brennan and see if she's made any progress. In the meantime I'll create my fake dog. It'll be a collie, of course.

"Where are you sending her?" I asked.

"To my cousin up north in Harrisville. I don't drive on freeways. That's why I need a transport service."

"How do you get around?" Harold wanted to know.

"On country roads," she said.

"All across the state? That's crazy."

She glared at him.

Helena sighed. "I was beginning to think I'll never see my collie, Arden, again, but this meeting, all of us in it together, gives me hope. There's strength in numbers."

I was glad she felt that way. For myself, I couldn't imagine a less convivial group of people. Unity was a foreign concept to them. Most dog lovers will go to any length when their pets are threatened. I understood. I felt that way myself. But Helena had gotten the saying wrong. There's strength in unity.

The Sea-to-Sea Transport case required a more subtle approach, and first, we had to find them.

Not knowing how to proceed yet, I set about to create my fictitious dog while Lyle and Harold argued about what breed of dog was best for pheasant hunting.

~ * ~

Harold was the first to leave, soon followed by Lyle and Marguerite. Helena and I offered to stay and help Sue with the clean-up which included vacuuming cookie crumbs the dogs had missed.

"That didn't go well," Sue murmured. "I don't know what I expected. Your plan might work, Jennet, if everybody does what you suggest."

We were to meet again in a week. It would be interesting to see if everyone had contacted the transport services.

"Your plan is too sophisticated for the likes of Harold Camden," Helena said. "I was thinking. He'd be attractive without that chip on his shoulder."

"Do you think so?" Sue took the vacuum from me and expertly wound up the cord. "When he called me Suze, I took an instant dislike to him."

"Well, he's a fellow victim," Helena said. "We can't choose our confederates."

She dropped the paper plates and cups in the kitchen basket and Sue shooed Scarlet away from it.

"I baked three dozen cookies," Sue said. "I thought I'd be sending some home with you ladies. Now I'll bet there aren't three dozen crumbs left."

Harold had eaten most of them and surreptitiously fed some to the dogs.

"There may be more of us who fell into the transporters' trap," I said. "We might be more effective if we were a larger group."

Sue nodded. "I'll ask Kate. Lyle is right about her. I think she should be doing more to help us. Thanks for your help tonight," she added.

"Thank you for hosting the meeting," Helena said.

Sue smiled. "You're welcome. Since you find Harold attractive, you can have the next one at your house."

"I didn't say that," she objected. "Not exactly, but I'm willing to do whatever it takes. I'll start making calls tomorrow."

We said goodnight and walked to our cars. Outside the house, it was marginally cooler. I took a long breath of fresh country air. It didn't matter that it came with a liberal dose of July heat.

"All I want is my dog," Helena said.

Fifteen

During the night the hot, muggy weather gave birth to a wild thunderstorm. I woke to lightning flashes and rain pounding on glass. Drat! I'd left the bedroom windows open. Halley whimpered and raised her head as I swung my legs out of bed and hurried to shut them. Misty raised her head, assessed the situation, and went back to sleep while I closed them.

Just in time.

Lightning slashed the sky, and at that moment I remembered a fragment of my dream, a sound of falling water. Like... I had to think. Like a powerful waterfall drowning out every other sound on earth.

Whatever other elements the dream possessed eluded me. There must have been more, though.

Halley nudged my hand, waiting direction.

"Go back to sleep," I whispered.

Bed for her and Misty was the doorway to our bedroom, which space they shared. They were our perpetual nighttime guards. What a pity they couldn't protect me from bad dreams because something evil had lurked in the dream water. Something to fear. Something I couldn't recall and probably never would as too much time had elapsed between the dream state and waking.

I used to love to listen to the sound of falling water.

Ever-changing images marched across my mind. Sagramore Lake. The stagnant water in Brent's pond... Coffee, tea, cookies—and water from Sue Appleton's tap. Or my own tap. I was making myself thirsty.

Finally I felt myself drifting off to sleep. Only then did I sense Halley returning to the doorway.

~ * ~

I didn't have a reason to return to Brent's house. On the other hand, at least a dozen household chores and errands awaited my attention, including further research at the library. None of these activities appealed to me, and none of them had to be done on this particular day.

You have dogs to take care of.

True, but it was too hot to drag them up and down the country lanes, or so they told me with elegant body language.

You have tonight's dinner to cook and nothing for dessert.

Yes, but it was too hot to cook or bake. If ever there was a day for Clover's take-out dinners and pie, this was it.

Lucy, the soul of Gothic utterance, would say that an irresistible force was calling out to me, that I had no choice but to answer it. She might also ask why I contemplated visiting the house without a companion—herself, Annica, or even Misty.

I had no ready answer for that. In truth I would have preferred to share the experience with a like-minded friend. Then I remembered the doughnuts that had disappeared from Brent's kitchen. Ah! The reason! I should replace them.

Suddenly filled with purpose, I bought a dozen orange-grazed crullers at the Hometown Bakery and, bearing gifts—or an offering?—drove to Loosestrife Lane where I parked in the shade of the weeping willow tree and walked through the gap in the picket fence. How peaceful this spot was, even with the condition of the water in the pond and the ruins that had once been a rock garden. The great weeping willow gave it an illusion of privacy, even though the road was fairly close to the lot line.

Something was different though. After last night's rain, the water level in the pond had risen. A few more rains and the water would spill over the bordering rocks. More leaves and miscellaneous debris littered the pond's surface. The flamingoes were gone from the rock garden, no doubt removed by Annica who planned to repaint them.

But none of these changes explained the difference I perceived in the scene.

A snarl invaded the stillness. The next moment a bedraggled collie leaped out of a stand of azalea bushes and landed on the ground not three yards from me. He looked familiar. My mind registered a dark sable coat and a narrow white blaze. His face was similar to the one that had replaced Misty's reflection.

The only dogs I feared were those who came out of nowhere, threatening to tear me apart. This dog looked more like a water monster than a collie. His long unkempt fur was drenched with vile smelling water. Bits of vegetation clung to his fur, and his teeth were bared in an unmistakable message: *Get out!*

"Good dog," I said softly.

I hoped he was a good dog.

Don't stare at him. Turn sideways. Walk slowly away. Slowly.

I couldn't move.

An unsettling suspicion broke through my terror. He might be rabid. On the heels of this very real fear came another thought. Could he be the dog from the fishpond? The phantom collie?

Whether he was a stray or a phantom who dwelled in the befouled water, he still posed a danger. Well, if he was a spirit, not so much.

Don't be silly, I told myself. *He's real enough.*

Instinctively I shoved my hand in my jacket pocket. On a cool day I would have worn a windbreaker with emergency bones or jerky treats in the pockets. Today the pocket of my denim skirt was empty. My arms were bare and the neckline of my blouse was cut low. I couldn't possibly be more vulnerable.

But wait! I still held the bag of doughnuts from the Hometown Bakery.

The collie shook himself vigorously. I stepped back from the shower of droplets, just a bit, and found my voice. "Good dog. Are you hungry? Do you want something to eat?"

Most dogs would react to 'hungry' and 'eat.'

He watched as I reached into the bag. My hands closed on two crullers. An enticing aroma of orange and sugar wafted through the air. He licked his chops. Good, he wanted them.

I pitched them as far I could—through the opening in the gap in the fence and onto the lane—where I'd never seen a walker or a runner who might stop and help me.

He bounded after the crullers and caught one in his mouth before it hit the ground. Now if only I could close the gap in the fence.

That wasn't an option.

I sprinted to the house. With a hand that trembled, I fumbled to unlock the front door.

Was the dog behind me intent on devouring the rest of the unexpected bounty? I didn't hear him.

At last the key turned. I pushed the door open and slammed it shut, leaning against it, trying to stop shaking.

That was close, but I was safe. For now. I took the bag to the kitchen. It would come in handy when I left the house in case the collie was lying in wait for me on the other side of the door.

I should have brought Misty. On second thought, maybe not. I didn't want either collie hurt.

A ghost dog can't harm a living one. Or you either. So calm down.

I sat in one of the hard, uncomfortable chairs Brent had brought up from the basement.

Rest, recover, think...

Did I just throw two crullers out to a phantom?

Don't be silly. A ghost wouldn't gobble down crullers.

My reasoning swung back and forth and finally settled on the most sensible fact. The dog who had wolfed down the crullers was as real as Misty.

Foxglove Corners had a large population of stray dogs, most of whom found their way to Letty and Lila Woodville at the animal shelter and from there to new homes. It made more sense that the collie was one of these poor abandoned creatures. Also, I'd already dealt with two phantom canines in the recent past. Surely that was anybody's limit.

I'd been letting my imagination and the vestiges of my fright color my thoughts. I needed to continue my planned investigation and give the ferocious dog plenty of time to move to another locale. In the meantime, I'd sample one of the miracle crullers for fortification.

I would have liked to explore the attic and the basement, but I would definitely need a companion, preferably Brent, to venture into those gloomy out-of-the-way places. In the meantime I could search the various rooms in the house, especially on the second floor, in case Annica and I had missed something like the tiny reinforcement that had fallen out of the thin air. So far that was our only tangible clue.

I paused on the landing to admire the stained glass window. It didn't communicate yesterday's terror to me, but a vague feeling of unease settled over me. It was a long way to the ground floor. Still longer to the front door. Could I make it in time?

Make what? And where had that thought come from?

I stood on the landing trying to catch strands that something—a force?—was trying to pull away from me in a bizarre tug-of-war.

It was no use. They were slipping out of my hands. I didn't even know what they were. Memories? Possibly, but not *my* memories.

Lucy had come closer to deciphering the secret of the wall. A woman frozen in terror, trapped in this small space where the colors of the stained glass provided the only brightness while the house swam in darkness.

I needed Lucy's talent and perception, but as she wasn't there. I climbed to the second floor and proceeded to look inside every room, even the closets. I found nothing more interesting than hangers, and nothing fell through the air. I even checked the bathroom with its outdated plumbing fixtures and faded wallpaper.

Nowhere did an alien thought break through my impressions of dust and stillness and emptiness. And thank heavens for that.

Last I went into the furnished room, telling myself that I would leave as soon as I'd searched it. After all, all decent clues are to be found in old attics, tucked away in trunks and chests and boxes. And old attics could wait for another day.

A scratching sound began, at first faint, barely discernible. Gradually it grew louder. It seemed to be in this room where a previous occupant had emptied drawers, stripped the bed, and left the furniture for another tenant.

Or above it, above the ceiling, which would be in the attic.

I thought immediately of Annica's rat. A giant rodent capable of making an unusually loud scratching noise. I didn't want to see a creature that could do that.

It was time to leave.

At the landing I had another fleeting thought, this one of distances. Of the way out.

Count the number of stairs to the ground floor. The number of steps to the front door. Will I have time to reach the outside?

Downstairs I made a quick detour to the kitchen, hoping the thing that scratched at wood hadn't devoured the rest of the crullers. Cautiously I opened the bag. They were all there, minus the two I'd thrown to the dog and the one I'd eaten.

On an impulse, I tried the back door. To my surprise, it swung open. Had I just discovered the secret of the missing doughnuts? Time would tell.

Before leaving, I made sure the door was locked. Now to head home, and I hoped nothing would happen to prevent it.

Sixteen

Later that afternoon I found both Brent and Annica at Clovers. Brent was eating apple pie while Annica hovered over him with a coffee pot. I also found our dinner featured at the top of day's menu board: Fried chicken and farm fresh string beans. That, with one of the apple pies in the dessert carousel, would make Crane happy...and me as well. Putting a savory meal on the table with little preparation would be a good ending to a trying day.

"Hi, Jennet," Brent said. "Join me."

"How about if I bring you a lime cooler?" Annica asked.

Having fallen in love with the delicious cooling drink earlier this summer, as had most of Clovers' other customers, I accepted happily, gave her my take-out order, and lost no time in telling Brent what was on my mind.

"You should check out that scratching sound in your house. I heard it again. A creature may have made its home there. A rat or something can do a lot of damage."

"I'll bring over one of the barn cats," he said. "Unless you think you're hearing a ghost."

"I don't know what it is. I saw a wet collie on your property, too. He might have been cooling off in the pond."

I omitted my earlier speculation that the dog might be the phantom. But Brent pounced on the possibility.

"Do you think you saw the phantom dog?" he asked.

"Not at all. I threw two of the pastries I was bringing you outside the fence. That gave me a chance to escape to the house."

"Escape?" he echoed. "You were afraid of a collie? Tell me you're joking."

"Well, yes. He might have rabies. He bared his teeth at me."

"Who has rabies?" Annica set my drink on the table. "Are you sure you don't want a piece of apple pie to go with it, Jennet?"

"Just a whole pie to take out. I saw a stray collie running loose on the grounds," I added.

"I'm going to fix the fence tomorrow," Brent said. "I meant to do it before, but I've been busy trying to find the right caretakers. Without them, my project won't get off the ground."

Annica glanced around. Seeing that all of her customers were engrossed in their dinners and conversations, she slipped into a chair.

"That sounds to me like a dream job for the right person," she said.

Brent nodded. "I'm including room and board with a nice salary, but my offer seems to draw the lunatic fringe of society. One guy who applied is a reformed hoarder who thinks he might be allergic to dogs. There's a lady who never had a dog in her life. Then there's a single mother with three kids. All brats from what I could tell. I wouldn't trust them not to hurt the dogs."

Annica gasped. "Surely not."

"By playing rough," he amended. "One little devil asked if he could ride the dogs." He ate the last bit of pie, a miniscule morsel of crust with a sliver of apple clinging to it. "Can I have another piece, Annica? That one was too small."

She rolled her eyes, turning her head so that Brent couldn't see the gesture. "Coming right up. Should I bring you two slices?"

"One'll do if you make it a decent size."

"While you're at the house, see if you can figure out where the scratching sound is coming from," I said. After a pause, I added, "If you can hear it, I'll know it isn't just me."

Annica was back in record time, setting a generous slice of pie in front of Brent and refilling his coffee cup. "Does this meet with your approval, sir?"

"Looks good," he said.

"I heard Jennet talking about that sound," Annica said. "For the record, I didn't hear it."

"When you take a break from interviewing caretakers, will you go with me up to the attic?" I asked. "I'm dying to know more about Lucy's frightened woman."

"I want to go, too." Annica sounded like a child in danger of being left out of an adventure.

"I'll take both of you if you promise to dress sensibly," Brent said. "Especially wear the right kind of shoes. The floor isn't stable."

"You've been in the attic already?" I asked.

"Before I bought the house, sure. It's loaded with stuff. The realtor said I could do whatever I liked with it."

Loaded with stuff. That was what I'd hoped to hear. Maybe we'd find a diary or old letters. Possibly newspaper clippings.

"How soon can we go?" Annica asked.

He consulted his phone. "Are you both free day after tomorrow? Say around noon?"

"I can be," Annica said. "I'll ask Mary Jeanne and switch shifts with Marcy. Marcy wants more hours anyway."

"It's a date," he said. "I'll have the fence fixed by then and maybe the pond drained."

With the pond cleared of debris and filled with fresh water, would I still see the phantom collie's reflection in the water? I couldn't wait to find out.

~ * ~

The high temperatures of the previous days dipped down to a more comfortable level overnight. I woke to a cerulean sky filled with white cotton candy clouds. The grass and leaves seemed greener, and Camille's gardens blazed with color. It was a picture perfect summer day when anything was possible.

When Crane left for his shift, I set out for a walk with Raven, Gemmy, and Star, leaving the rest of the pack with fresh water and toys. The ones left behind didn't fuss; they knew their turn would come. Thank heavens for summer vacation and the priceless gift of time.

A soft wind blew the myriads of floral scents of Foxglove Corners over the lane as we headed toward Sagramore Lake, one of the most popular gathering spots in the area. It was early, so I anticipated having the beach mostly to ourselves.

The water sparkled in the morning sun. My collies didn't like to get their feet wet but loved making tracks in the sand. An elaborate sandcastle, still intact, captured Raven's attention. As she nudged a turret with her nose, I guided my trio around it. Gemmy alerted me to a disturbance on the beach. Three figures were running toward us. One of them called my name.

It was my young friends, Molly and Jennifer, with the collie, Ginger. I tended to think of them as little girls selling lemonade and cookies, but they were in high school now, taller and wearing makeup. Both girls had long flowing hair. They were dressed alike in shorts and the shirts Miss Eidt had designed for her summer reading club. Not to be left out, Ginger proudly wore a pink and white bandana.

The four collies, old friends, greeted and sniffed one another and performed endearing play bows. Ginger's paws were wet. Here was one canine who didn't mind the water.

Molly brushed back her hair with her hand, her pink shell bracelet making a gentle clacking sound. Like Annica she favored jewelry with sound effects. "Do you have any mysteries to solve this summer?" she asked.

The girls fancied themselves amateur detectives and, in truth, had been helpful to me in the past. Because I couldn't see any harm in the mysteries of Brent's house—only ghosts—I told them about the phantom in the fishpond and the scratching noise inside that might indicate the presence of a rat or something more sinister.

What I didn't mention was the feeling of terror Lucy sensed on the landing.

Jennifer reacted for both of them. "Wow! Maybe a whole pack of rats lives there."

"I hope not."

"Where is this place?" Molly wanted to know.

"Not far. On Loosestrife Lane."

"We've seen it," she said. "Last summer when we rode our bikes that way."

"It has to be the spookiest house in Foxglove Corners," Jennifer added.

"Mr. Fowler is going to fix it up as a shelter for geriatric collies, the ones nobody wants."

"How sad," Molly said.

"I don't think so," Jennifer countered. "That's a wonderful idea. A house just for dogs."

"I mean about the ones nobody wants to adopt. Will Brent's house be just for collies?"

"That's what he says."

"Oh."

"What?" I asked.

"What will happen to other breeds?" she asked. "All dogs get old and sometimes their owners don't want to keep them. Like Sandy on our street."

"Lila and Letty Woodville welcome all dogs at the animal shelter," I told her. "Any breed, any age."

"Maybe not anymore," Jennifer said.

The animal shelter across from the municipal park was the library's neighbor. Like the library, it was an institution in Foxglove Corners. I knew the Woodville sisters well and felt bad that I hadn't visited them in months. I used to bring treats for the foundlings regularly.

"What changed?" I asked.

"Miss Lila said they may have to close the shelter," she said. "Then all that's left is the pound, and they kill dogs there."

Seventeen

"Back up, Jennifer," I said. "Why would the Woodville sisters close the animal shelter?"

"They don't want to, but Major March passed away. The legacy he left to the shelter won't be enough to feed all their dogs and pay for vet bills."

Soon after moving to Foxglove Corners, I had met charismatic animal activist, Caroline Meilland who had later been slain. In her memory, her friend, Major March, had established the shelter and recruited Lila and Letty Woodville to take care of the town's strays and find new homes for them. Without his financial support, they would soon be floundering.

"When did Major March die?" I asked.

"Last month," Jennifer said. "He was killed in a plane crash."

The Woodville sisters were my good friends. I should have known.

Not if you don't keep in touch with people, I told myself.

"We're organizing fundraisers for the shelter," Molly said. "Will you help us?"

"Of course I will. Whatever you need."

Jennifer said, "I knew you would. We're going to bathe dogs at Molly's house the first Saturday in August. We'll charge fifteen dollars for small dogs and twenty-five for big dogs like Ginger."

"And my job will be...?"

"To give them baths. We're getting soap and tubs and stuff from all over."

Oh, good grief. I had a fleeting vision of suds and water, struggling dogs, flying hair... Fleas? With seven collies of my own to groom, I usually took them, two at a time, to Marina's Pet Parlor."

"Miss Lila and Miss Letty are going to help," Molly said. "Do you think we should ask Mr. Fowler?"

Brent? I had to think about that. Brent usually hired others to do menial jobs or any jobs, for that matter. I knew that one of the young men at his barn was in charge of grooming Napoleon and his collies. I couldn't imagine Brent with his shirt sleeves rolled up, rinsing shampoo out of a dog's coat.

"He loves animals. I'm sure he'll make a donation to the cause," I said.

"We'll ask him then, and we have other ideas. We're going to learn how to embroider pretty collars. Can you think of anything else we can do?"

"Not right away. I can probably come up with something."

Or Sue would, or Ronda or Emma, my fellow Rescue League members. But whatever funds we raised couldn't compete with Major March's ongoing support. Perhaps the animal shelter, as we knew it, was doomed.

"They were going to turn away new dogs," Molly said. "But then someone left a cute black and white puppy on the porch, and they couldn't send him to the pound."

What if they had no choice? It might happen if all the fundraisers in town couldn't bail out the shelter.

We couldn't let that happen.

I gazed out over Sagramore Lake, trying to see the horizon as if the answer could be found in that barely discernible line.

In the short time we'd been talking, the lake had filled with watercraft, and sunbathers were claiming prized lying places on the beach. Like the animal shelter, I expected the lake and the beach to be there for us always. But suppose some future summer it was gone? The beach contaminated or the lake dried up?

"All we can do is try to save the shelter," I said. "All of us working together."

We said goodbye, humans and canines, and I took the collies home, filled a large brown bag with treats, and drove to the Corners. As I glanced at the yellow Victorian I remembered that Camille often gifted our dogs with homemade treats. Maybe she would be willing to make flavorful bones to sell at one of the fundraisers, along with handwritten recipes. She and Leonora could always arrange a bake sale.

Maybe all was not lost.

~ * ~

For once I bypassed the library and parked in front of the Foxglove Corners Animal Shelter. The house was another old white Victorian built around the same time as the library. Memories rolled over me.

The day I had seen a Christmas tree, decorated with vintage icicles, in the bay window of the house next to the shelter. A tree that subsequently, unaccountably, disappeared the next time I looked. Of Winter, the glorious blue merle I'd found lying as if dead on a snowy country road and taken to the shelter. My first rescue.

All the other strays I'd brought to the shelter, wholeheartedly welcomed by Lila or Letty. I could almost see Lila in one of her old-fashioned aprons offering me a piece of her homemade coffee cake, and Caroline Meilland who'd championed all the animals who share the earth with us.

Caroline had never seen the shelter, nor met the Woodville sisters, but from the first, she had been there in spirit.

The memories dissolved around me, and I was back in the present leaning over the gate to the shelter's spacious backyard. About a dozen of the Woodville's foundlings rushed the fence to welcome me, all noise and bright eyes and wagging tails. I wanted to greet them by their names but realized they were all new since my last visit. How long ago?

"Jennet," Lila called from the porch. "Don't stand out there. Come on in."

I did and found myself enfolded in Lila's grandmotherly embrace. She wore a voluminous apron that covered the bodice of her blue and white striped dress. From the wall in the vestibule, Caroline smiled down on us from her portrait.

"We haven't seen you in... How long, Letty?"

Letty emerged from the kitchen, carrying a coffee cup. "So long I can't remember. We've missed you."

There were minor changes like the highlights in Letty's pixie cut and a new hairdo for Lila, a short pageboy. The sisters fairly glowed with good health and energy, and neither one looked particularly unhappy.

"I ran into Jennifer and Molly on the beach," I said. "They told me about Major March's passing."

Lila said quietly, "He was a good man, gone before his time."

"I know what his loss means for the shelter," I added. "I'm so sorry."

"We've depended on his support for so long," Lila said. "It's hard to imagine any other way of life."

"Nothing lasts forever," Letty said briskly. "We need to cut way back on the dogs we take in."

I sensed that the sisters disagreed on that matter.

"How many dogs do you have now?" I asked.

"Twenty," Lila said.

"Twenty-one," Letty corrected. "Don't forget Gareth."

The puppy. I heard whimpering from the kitchen. It turned into a howl.

"That pesky pup," Letty said. "He chews everything in sight unless we watch him. And even then."

"That's what puppies do. Let's have coffee and cake. I baked this morning. It's nothing fancy, just a simple coffee cake."

So many problems could be solved or at least talked through over coffee and cake. I'd learned that from Camille in her cozy country kitchen.

The puppy's crate was next to the refrigerator. I talked softly to him while Letty brewed coffee and Lila brought forth the fruits of her labor, an apple coffee cake decorated with apple slices and walnuts.

"We could work harder to find homes," Lila said. "Doctor Foster gives us a discount for our dogs, but vet bills are sky high these days."

Letty set the table with dessert plates and coffee cups. "I don't know what more we could do. People who want a purebred dog tend to go to breeders or rescues. Not everybody, of course, and those dogs need homes, too."

My memory of the ghostly Christmas tree reminded me of the sisters' other neighbor.

"How is Henry McCullough?" I asked.

"He's fine. He went up north for the month of July. Henry pledged part of his pension to keep the shelter open," Letty said.

"I'm taking part in the girls' dog washing fundraiser," I said.

Lila beamed. "Molly and Jennifer are wonderful young women."

"We need Caroline Meilland," Letty said.

"We can't have her, but she sent Jennet in her place, along with a whole bunch of angels to show us the way."

Lila added, "While people continue to dump their pets on country roads and drive off."

I didn't want them to need me too much. True, I was on vacation all summer, but I had the fake transporters to track down, the phantom collie in the pond, and the other oddities of Brent's house. But...

"Foxglove Corners needs the animal shelter," I said. "The problem is how to keep it solvent."

"Not just for now," Lila added, "but forever."

Eighteen

I stood under the weeping willow tree gazing at the fishpond beyond the fence and marveling at its transformation. The water was fresh, its surface bright in the sunlight that made its way cautiously through graceful willow strands. All of the deteriorating mishmash of leaves and other debris had been cleared away, along with the weeds in the rock garden.

"It's so beautiful," I said. "Just the way I remember it."

Annica set the picnic basket from Clovers on the ground. "When did you see it before?"

"Oh..." Realizing what I had said, I rephrased my comment, "I was thinking about the pond at our house when I was a little girl. This one brings back memories."

"Are there any goldfish in it?" she asked.

"I can't tell from here."

We couldn't go any further as the new pickets were in place, accompanied by a 'Beware—Fresh Paint' sign. Brent would arrive any minute and unlock the gate and the door to the house.

"I guess we can't climb over it," Annica said. "I could have. Once."

"You'd impale yourself," I told her. "Brent shouldn't be long."

Annica glanced over her shoulder. "I don't see the rabid dog. I hope he's far away."

"If he shows up, we have plenty of food in the basket. He's partial to crullers."

We wore sensible clothes, as instructed, both of us in jeans and sneakers, to navigate the unstable attic floorboards. Annica drew the line at venturing out without her earrings. Today's pair were sequined seahorses. She twirled them absently. Unlike her other jewelry, they didn't make a sound.

In fact nothing disturbed the silence that lay heavily over us. Not even birdsong. The unbroken stillness was eerie, and I was grateful to have company.

"I hope we find something good in the attic," Annica said.

"Like hidden treasure?"

"Anything but the mystery rat. I can't understand why anyone would move all but one bedroom suite out of the house and leave stuff in the attic. I wonder if we'll find the rest of the furniture up there."

"I hope not. I'd like to find—"

What did I hope to find most in the attic? Something that belonged to a former resident, perhaps the frightened woman whose terror lived on in the walls. Something, an object, perhaps, with a story to tell.

"A diary," I said.

"How cliché. Every mystery worth its salt has a diary in it."

"How else can a reader know about events that happened a hundred years ago? Maybe old letters?"

"Another cliché. Besides, this isn't a book. It's real life."

I glanced at the pond, wishing myself inside the yard with Misty at my side. Would the phantom collie still be reflected in its surface if Misty looked into the water? Why had I only seen him twice?

Because I needed Misty?

"There's Brent," Annica announced as a green and white vintage Plymouth pulled up in front of the gate. As he got out of the car and waved to us, the sun struck lights into his dark red hair. He wore a green shirt. Brent must have a closet full of green to set off the unusual color of his hair and pay homage to the earth mother.

"Let the fun begin," I said.

We met him at the gate.

"Were you waiting long?" he asked as he took the picnic basket from Annica.

"Not long," I said. "We were admiring the pond."

"This is only the beginning. Wait till they get started inside the house."

"Did you buy the goldfish yet?" Annica asked.

"Not yet. Maybe I'll leave the pond the way it is. Are the flamingoes ready?"

"I gave them two coats of paint, but they need another day to dry."

"There's no hurry," he said. "I still haven't found my caretaker. Once the word was out that I needed one, somebody let all the inmates out of the looney bin. This basket is heavy," he added. "What's in it?"

"Ham sandwiches, blueberry muffins, and fruit," she said. "And it's staying where I can watch it. We don't want a repeat of the doughnut caper."

"It'll be okay in the kitchen," he said. "I made sure the back door was locked before I left. We won't be bothered by vagrants drifting in from outside."

"Can we go right up to the attic?" I asked.

"As soon as you girls are ready. I brought flashlights and extra batteries."

He unlocked the door. I took my last breath of fresh air for a while and followed them inside.

~ * ~

The house didn't welcome us. We walked into the usual close, stale air, anemic light that filtered through grimy windows, and emptiness. Only the truly imaginative could see a warm and welcoming place where a dog could sleep freed from the fear of being disturbed.

But Brent had turned the fishpond into a thing of beauty. He could work his magic again inside with paint on the walls, rugs on the floors, and new windows. Annica was going to help him furnish the house.

He strode into the kitchen and set the basket on the counter next to the coffeemaker, an array of bottles, and five flashlights.

"I sent one of my men over earlier with water and pop," he said. "Or we can have coffee. Everyone, take a flashlight. The entrance is on the second floor next to a linen closet. It's locked, but I have a key."

Annica patted her red-gold hair. It had a freshly washed sheen. "I wish I'd thought to bring a scarf. For the cobwebs. Oh, well…I can't imagine why the realtor didn't examine what was up there before saying you could do whatever you wanted with it," she added.

"I can. It was too much trouble. He'd rather unload the house and whatever was in it and forget about it."

"You can have a yard sale," I suggested.

He opened the attic door to a rush of cold air and darkness. You'd never think that outside the walls of the house, summer sun warmed the air, and flowers bloomed. I shivered. Annica wished for a scarf; I would be happy with a cardigan. But we were exactly where we wanted to be—in the attic, about to embark on an adventure.

"The stairs are narrow, and there's no hand rail and no light," he said. "I'll go first."

He switched on his flashlight, and shadows came to life, rising above mounds of boxes and large objects with amorphous shapes. It looked as if all the house's unwanted furniture from past decades had been relegated to the attic, most of it covered with yellow sheets.

"It's spooky," Annica said, "and quiet."

"Like a typical attic," I told her. "That's what we wanted."

"What should we do now?" Annica asked. "I don't have a plan."

"What do you want to do?" Brent asked.

"Open something. One of those boxes. Or that trunk."

She pointed to an ancient trunk at least a hundred years old and probably more. Once it had been shades of gray or brown, but its color had faded, and the brass hardware was dull.

He handed me the flashlight and pulled the trunk into a dim circle of light.

"It isn't locked." He pushed open the top, and a strong, rank odor assailed us. Mothballs or…Can mustiness have a smell? Or age, long sealed in place?

He lifted a tray with three divisions, all of which wre empty and set it on the floor. Beneath it lay an unsightly jumble of loose papers. He scooped up a handful of memorabilia and unearthed a calendar, every square of which was covered with writing.

"Treasure?" Annica murmured. "I don't think so."

I aimed my flashlight on the calendar. It was large, eight and a half by eleven, and opened to the month of August. The month's picture was a girl sitting in a rose arbor with a book. After the fifteenth of the month, the spaces for the days were blank.

"Don't be so sure," I said.

Nineteen

Annica peered over my shoulder. "Why do you say that?"

"Never underestimate the power of the written word," I said. "This calendar could tell us everything we want to know."

"But all this writing—it's just appointments and reminders."

"Maybe I'll find a name. Is it all right if I hold on to the calendar, Brent?"

"Be my guest," he said.

"It's for 1998, and there are no notations for the second half of the month. That tells us something happened on August fifteenth or shortly after that day." I flipped through the remaining pages. "Whoever owned the calendar didn't write anything after that date."

"Oh," Annica said. "I get it. Something prevented her from writing, and we need to find out what. But how on earth can we do that?"

I didn't have an answer for her. Not yet.

"Do you want to take anything else?" Brent asked.

"Maybe," I said. "Let's come back to the trunk. We can open some of these boxes."

Stepping carefully, Annica approached a neat stack of boxes in a corner. On the sides someone had written 'Holly' in red magic marker.

Who was Holly?

"I hope we haven't discovered a cache of Christmas decorations," Brent said.

The boxes had been secured with masking tape which had come loose over the years, or string, simply tied. Annica lifted the top box to the floor and opened it.

"It's full of clothes. Skirts, blouses, dresses, underwear..."

Holly. These were Holly's belongings.

"Most people donate old clothes," Brent said.

"These are in good condition," Annica pointed out. "Some look like new." She unfolded a white tank top. "This one still has its tag."

I said, "Maybe Holly died and her family couldn't bear to donate her clothes. They brought them up to the attic to decide another day, but that day never came."

"But why would they go away and leave them up here?" Annica asked. "Because no one has lived in the house for decades."

The house's history was a stumbling block. People and events tend to lose themselves in time. We would be lucky if we found additional information.

"Maybe by the time they left the house, their grief had worn away. They may have forgotten about the boxes. Or whoever stored them here died himself. We'll never know."

Annica unfolded a short aqua dress with a high waist. It was sleeveless with narrow brown trim and tiny brown buttons on the bodice. Cute but fussy, and possibly dating from the nineteen seventies, although I wasn't knowledgeable about yesteryear's fashions.

She held it up against her body. "How do I look?"

"Pretty," Brent said.

"Vintage," I added.

She refolded the dress and rifled through the folds. "These are mostly summer clothes. Shorts and pants and shirts. Here's a raincoat. Such nice things left to fall to pieces."

Turning away from the opened box, we concentrated on Holly's other possessions, most of which contained personal grooming articles—even makeup—and paperbacks. Oddly, the paperbacks were old Gothic novels in pristine condition. I felt an instant affinity for the unknown Holly.

"Miss Eidt would be ecstatic to have these for the Gothic Nook," I said.

Annica opened another, smaller box. "Look, a typewriter! I've only seen them in pictures. It still has the ribbon in it."

"This box has about a zillion copies of the same book," Brent said. "*The Ghost of Sunburst Plantation.*"

It had an intriguing cover. An imposing Tudor mansion with a lady in white walking toward the house. In my years of collecting Gothic novels, I'd seen countless variations of it. Usually the heroine was running in the other direction.

The author was Holly Wickersham.

"It's her book," I said. "Holly's. The girl who had the calendar."

"Wow!" Annica reached for a copy. "She was a published author."

I had another thought. Had I found the terrified woman standing on the landing of Brent's house, frozen in fear?

I pushed a cobweb off the return address on the box, just to be sure. It had been shipped from Starbright Publications.

"Her publisher sent her these books probably for promotion, but they ended up stored in the attic. I'm going to take one, Brent, okay? This is my kind of book."

And possibly it would tell me something about Holly.

"Take 'em all," Brent said.

"So all this stuff belonged to a writer," Annica said. "She must have been one of the previous tenants."

"Let's see if we can find something more personal, like a diary."

Annica muffled a cough. "You don't give up, do you, Jennet?"

"No, and that's why I'm the head sleuth and you're my humble assistant."

"Yeah. Right."

Between us we covered every inch of the attic, removing dust covers and opening other boxes. We didn't find a diary or anything belonging to the tenants who preceded Holly. That was strange, considering the age of the house. But on second thought, all it meant was that the others had taken all of their possessions when they left, as one would expect.

All but the furniture. Chairs, end tables, lamps, beds, rolled-up carpets, and empty suitcases filled the attic, leaving us barely enough room to maneuver between them.

I shone the flashlight on my watch and noted that we'd been wallowing in the dust, exploring, for almost two hours. This project had taken longer than we'd planned. I for one was ready for light and air, and I had chores to do at home.

Brent replaced a dust-coated sheet on a green velvet love seat. "I can furnish whole rooms with this stuff."

"Or you could sell it," Annica suggested.

"What's the point of getting rid of furniture I'd have to buy?" he wanted to know. "Let's eat," he added.

In the kitchen Annica appeared to be amazed that the picnic basket sat on the counter where Brent had placed it, and, moreover, that the contents were still inside.

She unfolded dinner-sized napkins for place mats and unpacked the sandwiches. In the meantime, Brent brought up two more chairs from the basement. We washed our hands over the sink near which someone had left a fresh bar of soap, and sat down to our indoor picnic.

Which was the best kind to have. In the attic we'd been in a different world, oblivious of drastic weather changes in the real one. While we'd been working in darkness, the sun had vanished behind dark clouds. It was raining, and the wind was blowing.

"We need candles," Annica murmured.

"Why?" Brent asked. "We have electricity."

"For atmosphere. Don't you agree, Jennet?"

I bit into a ham sandwich and thought about it. "I've had enough atmosphere for one day, but candles would come in handy in a power outage."

"I'm thinking about buying a generator," Brent said. "I have one in my house. Then you don't have to worry if the lights go out."

Slowly I became aware of a sound. A distant wail broke through the drumming of rain on the windows. Could an ambulance be rushing to an accident? That didn't happen often in Foxglove Corners. It didn't sound like an ambulance siren. It sounded like...

Before I could complete the thought it ended abruptly in mid-wail.

"Did you hear that?" I asked. "I wonder what happened."

"I don't hear anything," Annica said. "Only the wind. It's picking up."

"It wasn't the wind."

The wind wouldn't just stop as if someone had pulled its plug. But the ambulance might have reached its destination.

Okay. That's what happened. Don't look for a mystery.

"The rain isn't going to stop anytime soon," Brent said. "But we're through here for today. I'll come back and take inventory of the furniture in the attic in a day or two. I'd like to have at least the living room furnished before I open the doors."

"I'll buy some bedding at the mall," Annica volunteered. "You'll have a bedroom for your caretaker at least."

"And a workable kitchen. Then all I'll need is the caretaker."

I finished my sandwich and wandered to the window. Rain fell on the fishpond, and the wind tossed willow strands to and fro. The sound was soothing and at the same time unsettling. How could that be?

I didn't waste time puzzling over it. It just was. Just a feeling. I thought about the phantom collie in the pond and wondered if I'd ever see him again. I'd hoped to, and possibly I would, even though the pond had been cleaned of its befouled water.

You don't clean away a spirit.

"You didn't hear that scratching sound today," Annica said. "And I didn't feel anything when I stood on the landing like Lucy did. Now that we have some answers, maybe the haunting has gone away."

"What answers?" Brent countered. "All we have is a calendar and a book."

"And a name, Holly Wickersham," I added. "As for the haunting, I think it's still here. It's just resting."

But who could know for certain?

Twenty

Brent and Annica came over that evening with barbecued chicken and carrot cake from Clovers, which gave me a chance to tell both of them about the animal shelter's dilemma and the girls' fundraiser. Neither one was aware that Major March had passed away. I imagined they had never met him or realized that he had generously supported the shelter since Caroline Meilland's death.

"Count me in," Annica said. "I've gotten to be an expert at bathing dogs. I can't afford to take Angel to a groomer."

"It'll take more than an occasional fundraiser to keep the shelter afloat," Brent pointed out."

"Letty wants to cut way back on the dogs they take in," I said.

"Then what happens to the others?" Annica asked.

"They go to the pound, I'm afraid."

"I usually come across one or two stray dogs every week," Crane said. "The Woodville sisters make them welcome. Often they find new homes for them, especially the puppies."

All those misinformed people who thought some farmer would gladly adopt their discarded pet. All those new orphans.

I knew Foxglove Corners had more than its share of stray dogs. But two a week?

I unpacked the chicken and placed it in baking dishes to keep warm in the oven. All I needed to do was toss a salad, but thoughts of dogs being turned away tore at my heart. Two a week? Eight a month. How could there be that many homes?

"The pound is a far cry from the Woodvilles' place," Annica said, "and they may put the dogs they can't take care of to sleep." She turned to Brent. "Couldn't you make room for them in your new house?"

"I'm not opening an all-breed shelter," he reminded us. "The house is for geriatric collies that haven't a prayer of being adopted. They're important, too, and that's my mission. Of course I want to help…" He paused, considering. "In some way."

"You can sign up to wash the dogs," Annica said.

"Mmm. What else can I do? They'll need plenty of shampoo and all sorts of things like dryers and brushes."

"Money most of all," I said.

He agreed. "Like money. I'll write a check tonight."

It was as I'd thought. I'd never see Brent roll up his shirtsleeves and squirt shampoo into a dog's coat. But he'd be generous with his funds, if not his time.

"One of the men at my barn is crazy about collies," Brent said. "He even shares his dinner with them. I'll see if he wants to volunteer."

Annica smiled at him. "The more the merrier."

"How about you, Sheriff?" Brent asked. "What are you going to contribute to this enterprise?"

"I'll be busy keeping the bad guys away," Crane said.

"What bad guys? There's been zero crime in Foxglove Corners this summer."

"Don't forget the transport scam," I said.

"Crime is down because we deputies are so good. Jennet will represent our family."

"While Crane keeps the home fires burning," I added. "I suspect you men think taking care of animals is women's work."

"Isn't it?" Brent asked.

Instead of challenging him, I said, "It's everyone's duty to do everything in their power to help the animals that share the earth with us. You may remember Caroline Meilland used to say that. It's just as relevant today."

Brent sprang to his own defense. "My animals have a good life."

Nobody could deny it.

"Well, I hope Jennifer and Molly thought of advertising their fundraiser," Annica said. "This is the first I'm hearing of it. People have to know when and where to bring their dogs and how much it will cost them."

"They're setting up on Sagramore Lake Road the first Saturday in August. That's where they used to sell lemonade and cookies. You're right, Annica. We can all help them spread the word."

"Yeah," she said, "or they'll be no dogs to wash. Just unopened bottles of shampoo."

~ * ~

After our company left, Crane watched the late news while I straightened the kitchen and refrigerated leftover chicken, giving occasional handouts to the collies astute enough to follow me. Candy had her eye on the carrot cake, but I had my own plans for it.

"You'll want to hear this, Jennet," Crane called from the living room.

I joined him to see Kate Brennan on the screen. She stood on a country road where a smashed van lay on its side in a ditch. Near her a state trooper cradled a shivering Siberian husky puppy. The van was in sad shape, definitely totaled, but the writing on its side was visible: *Sea-to-Sea Transport.*

Kate was saying, "Sea-to-Sea is the subject of an active *Kate in Your Corner* investigation. The scammers are contracted to deliver pets to a new location for a hefty fee. Instead they abscond with the dog and the owner's money. The driver of this van apparently fled the scene, leaving this puppy behind in a crate."

The camera focused on the pup who looked terrified.

"Anyone with information about the crash or the driver is urged to contact us here at *Kate in Your Corner.*"

The segment ended with the number of the station rolling by at the bottom of the screen.

Crane turned the volume down. "This happened earlier today north of Maple Creek. The lanes were dry. There was a light drizzle but nothing to cause a driver to crash his van."

"He must have been drunk," I said, "or he might have had a medical problem."

"It didn't interfere with his running away from the scene," Crane pointed out.

"And leaving the dog in a crate. That's how Sea-to-Sea takes care of their pets. I hope the husky's owner is watching."

"They'll find his family," Crane said. "I'll bet it's a Michigan company."

"Now maybe we can find out what happened to Helena's Arden and the other missing dogs."

My phone began its rippling notes. I glanced at the number. It was Helena. Her voice was higher than usual, and her words were rushed. "I just saw Kate's report on the news," she said. "We got him."

"I thought he ran away from the scene—or walked or crawled."

"He took off, but how far can he go on foot? He must have been banged up. I hope so. Did you see the condition of that van?"

"Sooner or later they'll find him or his body," I said. "It's unlikely he escaped without a scratch."

"Doesn't he have a partner?" Helena asked. "Maybe he was able to call him. At least Kate has a lead. I wonder where Arden is in all this mess."

"Hopefully in a place where we can retrieve her," I said. "First, they have to find the driver. Then—"

An annoying beep alerted me to another call.

"I'll talk to you tomorrow, Helena," I said. "By then we may know more."

It turned out I had multiple calls, one after the other. Everyone who had lost a pet to Sea-to-Sea Transport must have seen Kate's segment tonight, as well as those who had been at the meeting at Sue's ranch. Including Sue. But no one had any additional information. Yet.

"I'm going to turn the phone off tonight," I said. "What famous person once said, Tomorrow is another day?"

"You say that," Crane answered. "Let's go to bed. I'll take the dogs out."

Amazingly, most of them understood what he'd said. Candy rushed to the side door, and Sky emerged from her den under the dining room table. The others materialized at Crane's side like shadowy ghosts. They all went outside quietly, and I moved through the first floor rooms turning out lights.

I silenced my phone and dropped it into my purse. It was later than our usual bedtime. In fact, tomorrow was only an hour away. The next day promised to be busy in a good way.

~ * ~

I was so tired that it took me a while to fall asleep. I could turn out the lights in the house but not the one that shone in my brain. Question after question paraded through my mind.

Where had the driver of the transport van taken refuge? Would the state police find him? Who was missing money and a husky puppy? And where were Arden and the other dogs stolen from their trusting owners?

Finally I fell asleep only to wake about an hour later, having escaped from a terrifying nightmare. I lay still, wanting to forget it, but at the same time thinking parts of it were worth remembering.

I was back at Brent's house walking alone in the vast wilderness that was his yard. Annica and Brent had left. I had tried in vain to keep up with them, but they were too fast for me. They'd gone through the gate and disappeared from my view.

Loosestrife Lane was a singularly dark road. I couldn't see my car, but there was the pond in all its newly-restored glory, illuminated by a light from...somewhere. The moon, perhaps? But since when did the moon spill eerie yellowish-green light on the earth?

A sound of water broke through the silence, a loud splashing. A creature emerged from the pond. Seaweed hung from its fur like an uneven fringe, but its form was clear. A dark sable collie stood in the weeds and shook himself vigorously.

I felt the drops of water on my face and on my arms. And I was afraid.

Twenty-one

In the end, the day that had promised so much proved uneventful. The state trooper had taken temporary custody of the husky puppy, as his owners apparently were the only people who hadn't seen Kate Brennan's segment. The scam artist hadn't been found, but there were plenty of places to hide in the woods of Maple Creek.

The van was, as I had suspected, totaled. With the Sea-to-Sea case out of my hands, I turned my attention to the mystery at Brent's house and the search for Holly Wickersham.

Really, this summer would go down in my history as the summer of the myriad mysteries. I relived our exploration of the attic and ignored the weird ending my dream had conjured.

The makeup I assumed belonged to Holly bothered me, as did the comb and a toothbrush, along with a half-empty tubes of toothpaste. More than anything else we found in Holly's boxes, the discovery of those essentials convinced me that Holly had left the house suddenly and perhaps not of her own will.

Or had she planned to return in an hour or two, then something untoward had happened?

We hadn't found her handbag, which suggested that she had taken it with her.

A common thread ran through these speculations, the image of Holly trapped on the landing in the grip of terror.

I could create scenarios all day, but what I needed were facts. Fortunately I found a few informative sentences in a short biography at the end of Holly's book, *The Ghost of Sunburst Plantation*.

Born in Oscoda, Michigan, Holly Wickersham had attended Michigan State University. She began her career as a journalist but soon discovered she preferred to write fiction. Her hobbies were folk music and traveling. Her next book, a supernatural mystery titled *The Edelweiss Lure*, was scheduled for release in 1990.

Had that book ever been published? I could easily find out.

The biography included a black and white photograph that might have been taken on the porch of Brent's house. Holly wore a dark dress with cap sleeves, possibly black, and her shoulder-length blonde hair was slightly tousled...as if a wind gust had passed by at the very moment the camera captured her likeness. She was an attractive woman with the ghost of a smile on her lips.

Armed with a name, I searched the Internet and found that Holly had written seven novels of romantic suspense. Then in the summer of l998 she disappeared without a trace, like one of her own heroines. I had a good idea of the date—August 15th, the day when she had stopped writing notations on her calendar.

Holly's life had turned into one of her own mysteries.

Had she been murdered or perhaps arranged her own disappearance? Or could she have lost her memory in an accident? None of her contemporaries seemed to have speculated on her fate. Eventually her books went out of print and her brief sojourn on the mystery scene slipped out of the public's consciousness.

As Holly had lived in the house on Loosestrife Lane at one time, I thought Miss Eidt might have met her. She liked to showcase local authors. I might find other Wickersham books in the Gothic Nook. Therefore, a trip to the library was my next logical step.

Afterward, I planned to visit Lucy at Dark Gables. Now that I knew more about Holly and had access to her possessions, I could give Lucy more to work with. I suspected it was Holly's emotions, her fear, that had seeped into the walls of the Brent's house. With Lucy's affinity for supernatural oddities, perhaps she would be able to add to our slowly forming picture of Holly Wickersham and with luck, we would be able to solve the mystery of her disappearance.

That was the project I would pursue while the authorities tried to track down the Sea-to-Sea man and return the missing dogs to their families.

~ * ~

At noon the Corners drowsed under an unrelenting sun. After a brief respite, we were back in the hot zone. The line in front of The Ice Cream Parlor was long, and the library's parking lot was practically empty. I imagined Sagramore Lake would be crowded, but since I needed quiet, if not solitude, a sparsely peopled library appealed to me.

Dodging the reach of the sprinkler, I paused to give Blackberry the cat my customary greeting. She didn't stir from her perch on the wicker chair but returned it with a cold, inimical stare that neither welcomed me nor warned me away from her domain.

I pushed open the door and was welcomed instead by cool air circulating in the large quiet space.

Miss Eidt was shelving books in the paperback carousel to the right of her desk. She always looked cool and lovely, especially in one of her pastel shirtwaist dresses, today the color of a clear blue sky.

"Are you changing the carousel theme?" I asked.

"Yes, to science-fiction," she said. "I have a nice mix of classics and new releases. What are you in the mood for today?"

"Research. I'm still hoping to solve the mystery of Brent's house on Loosestrife Lane. I'd like to use your marvelous vertical file."

"Are you talking about the ghost in the pond?"

"This is something else. Did you ever hear of a Michigan author named Holly Wickersham? She was writing mysteries and Gothics in the nineteen-nineties."

"I'm afraid not," Miss Eidt said. "But Debbie and I aren't finished cataloging the books in the Gothic Nook yet."

"I should start there then."

"What does this author have to do with Brent's house?" she asked.

"She may have disappeared from there. When Lucy and I were on the staircase, she became aware of a disturbance."

"Lucy is so lucky to be able to tune into the other world," Miss Eidt said.

"In a way." I doubted that Lucy thought of sensing an unpleasant, long-departed emotion as lucky. "The problem is she can't tell the cause of the disturbance."

"I hope this hapless writer wasn't walled up alive," Miss Eidt said, revealing her rarely seen macabre side.

"Doesn't that just happen in historical fiction?" I asked.

"It must have happened in real life. Somewhere. Sometime."

"Well, I don't think it happened in Foxglove Corners in the twentieth century."

Now that Miss Eidt had brought it to my attention, though, I could only hope Holly's fate hadn't been that gruesome.

~ * ~

I had the Gothic Nook to myself. Readers who weren't devoted to the genre would take one look at Miss Eidt's collection and head for the flashy new offerings in the front of the library. They wouldn't see the chocolates Miss Eidt had set out in antique candy dishes on vintage tables.

The collection had steadily grown as Miss Eidt and Debbie haunted estate sales and bookstores far and wide. Old paperbacks with small print and yellowish pages. Intriguing covers promising a world of Gothic thrills. Occasionally carefully mended covers. Hundreds of them. No wonder they were behind in their cataloguing.

The books weren't shelved in alphabetical order. Mary Stewart shared space with Mary Higgins Clark and *Rebecca*. One could tell that some books were better than others, but here in the Gothic Nook all were equal.

The only way to find a specific title was to dive right in. As many covers resembled one another with a castle and a damsel-in-distress, I searched for the author's name, Wickersham. Eventually I found

The Edelweiss Lure, a novel of romantic suspense possibly published around the time of Holly's disappearance.

This cover was different, depicting a German cuckoo clock and a girl in a long pale yellow dress. She held a tan dog in so close an embrace it seemed as if she would never let her go. All three spun around in a whirlwind that held them in captivity.

The cover art suggested time travel. It would make a provocative painting.

Twenty-two

By the time I reached Dark Gables, the sky had darkened, and thunder rumbled high over my head. I didn't intend to stay long, only long enough to have my tea leaves read and convince Lucy to accompany me to Brent's house.

Sky was watching my approach from the window, and Lucy stood in the doorway. I tucked *The Edelweiss Lure* into my purse, grabbed the umbrella, and walked quickly up to the porch, well ahead of the first raindrops.

"My goodness," Lucy said. "You came out in the storm?"

"I was already out."

She scanned the sky. "Nonetheless, you'll stay till it blows over. Hurry inside."

Sky circled happily around my skirt, nudging me playfully, adding her invitation to Lucy's.

"I have a favor to ask you," I said. "Your participation in an afternoon of ghost chasing. Not today though," I added as a bolt of lightning zigzagged across the sky.

"That sounds intriguing. Let's have tea and you can tell me about it."

In the sun room, Lucy lit a crystal banker's lamp that sat on her desk and turned on the teakettle.

"What ghosts are we going to catch?" she asked.

"The spirit of Holly Wickersham. Maybe. She lived in Brent's new house a long time ago."

"Are you sure she's a spirit?"

"Pretty sure."

I took *The Edelweiss Lure* out my shoulder bag and watched Lucy study the clock, girl, and dog swirling through the air on the cover.

"So Holly Wickersham was an author. Have you read it?"

"Not yet. I will tonight. I found a box of other books, all the same. They must have come from the publisher."

Lucy nodded. "For promotion. What else did you find?"

"Probably everything that belonged to her. It was packed away and apparently forgotten."

"I assume that's why you think she's deceased."

"She must be."

"Do you think she's haunting the house?"

"I haven't seen anything ghostly. Haven't heard anything... Wait, that isn't true. There was a scratching sound and the terror you felt on the landing. And the collie in the pond. One time I heard a siren. I'm not sure that could be classified as ghostly."

"That's plenty," Lucy said. "You want me to go back to the house with you and see what else I can find or perhaps sense."

"If you would. Two searchers are better than one."

"We'll have to have Brent's permission," she reminded me.

"He'll give it. He may even offer to go with us. Will you come?"

The teakettle whistled. Sensing treats, Sky began to whine.

"I'd love to know more about a fellow author," she said. "Especially if she experienced a traumatic happening that keeps her earthbound. When shall we go?"

"Is tomorrow too soon?"

Lucy nodded in agreement. "The sooner the better. Before the place is overrun with contractors. They can be loud enough to scare the most desperate ghost away."

"I had the same thought."

~ * ~

After dinner that night, I settled in the rocker with a cup of hot chocolate and *The Edelweiss Lure*. The old paperback was all I had to show for an hour and a half of library research. This book with its unique cover seemed to call to me. Besides, it was a time travel, which was one of my favorite genres. I would read the other book another day.

Misty padded into the living room and lay at my feet, followed by Crane with the *Banner*. This, I reflected, was a perfect way to end the day, with a good dinner, a better dessert—apple pie—and quiet time without interruption.

I turned to the first chapter and started reading.

I woke to the ticking of a clock in the adjoining room, lay still, and listened. Where did that sound come from? Nothing in the living room was capable of ticking, except the ornate cuckoo clock that hadn't been working yesterday when I'd moved into the cottage. And even before that, according to the realtor.

"The clock comes with the house," she'd said. "It starts and stops at odd times, so you can think of it as a wall decoration. Or you could have it repaired."

"It's magnificent," I said. "I've never seen a cuckoo clock like it."

"Oh, it's different all right. There's a story attached to it. You can take it with a grain of salt." She paused, glancing at me as if seeking permission to continue. "The clock has to stay with the house. If it's moved, bad luck will follow."

"Bad luck for whom?" I asked.

"For the current tenant," she said. "That's you."

I believed she was having fun at my expense and changed the subject.

The clock seemed to be fine now, rhythmic beats like water dripping from a downspout. What had brought it to life this morning? Didn't someone first have to start the pendulum moving by hand? I might as well get up and see.

Heat pressed down on me as I swung out of the tangled sheets that had been clean and crisp seven hours ago. It was hot and muggy in the bedroom. The cottage had no air conditioning, only a small fan, but it was a house, snug and pretty with pale yellow siding and white trim. Best of all, it was mine for the summer. I crossed the small living room and stood in front of the clock. It was definitely working, its pendulum swinging languidly to and fro, the weights lower than they'd been last night.

~ * ~

"Is your book good?" Crane asked.

I looked up. "Well, I just started it. It's about a clock."

"Strange subject."

"A *haunted* clock," I added. "It's supposed to be a time travel, but it sounds more like a traditional ghost story."

"It's your kind of book then," he said.

"I think it will be."

He turned to another page of the *Banner*. "I'll let you get back to it."

~ * ~

I couldn't help but admire the clock's workmanship, even though it was too large and heavy for the wall, too imposing for the small space. Unlike the classic cuckoo clock adorned with branches and birds, it invoked images of the sea.

At the top a mermaid with streaming hair reclined on a rock. Sea shells and sea horses cascaded down the sides. At the base sat an ornate treasure chest. Delicate edelweiss flowers shone like white stars amid the aquatic decorations. The clock supposedly played "Edelweiss" on the hour, according to a square of faded paper on the side.

The clock was ticking, but the time was wrong. The hands, previously frozen at one-thirty, had been advancing slowly. I moved them to the right time, six forty-five. Now, in fifteen minutes, the cuckoo would emerge from its house, the miniature Bavarian figures would twirl on their pedestal, and I would hear music.

I wondered. By what magic had the clock suddenly start running?

~ * ~

I took a sip of hot chocolate. It was just right, but it wouldn't be for long if I let it set.

I would love to have a clock like that. But not one with a mind of its own. I already had a watch whose hands had run backward—until one day they stopped moving entirely. My timepiece had been found in the wildflower field on Huron Court, which says everything one needs to know about the object. I'd never understood its proclivity, but sometimes I wore the watch as a bracelet.

Perhaps Holly's heroine—whatever her name was—would have better luck with her cuckoo clock.

I turned back to my book as my cell phone started ringing. I considered ignoring the call but couldn't do that. There was too much going on in my life this summer, and all of it was important. I checked the caller ID. Sue Appleton.

"Were you watching the news?" she asked.

"No, reading."

"It'll be over now. The Sea-to-Sea man turned himself in this morning. He needed medical care."

"Did he say what he did with the missing dogs?"

"He claims they were all delivered to their new owners."

"That's a lie," I said.

"He also claims that a truck forced him off the road and drove away, leaving him trapped in his vehicle."

"It could have happened that way, but obviously he got away. What about the husky pup?"

"That he couldn't help him. The puppy was to have been delivered to a family in Ohio."

"That state trooper who took him home will sort it all out," I said.

"And in the meantime Kate Brennan will question him. There's something else," Sue added. "He says he doesn't have a partner. He works alone."

"Doesn't he realize that people saw his website? It clearly stated that Sea-to-Sea had two owners."

"He'll be a tough nut to crack," Sue said.

Her comparison made me feel like laughing, although there was nothing humorous about what the man had done.

"Where is he now?" I asked.

"Still in the hospital."

"Let him stay there till he answers our questions truthfully," I said.

"You mean Kate's questions."

"Of course. He has to pay for all the grief he's caused and give the dogs back to their owners."

"If he can," Sue said.

Twenty-three

I set *The Edelweiss Lure* aside and let it slide to the back of my mind but only for the moment. I didn't intend to procrastinate indefinitely on the off chance that Holly might have left a clue to her fate or even her frame of mind in her book. Writers did that sometimes, I believe.

I'd already studied her calendar, reliving her year month by month...until August when she stopped making notations. It was similar to my own with appointments, reminders of engagements, and occasional comments about the weather with which she seemed to be obsessed.

She also kept track of her writing progress. For example, she completed a science-fiction short story on the first of May. In mid-June she started a new book. She also noted the receipt of a contract and the notification of an award.

The mention of 'Lorin' to whom she'd dedicated both of her books didn't help as she hadn't included a last name. I stashed the calendar in my desk drawer for possible future reference and resolved to look through the old trunk for a more promising source of information.

I didn't have time to spare in the next few days. The people most affected by the Sea-to-Sea scam kept me busy talking on the phone. It seemed to ring constantly. Lyle wanted to know if I possessed any inside information; Helena invited me to meet her for coffee and a strategy session; Sue kept me in the loop and Lyle, on still another call, wanted all of us who had been victimized by Sea-to-Sea Transport to get together again.

"There's strength in numbers," he said. "All of us together, we can take him down. What does the jerk call himself?"

"Duncan O'Meara," I said.

"That's a fake name. I saw his picture on the news. He isn't the man I dealt with."

Nobody, least of all Kate, believed that Duncan O'Meara was a new hire under the impression that Sea-to-Sea was a legitimate company. Still, no one contradicted him. No one corroborated his version of events either.

"He's going to walk free," I said, "possibly with the proverbial slap on the wrist."

"One way or the other, that's not going to happen," Lyle said.

Recalling Lyle's passion for carrying arms, I knew what he meant. I'd cautioned him once about his threatening stance, but obviously he planned to go on his merry way with his gun beneath his vest.

Helena was deeply disappointed. "It isn't that I thought Arden would be in that van, but I counted on the man talking, if only to save his neck."

"Oh, he's talking. He's just not saying what we want to hear."

"What does your husband think?" she asked.

"You understand that Crane is all for law and order. He's pretty sure Duncan, or whatever his name is, will slip through the cracks. Sometimes it happens."

"Where does that leave me and the others?"

"Last night on her segment Kate said one of the victims identified Duncan as the company's owner," I said. "Well, the person is ninety percent sure, which leaves room for doubt. Lyle says it was another man who picked up his dogs."

"Even with the van turning up, we're back at Square One," Helena said. "Are you going to the get-together?"

"I'll be there."

"I'm hosting this time. On Friday at seven."

"Would you like me to bring something?" I asked.

"I have it covered... Oh, wait, with that gang, we can always use more cookies."

I jotted down directions to Helena's house. "I hope something turns up by then," I said in parting.

My seldom heard inner voice chimed in, *Don't count on it.*

~ * ~

Once again we waited for Sea-to-Sea Transport to make a move. Duncan O'Meara was released from the hospital and promptly dropped out of sight. I imagined the company would lie low for a while and perhaps change their method of operation. They must have another van and would certainly choose a different name.

But would they repeat the pet transport scam? Not if they were smart.

Kate's audience was now aware of them. Dog owners would be leery of all transport services in the future. That was unfortunate, as some companies were honest and the service they offered was helpful.

Still, none of this brought the stolen dogs home.

With the Sea-to-Sea mystery in Kate's hands, Lucy and I turned our attention to what Lucy called "the haunting of Holly Wickersham."

"That's a great title for a book," Lucy said.

"I agree. Do you think you'll use it?"

"I may. But I'd like to solve the mysteries first."

Seized by the imp of the perverse, I imagined how surprised we all would be if it turned out that Holly was alive. But what woman would leave all her belongings behind?

Before moving on to the house, Lucy wanted to see the restored pond in all its glory. We stood at the rock border enjoying the beauty of that well-shaded part of the property. New plants flourished in the rock garden, and the freshly-painted flamingoes overlooked the clear water. It seemed impossible that once a strange collie had supplanted Misty's reflection in its surface.

"I don't think any otherworldly creature lurks in the pond," Lucy said, "but there's something that never left. It's been here for a long time. It's a feeling. Very faint."

"Like the feeling on the landing?" I asked.

"Not exactly. I sense loss and sadness."

As we made our way through overgrown grasses to the house, I said, "How common do you think it is for a person to leave her emotions behind when she passes from this life?"

"Not very, I'd say. Perhaps if her passing were violent. What is uncommon is for somebody to be aware of them."

"Somebody like you," I pointed out.

"Or you," Lucy said. "You've sensed things and heard sounds."

I had. The scratching that Annica said was a giant rat. And the siren that cut off in mid-wail. Neither Brent nor Annica had been aware of it. I assumed it was part of the ghostly trappings.

"I hope the ghostly sounds will be gone by the time Brent is ready to open his shelter," Lucy said.

That would be ideal, but we didn't have much time to accomplish that.

Brent had promised to meet us at the house after he interviewed a new applicant for the caretaker position.

"When he gets here, we can go up to the attic again," I said.

"An old attic—yes. That mystery story staple."

"All of Holly's possessions were dumped up there," I said. "I'm sure we'll find something else."

~ * ~

Lucy stopped on the landing and recoiled as if someone had shoved her. She grabbed at the wall for balance. I steadied her.

"What's wrong?"

"Some force." Her breath came in gasps. "I felt somebody push me and..." She held onto the railing and sat on the closest step. "There's darkness and confusion. Motion. Things are flying around the house."

"How can you tell?" I asked. "We're on the stairs."

"I can see it in my mind's eye. For just a moment, I felt like I was falling."

"Sit here for a while," I said. "I'll make you a cup of tea or…" I recalled I wasn't at home but in Brent's house on Loosestrife Lane. "Coffee maybe," I added, thinking of the coffee maker in the kitchen.

"The images are beginning to fade," Lucy said. "They're fuzzy."

I'd rarely seen her so shaken.

She described the experience again, the eerie sensation of being shoved into a maelstrom of hard objects, of losing control, and of being a little nauseous.

"It was so real."

I may have heard scratching and a siren, but at present everything in my environment was stable. Except…

The stained glass window. Were the colors running? Was it— melting? I looked again. No, it was intact with the sun turning the multi-colored panes to rare jewels. Everything was still and quiet.

The power of suggestion? The calm before the storm?

"Let's get away from this landing," I said.

Twenty-four

I sat at the table in the kitchen sipping tepid coffee and listening to Lucy rehash her experience on the landing. She hadn't touched her own coffee, but she appeared calmer. An anonymous benefactor—Brent?—had left a box of jelly doughnuts from the Hometown Bakery on the counter.

Now that we all made sure the back door was locked, food had stopped disappearing.

"Strawberry," Lucy said. "My favorite. This will go a long way toward restoring normalcy. Whatever happened on that landing was too intense to fade away with time," she added. "On the contrary. It's growing stronger."

"You'd think the whole house would be affected."

As a drop of strawberry jelly escaped from the doughnut, Lucy reached for the napkins. "What happened was like the cover of Holly's book with leaves, a girl, and a dog all caught up in a whirlwind. It left me with the kind of sensation you sometimes experience when you ride in an elevator."

"You spoke of furniture flying through the air," I reminded her.

"That's what I saw. But what happened—really? Will we ever know?"

"I hope so."

I took a few more sips of coffee, the last few drops in the cup. Ordinarily I'd never drink coffee that cooled so drastically, but my throat was dry. From trauma, I suspected. Nothing in my world had flown out of its appointed place, but in a way I had shared Lucy's experience.

"Brent's house is haunted," I said. "There's no doubt about it."

"But not necessarily by a traditional spirit. At least I didn't see an entity wandering through the rooms."

"Because she isn't dead?"

"I can't say. Perhaps we'll know some day."

"Then why can't you pass the landing without being trapped in an upheaval from yesteryear?" I asked.

"That's what I have to find out," Lucy said.

"You'll have to pass the landing en route to the attic."

Lucy sighed. "I'm not quite ready for a repeat performance, Jennet. I'm just now feeling grounded."

I started as I heard a commotion in the living room: A stomping of boots on hardwood, a ping of an object falling to the floor, a loud curse. Brent had arrived.

"Where is everybody?" he called. "Lucy? Jennet?"

"In the kitchen," Lucy said.

He came in, jingling his house key. "Are you girls through exploring?"

"We never started," I said.

He made a show of consulting his watch. "What have you been doing all this time?"

"Lucy sensed something on the landing," I said. "She's been recovering. I've been monitoring her progress."

"What's this about the landing?"

"You know what I believe about certain events imprinting themselves on the walls of a house and echoing through the ages?" Lucy said.

He frowned. "Maybe. Tell me again."

She did.

"That's weird," he said. "If something bad happens, you want it to be over and done with. Not to happen over and over again."

"Not everyone will be aware of it," Lucy pointed out. "Something frightening took place on that landing—who knows how long ago?"

"What can happen on a landing?" Brent asked. "It's so small."

"Anything," I said. "Like murder. We haven't scratched the surface of the psychic activity in this house yet."

"Then hurry the investigation along. Next week the kitchen renovation is scheduled to start, and before next month, I want to move my senior collies into the house."

"Did you find your caretaker yet?" I asked.

"I think so. It's a nice couple, the Ralstons, who lost their own collie a few months ago. They think they're too old to raise another puppy. Turns out they haven't had any luck finding a rescue, not even from Sue Appleton. My job is ideal for them. They'll sell their house and have a nest egg for their future."

"That's good," I said.

"Except..." Lucy corralled the crumbs and powdered sugar onto her napkin. She paused, frowning.

"Except what, Lucy?" Brent asked.

"Don't you want to start with a clean slate?"

"What do you mean?"

"Without any leftover shadows to cause difficulties."

"What could they do?"

"Who knows? A severe fright could give an older person a heart attack. A fall down the stairs could kill somebody. Luckily Jennet was with me earlier or I might have been hurt when I lost my balance."

"I'm not saying you're wrong about something bad hanging around the place, but I never saw anything out of the ordinary," Brent said. "And Jennet, no one else ever saw a dog's reflection in the pond, before or after I had it cleaned."

That ghastly reflection. It seemed to have happened a long time ago and had only occurred twice. Still, I wasn't ready to assign it to imagination.

"Don't you believe us?" I asked.

"Sure, but I can't abandon my project at this stage. I don't want to. I'm keeping six senior collies at the barn just waiting to move them to the house. Now that I found the caretakers, it's all coming together."

"So you're going ahead, no matter what?"

"Maybe I'll get a priest to bless the house," he said. "Would that help, do you think?"

"It couldn't hurt."

Lucy stood and took our cups to the sink to rinse. "Then we have to solve the mystery quickly."

"Do you still want to go back up to the attic today, Jennet?" Brent asked.

"Yes. Now more than ever."

"Lucy?"

"If I could get there without setting foot on the landing... If I could fly across it..."

"I can carry you."

"Thanks, but I think I'll stay downstairs and make more coffee. You and Jennet go ahead. Jennet won't be in danger."

I nodded. "I'll be all right, and we have to explore every avenue. Let's go."

~ * ~

Oddly enough, the old attic appeared to welcome us, even while the house below didn't. I took Brent's hand and stepped up onto the uneven floorboards. Why did builders take such care when constructing a house and leave the attic floor, walls and ceiling unfinished?

The chill that permeated the stale air was perhaps a bit less unpleasant today, and it seemed that more light filtered through the small windows. But this was our second foray into the uppermost story of the house. The thrill of first discovery was over. It was time to focus: on Holly, on her memorabilia, on a clue to her fate. Any clue.

"I'd like to go through the trunk again," I said.

Brent pulled a book of stickers out of his pocket. "I'm going to tag the furniture I want moved downstairs. Be careful. Watch where you walk."

"I will."

I opened the trunk and began to shift through the material stuffed inside. Paid bills tied together with string, an address book with a smudged cover—I set that aside—pages torn from a magazine on a variety of unusual subjects, probably story ideas for a dry spell, and greeting cards for every conceivable occasion. Did she never throw a card away?

Brent called from the northernmost corner. "Here's a small piano. How did they get it up in the attic?"

"Is it a spinet?" I asked.

"I don't know what a spinet is. So, maybe yes. It could be a kid's toy, too."

"Does it play?"

He struck a note, then a whole chord, then another. A shiver cut through me. The resulting melody, developed from keys played at random, sounded like a refrain from a macabre tune.

"I don't think a piano would add to the quality of a collie's life," I said.

"Not true. Some of the collies at the barn like music. A couple of them watch TV. Ray brought Lassie videos in for them."

"Mmm."

I stopped listening. At the bottom of the truck, under a folded patchwork quilt, I saw an album. As I lifted it, a photograph fell out. I picked up a picture of a man and woman standing on a beach. The man was tall and fair-haired, and handsome with rugged features and a half smile. The woman about a foot shorter, had dark hair blowing in the wind.

The woman was Holly Wickersham.

Twenty-five

"Brent, come look at this," I said.

He clomped his way across the boards. "What did you find?"

"A picture of a man and woman. It's Holly. I recognized her from the photo on her books."

Brent shone the flashlight on the photograph. "She was pretty, wasn't she? Who's the man?"

I turned the photo over and saw the date on the back written in faded ink—July, 1987, and beneath it, neatly written: Me and Micah.

"Is that Sagramore Beach?" Brent asked.

"It could be. Or it could be any lake, any beach, I suppose. She didn't paste the picture in the album, and it fell out."

"Then, after Holly vanished, someone threw it in the trunk with the rest of her things and took the trunk to the attic."

"I guess that's what happened."

I remembered the tiny gold reinforcement I'd found in the furnished bedroom. Holly must have kept the album in that room, but I couldn't explain why this one picture was separate from the others.

She looked happy, I thought. Or rather she was smiling. Don't people usually smile when they're having their picture taken, no matter what their true feelings are? And the tall, blond man—was this the only picture of him? He must have been important to Holly at one time.

"They're not wearing swim suits or sports clothes," Brent pointed out.

I'd noticed that. Holly wore a white sundress with a gold cross on a chain. Her companion was dressed in tan slacks and a blue-striped shirt.

"It looks like they were at the lake, say at a lakeside restaurant, and wanted their picture taken," I said.

"There's no restaurant anywhere near Sagramore Lake."

"It was taken at another lake then. I'll check out the other photos in the album."

"Another guy to look for," Brent said.

"This could be the breakthrough we're waiting for."

"What else do you want to take out of the attic?" he asked.

"For now, just this. Can we come back?"

"If we do it soon."

"I don't see how our being here will disturb your contractors," I said. "They'll be working in the kitchen."

"It won't. But Lucy may be right. If there's anything harmful in the house, we should get rid of it before I bring the collies to their new home."

"I don't think we can solve a mystery in an artificial timeline," I said.

"You can try, and we'll take it from there."

He picked up the album and address book; I held on to the picture.

"Let's see how Lucy's doing," I said.

~ * ~

She didn't look very happy. "I decided I have to return to that landing again. How else will I know what's going on?"

"That's the best way," I said, "and don't worry. We'll both be with you."

"I won't do it today, though," she added.

I was happy to wait for another day. It seemed as if I had spent an inordinate amount of time in Brent's house. With work to do at home and dogs to take care of, I felt a little guilty.

"Did you make more coffee, Lucy?" Brent asked.

"There's some for you and Jennet." She pointed languidly to the stove, and the Zodiac charms on her bracelet jangled. "I don't want anymore."

I showed Lucy the picture while Brent poured two cups of coffee.

"Jennet found a photo album and an address book, too," he said.

Lucy brightened. "Then maybe we can trace the man. That's assuming he's still alive." She held on to the picture for a moment. "He looks familiar."

"Do you think you might have met him?" I asked.

"It's possible, but more likely I saw him at one of my book signings. He's attractive, and with that height, he'd stand out."

"That won't help us trace him," I said.

"No, but if you find him, he can't deny he knew Holly. You have the proof right here," Brent pointed out.

"Why would he deny knowing her?"

Lucy turned the picture over and over again. "It feels just like paper. At times I can see more than is there."

"Come again?" Brent said.

"When I handle something that belonged to a person, sometimes I can sense something about her. Not this time, though."

I studied the picture. "It looks like a stormy day," I said.

Brent peered over my shoulder. "How can you tell?"

"Elementary," I said. "Because of all the clouds."

"It wasn't a good beach day, then."

"It was another summer," Lucy said.

"Well, sure it was. She wrote the date on the picture." Brent looked puzzled. "Or is that a special Lucy comment?"

"It was just a random thought that came into my mind."

She didn't say anything more.

~ * ~

At home I looked through the album but didn't find another photo of the man on the beach. Holly had taken pictures of the house, of banks of tall pink loosestrife, and of the pond before it deteriorated into a sodden mess. Purple pansies bloomed in the rock garden, and the flamingoes stood closer to the pond's edge than they were now.

Apparently there was no one around to take pictures of Holly.

I imagined that at the time she was new to the house on Loosestrife Lane, perhaps a summer tenant whose belongings, unclaimed, had been stored in the attic to make way for the next resident. But I had high hopes for the address book, and soon after I opened it, I found an entry for Micah Frost in Maple Falls and an address.

What were the chances Micah Frost still lived in Maple Falls and had the same phone number? How unlikely it would be if this number were still in service? It would be fun to dial it. And say what?

I'm investigating paranormal activity in an old Victorian house on Loosestrife Lane in Foxglove Corners. Did you ever know a writer named Holly Wickersham? I think she may haunt the place.

If by remote chance Micah answered his phone, he'd no doubt hang up on me thinking a lunatic had dialed his number.

When I first came to Foxglove Corners, I thought nothing of taking a day trip up north. I was single then. I didn't have a husband and seven dogs to feed. My life had since changed. A three or four hour drive was doable, but I would have to make arrangements ahead of time.

Okay. I'd make those arrangements. But where to start?

I kept coming back to the picture of Micah. With his good looks and slightly old-fashioned air, he looked like a man to whom any girl would be attracted, especially one who created dashing heroes for her living.

Micah Frost was definitely a man to investigate.

Twenty-six

By the time I dialed Micah Frost's number I had my introduction in place, even though I hadn't had a chance to use it yet:

I'm trying to contact Michigan author Holly Wickersham and believe that you knew her at one time.

(Three decades ago.)

Then the ball would be in his court.

I had added to my information by searching the Internet. I'd discovered that Micah Frost owned a camping supplies store in Maple Falls. It sounded prosperous, judging by an elaborate website ad and a half dozen glowing reviews. He had a different phone number.

When I called, he was out to lunch. I said I'd like to speak to him about a personal matter and would call again. I'd given the collies their noon meal but hadn't realized I was hungry as well. The thrill of the quest, an elusive man from Holly's past, had driven hunger temporarily out of my mind. I sensed that I was on the brink of a discovery, that my luck was about to turn.

Of course Micah might say he didn't remember Holly, implying that she was one of his many girlfriends over the years. But Holly wasn't just any girlfriend. She was a published author who had enjoyed a modicum of fame. For that reason alone, she should stand out in his memory.

Unless she was indeed one of many, and that snapshot of Holly and Micah at the beach captured a one-time encounter.

But what was the point of idle speculation? With luck, I would soon know.

Look on the bright side, I told myself. Micah Frost might lead me to Holly. I ate a quick lunch and called again. He hadn't returned yet. Apparently the owner of the store could take long lunch breaks.

The clerk who answered the phone offered to have Mr. Frost call me.

"I'll try later." I sensed that I wasn't going to make contact with Micah Frost today. Or perhaps he was there but avoiding anyone who claimed to have personal business with him.

Maple Falls was located up north in the Lower Peninsula, near Lake Huron. We could drive there in a day and be back home before dark. I'd ask Annica to go with me.

I didn't reach him until the following morning.

"Frost Sports Center." He had a deep voice, clipped and not particularly friendly.

I told him my name and recited my set piece.

"Holly Wickersham," he said after a moment. "You're going a long way back. I haven't heard that name in ages."

"You knew her then," I said.

"I did. May I ask what business you have with Holly?"

Here I had to be careful. I couldn't launch into a wild tale of hauntings in an old house and of feelings that refused to die. Even though it was true.

"My friend purchased a house in Foxglove Corners where Holly once lived. She left some personal possessions behind. I assume she'd like to have them."

"What does that have to do with me?" he asked.

I'd have thought that was obvious.

"I'm looking for people who knew her." I might as well give him a grain of truth. "One of the items was her address book which is where I found your name."

I thought it best not to mention the picture.

"Holly is dead," he said. "Obviously she won't be needing an address book."

In a way I'd expected that. Still, it came as a shock, a sense of loss for a woman I'd never met.

"I hate to throw her belongings away," I said, adding, "My friend has plans for the house. He wants everything cleared out of it."

After a pause that lasted a bit too long, Micah said, "There's nothing stopping him. If he doesn't want to throw Holly's stuff out, he can donate it to a charity. Does that help?"

His question held an air of finality. I couldn't let the conversation end here.

"Did she have a next of kin?" I asked.

"One."

"Could you tell me his name? I'd like to contact him. Or her."

"Look," he said. "I can't talk about this over the phone. Can you stop by the store sometime?"

"Sure. Any special time?"

"On Friday. We close early. I can give you about a half hour."

"That'll be great. I'll bring a friend with me," I added.

There was another pause. "The new homeowner?"

"Someone else," I said.

~ * ~

The someone else nodded her head vigorously, setting her wind chime earrings to ringing. I'd just asked her if she'd accompany me on a little day trip.

"You bet," she said. "Where? When?"

That was Annica. She could detect my inner excitement and wanted to play a part in the coming adventure even before knowing what it might involve. She slid into the booth opposite me and picked up her lime cooler.

"Nothing tastes better on a hot day," she murmured. "Tell me. Where are we going?"

"I plan to drive up north to Maple Falls on Friday," I said. "I have a lead on Holly Wickersham."

"The lady who left her emotions in the walls of Brent's new house?"

"No, but a possible friend of hers. I found his picture with Holly in the trunk."

I summarized my conversation with Micah Frost. "He said Holly's dead."

"Well, she'd have to be if she haunts the house, wouldn't she?"

"Yes, I guess so."

But... An idea I'd had earlier resurfaced. What if she wasn't? Could she still leave her feelings of terror trapped in the walls of a house? I'd asked Lucy about that once, but she hadn't given me a definitive answer. She didn't know.

"What are we looking for?" Annica asked.

"Any information about Holly Wickersham that can help us understand the phenomena at the house," I said. "So far Micah Frost is our only connection to her."

"Why do you think he didn't want to talk about her on the phone?"

"I suspect there's something about the matter that isn't generally known."

"Secrets! Ah."

She sipped her drink and gazed across Crispian Road at the woods with their green sparkle in the sunlight. The woods were forever, green in the summer, ablaze with color in the fall, gaunt and draped in snow in the winter. This mystery might be forever, too, if we didn't take steps to solve it.

"Crane is okay with my leaving for the day if I don't go alone," I said, "and Camille will take care of the dogs."

"I'll have to ask Mary Jeanne for time off, but she won't object. Business has been slow."

"It's all set then."

She turned away from the window, her expression suddenly grim. "Brent said Lucy had a traumatic experience on the landing. She doesn't want to set foot in that part of the house again. What exactly happened?"

"I'm not sure if I can explain it," I said. "She felt that somebody shoved her. She might have fallen down the stairs if I hadn't been there. Then she talked about furniture moving through the air and herself spinning around with it."

"Like clothes in a dryer?"

"Something like that."

Annica set her spoon spinning through what was left of her drink. "Like that. Weird. Do you think we could be dealing with an evil spirit?"

"At this point, I don't know. I've been thinking of Holly Wickersham as a victim."

Possibly as a woman who had been slain, whose murder had been covered up, all traces of her existence erased. For some reason.

"But you don't know," Annica said.

"No." I drained my glass, not wanting to waste a single drop. The trouble with Clovers' lime coolers was that they didn't last long enough.

"But let's hope Micah Frost does."

Twenty-seven

We stood in front of Frost's Outfitters on Main Street within walking distance of Lake Huron. Surprisingly it was almost as warm in Maple Falls as it had been this morning in Foxglove Corners when we'd set out on our trip. I brushed my bangs off my forehead; they were damp. Feeling crumpled and not at my best, I surveyed our destination.

The store stood close to an imposing blue Victorian house at which point elegant private residences in pastel colors gave gradual way to businesses. Micah Frost's window display was a clever re-creation of a well-equipped campsite over which an oversized black bear, a marvel of taxidermy, loomed in a menacing manner.

"Surely they're not that big." Annica patted down her long denim skirt which had acquired a sheen of wrinkles as we made our way up to the North Country. "Just the thought of bears would discourage me from camping—ever."

"I guess that's why they sell shotguns and rifles here," I said. "For me it's snakes. I couldn't close my eyes if I thought snakes were slithering past my tent."

"Well, no one ever accused us of being outdoor girls." She moved closer to the window. "Do you think that was a live bear once or a statue in a fur coat?"

"It's hard to tell. I'd say it was live, but you can ask."

"Uh, no. I'd sound like a jerk."

"I'll sound like one when I start talking about haunted houses."

Fortunately we weren't at Micah Frost's store under false pretenses because we would never fool anyone if we pretended to be shopping for camping supplies. Micah knew what we wanted; he was expecting us. Now that we were in Maple Falls, I anticipated great developments to grow out of our meeting. I would be disappointed if we didn't learn anything new.

A quick glance at my watch told me we were a half hour early, which was somewhat a miracle, considering all the road construction we'd encountered on the way.

"We might as well go in." I pushed the door open and stepped into a blast of cold air and aisles filled with sporting goods in neutral, uninspired colors. I didn't see any customers, then remembered the store's three o'clock closing time.

Micah Frost was waiting for us, possibly having watched through the window as we gazed at his display. Strangely, he hadn't changed much from the day all those years ago when he posed on the beach beside Holly except for fine lines around his eyes and mouth. His hair had more gray in it than blond and the color of his eyes were the clear blue of a summer sky. Ironically, he wore the same kind of shirt, blue and white striped with sleeves rolled up to his elbows.

I stepped forward. He held out his hand. "You must be Jennet Ferguson and this is…"

"My friend, Annica."

"Come into my office." He led us to the back of the store and ushered us through a half-open door. "Have a seat. Care for some coffee?"

"None for me," Annica said.

"I'd like a cup if it's no trouble," I said, suddenly aware of a dryness in my mouth accompanied by a stab of uncertainty. Would this meeting lead to a solution of the Holly Wickersham mystery?

I looked around the office trying to form an impression of Micah Frost. His office was small with a large desk and three plain chairs. There was clutter everywhere and a coffee machine on a small table near a window. On the walls, deer, bear, and wolf heads, stuffed and mounted, looked pathetic with their unseeing eyes.

He poured two cups of coffee and seated himself behind the desk. "After we talked, I got to thinking," he said. "How did you ladies get involved in a house downstate? In Foxglove Corners, is it?"

He fixed his gaze on Annica. She cleared her throat and glanced at me. We'd agreed that I would lead the conversation.

"We live in Foxglove Corners," I said. "A good friend of ours bought a house on Loosestrife Lane. In the course of preparing it for occupancy, we discovered Holly Wickersham's possessions in the attic, including boxes of her published books."

"You've come a long way for this meeting," he said.

"It's important."

"I'm surprised anything of Holly's is still there. Now, how can I help you?"

"You could give me the name of Holly's next of kin. I don't want to make the decision to discard her belongings if there's someone who'd like to have them."

"There's a cousin, Jane Wickersham." Obviously prepared for our visit, he pulled a slip of paper from under his blotter. "I don't know if this address is current."

I glanced at it and slipped it into my shoulder bag. Holly's cousin had once lived in Maple Creek which was closer to us than Maple Falls. I hoped she was still there.

"Is there anything else you want to know?" he asked.

Realizing it was too early for ghost talk, I said, "Were you and Holly good friends?"

"Fairly good."

"You must know how she died then."

"No one does for sure," he said, "but it was assumed she died in the tornado."

"Tornado?"

Grim memories of my own experience in the Oakpoint tornado rolled over me. The darkness, the siren, the terrifying sound of a hundred trains barreling down on me, holding fast to Halley while the giant poplar tree in my backyard crashed into my house.

A puzzle piece slipped smoothly into place: Lucy's sensation of spinning around in the air with the furniture. She had been caught up in a remembered funnel.

"Foxglove Corners took a direct hit," he said. "In the aftermath, Holly went missing. They thought she was away from home when the siren went off. They never found her body," he added, "and they never found her."

I hadn't known that Foxglove Corners had experienced a tornado. With an effort, I found my voice. "Was Holly declared legally dead?"

"Possibly. I don't know for certain."

"Then she could still be alive," Annica said.

Micah stared at Annica. "It's hardly likely. Nobody ever saw her or heard from her after that day. Her dog disappeared too. Two other people were killed."

"She had a dog?" I asked.

"A collie. She gave him a fancy name. Something medieval sounding. Oh, yes. Tristan."

Something of the collie, Tristan, lived on in the fish pond. It had stared up at Misty as she'd looked down into the water. But I didn't want to bring the phantom dog into an already difficult conversation.

I said, "Didn't anyone search for her?"

"Of course. The police investigated. They had an idea that she might have met with foul play."

Foul play covering a multitude of violent acts, perhaps committed with the knowledge that the storm could easily take the blame for a random murder.

"Why did they think that?" I asked.

"It was Jane Wickersham's insane idea totally based on the plot of one of Holly's books. They took it seriously."

"Which book?"

"I don't remember. The idea was way out in left field, anyway, something about a murder that took place during a tornado. They said I was the last person to see Holly alive, and there was that incriminating book, so I was questioned.

"Did they think you killed her?" Annica asked.

"I was exonerated," Micah said, "and you can understand why I don't care to relive those days. Don't let this story go any further."

"This is for my own information," I assured him.

But at the time there must have been stories about a missing woman in the newspapers and almost certainly news about possible suspects. I could see myself spending more time on research.

"Now you know where to inquire about Holly's belongings," he said.

"Huh? Oh, yes."

He started to rise. "Well, if that's all…"

It wasn't. Remembering the mysteries that swirled around the house on Loosestrife Lane, I said, "No," too quickly, too forcefully.

He frowned. "Is there something else?"

"Some people think Holly's spirit haunts the house," I said. "That she never left it. Or that she came back."

He suppressed a laugh. "Holly Wickersham a ghost? That's pure nonsense."

"That's Foxglove Corners," Annica said.

"What?"

"Our little town has an occasional ghost story associated with it," I said.

"We call it Halloween Town," Annica added.

"Holly wrote about ghosts, but she was a hundred percent down-to-earth. Did someone actually see her floating around in a white sheet?"

I smiled at his naïve image of a haunting spirit. "Not that I know of."

It was easier to say that than to explain about Lucy's trauma on the landing or the unnerving scratching sound. Or the phantom collie in the pond, whose name I now knew.

"But it's not beyond the realm of possibility," I said.

Micah *did* rise this time and walked to the door, not bothering to mask his amusement. "I think we're finished here, Mrs. Ferguson. Have a safe trip home to your Halloween town."

All we could do was thank him for his time and leave.

Twenty-eight

"He seemed nice," I said.

Annica nodded. "Not bad looking for an old man."

"But I don't like him. That condescending jab about Halloween Town. I'm not sure he's trustworthy."

"Because of that?"

"No, because I have a feeling he was holding something back. What if he did kill Holly?"

"Then he wouldn't have told us how she died or that the police questioned him. He wouldn't have agreed to talk to us at all."

"I'm not sure. It was a good way to throw us off the trail. If we investigated, we'd find out the police didn't think he was guilty."

I turned on the air conditioning and drove away from Frost's store. We had decided to stop for a late lunch before embarking on the long drive home.

"I wish I'd asked him why they thought he killed Holly," I said.

"Ah yes, the motive. It's missing. Why would a man kill his girlfriend? I can think of lots of reasons."

"He didn't say she was his girlfriend," I pointed out.

"I noticed that."

I spied a small picturesque restaurant ahead and slowed down. *Open 24 Hours,* proclaimed a sign.

"Let's stop here," Annica said. "I'm starving."

I was hungry, too, and I didn't have to make dinner tonight. Crane was bringing a pizza home, and Camille had promised us one of her fresh peach pies. Hurrying inside, we found a booth and ordered fried perch with French fries and iced tea. Annica selected a cloverleaf roll from the breadbox to nibble on, and we returned to discussing our visit with Micah Frost.

"I can't wait to read the book Micah talked about," I said. "I hope it's one of the two I have."

If it wasn't, I'd have to search for it and hope a copy existed somewhere.

"I think it's too much of a coincidence that Holly wrote about something that ended up happening to her in real life," Annica said.

"They say life imitates art. Or is it art imitates life?" I shook my head, attempting to dislodge the mental block, deciding it wasn't important. "I agree, unless she wrote the book to leave a clue."

"What author does that? And why? She'd have to have anticipated her murder and known her killer."

"I guess it isn't possible, unless she planned to disappear in the tornado."

That also seemed unlikely. Would anyone wait on a tornado warning to drop out of sight?

"We have all sorts of additions to our mystery," I said, "along with another person to find, the cousin who believed Holly was murdered. I'm glad we came here today."

Our lunch arrived, and we fell quiet, enjoying our first full meal of the day. As I ate, bits and pieces of our conversation with Micah Frost replayed in my mind, occasionally overshadowed by images of the tornado I'd survived.

I thought about Lucy, affected by the emotions that lived on in the walls of Brent's house and imagined Holly, alerted to worsening weather, frozen in terror on the landing, looking through the stained glass window as the tornado swirled closer on its path of death and destruction.

What could she see through the rainbow explosion of color? Would she make it to the basement before the tornado touched down? And where was her collie?

I finished eating before Annica, not looking forward to being on the road again, yet longing for home.

East, west, home is best, I thought.

~ * ~

Home was Crane waiting for me in our green Victorian farmhouse, a pizza staying warm in the oven, and seven collies falling over themselves to welcome me back to the fold.

I'd dropped Annica off and barely kept my eyes open as I drove the last miles to Jonquil Lane. A dose of fresh air and being home revived me.

The dogs had a grievance to air. I'd been gone too long. So long they were afraid I wasn't coming back. They converged on me in an extravaganza of wagging tails, playful nips

And yips. At one point Candy backed into me, sending me into Crane's arms. That was fine with me. I stayed there for a few extra minutes.

"Did you have a successful trip?" Crane asked when our greetings were completed.

"An interesting one. I learned how Holly Wickersham died and found out the name of her cousin. I'll tell you about it later."

"Are you hungry?"

"A little." Our late lunch at the restaurant was hours away. Crane took the pizza out of the oven. The table was already set, and I spied Camille's peach pie set far back on the counter out of the collies' reach. He brought two bottles out of the refrigerator. I bit into the pizza, trying to ignore the seven pairs of collie eyes fixed on my dinner.

"I watched *Kate-in-Your-Corner* for you tonight," Crane said.

I looked up, pizza momentarily forgotten. "What did I miss?"

"One of the missing dogs is home. A man who's been following the story saw a picture of his new German shepherd on TV and contacted

Kate. The dog was supposed to have gone to a man in Florida, but after this trouble, the owner changed his mind. O'Meara sold the dog for fifteen hundred dollars with a fake registration and collected nine hundred for his transport."

"So that's O'Meara's game. He gets paid to transport a dog, then sells the dog to someone else and collects more money. Did they catch him?"

"He's lying low."

"There's hope for all the missing dogs then. Helena may have her Arden back."

"O'Meara picked up and sold the shepherd to a man in Michigan. Maybe Arden is closer than we thought."

I'd have to call Helena in case she hadn't watched the segment. Helena... I glanced at the calendar hanging on the wall in my view. "Oh, darn, darn, darn!"

"What?"

"The meeting tomorrow at Helena's. I forgot all about it."

"Well, it wasn't tonight."

"Thank heavens for that. I'd be extremely unpopular if I missed it. Oh, and I promised to bake cookies."

"I don't see what the problem is," he said.

"Just that I wanted to do some research on Holly Wickersham tomorrow."

While I finished my pizza, I told Crane about the Foxglove Corners tornado and the suspicions surrounding Holly's disappearance.

"And I have to track down one of her books that may contain a lead. It's out of print, so it may not be easy. Apparently the plot was provocative enough to convince Holly's cousin, Jane Wickersham, that she had been murdered."

"You'll do it all," Crane said. "I have faith in you." He covered my hand with his. "Just do it from home. We all missed you."

"If possible. I won't go up to Maple Falls again, but Holly's cousin lived in Maple Creek. That's closer to home."

I set about tearing crust off the uneaten pizza. The dogs moved even closer to me. This was what they had been waiting for.

Crane said, "This man you saw in Maple Falls, Micah Frost, do you think he's a killer?"

"There's a chance he could be. The police didn't think so. No one knows for sure if Holly is dead or alive."

"Nothing is more dangerous than a man who's gotten away with murder for years. He won't like you and Annica raking up the past."

I sensed that Crane was on the verge of warning me to be careful, or perhaps of suggesting that I abandon the mystery of Holly Wickersham. Quickly, I said, "We won't see him again. The only danger might be for Lucy reliving an old traumatic experience that wasn't even hers, and I don't think she'll go to Brent's house again."

That wasn't the whole story, of course, but why borrow trouble? It was counter-productive to worry about something that might never happen. In the meantime, we had a bona fide villain to apprehend.

Twenty-nine

Everyone at the meeting had heard the story of the recovered German shepherd. Because of this development, the others were hopeful of finding their own lost dogs. Lyle's anger had increased ten-fold.

"I've been looking all over town for that no-good varmint who stole my animals," he announced, as I added two dozen oatmeal cookies to the impressive display on Helena's buffet.

"I'm curious," I said, taking a chair next to the fireplace. "Where are you looking?"

"In bars mostly," he said. "I heard about a place he goes in Rochester. One day I'll see him there and all hell will break loose."

Recalling his previous threats and his fondness for carrying concealed weapons, I knew how Lyle planned to accomplish this. Naturally I was hoping for a more civil outcome.

Helena set a large coffee pot on the table. "Let's leave O'Meara to Kate and the police. We're getting close to a solution. I feel sure of it."

"Well, I don't," Harold Camden said. "Kate is getting nowhere fast. How long do we have to wait before we find out what happened to our dogs?"

"You may have to be patient a little longer," Sue Appleton suggested.

The group was in no mood to hear this. Lyle, the hothead, took particular exception to Sue's call for patience.

"Easy for you to say. You don't have a dog missing."

"But I have in the past," Sue said. "I know how helpless you all feel."

I wished I could contribute something positive to the discussion, some clue or even a rumor. But O'Meara and his partner remained elusive. I could hardly go bar hopping in pursuit of him. In any event, I wouldn't want to.

As I didn't have anything to say at the moment, I gazed at the oil painting centered above the sofa. A slightly younger Helena rested her arm on the neck of a silky black horse. Helena's eyes shone with pride and I detected a glint of mischief in the horse's bright eyes. The pair reminded me of a favorite childhood book, *Black Beauty,* and my own love of horses.

I imagined a companion painting hanging on the wall. Helena and her tricolor collie, finally found.

"What's the name of this bar?" Harold asked. "I could go there on different nights at different times. One of us is bound to run into him."

"It's called Chances," Lyle said.

His wife, Marguerite, spoke up, which was a rare occurrence for her. "I agree with Helena and Sue. We can wait—"

"I don't wait," Lyle countered. "You know that."

Harold topped off his coffee and plunked three of my oatmeal cookies in a paper plate. "You gals sure know how to bake."

Gals?

Helena smiled, blushing faintly as she thanked Harold for the compliment. It seemed she liked the man in spite of his roughhewn appearance and that long ginger beard. Or perhaps because of them. Well, to each her own.

"So," Lyle said. "What else are we going to do to? Does anybody have any bright ideas?"

All of a sudden I remembered the plan I'd suggested at our last meeting.

"Everyone was going to contact one of the transport services with a request to relocate Rover. What happened with that?"

"Rover?" Harold said. "Rover who?"

"A make-believe dog."

"I talked to a company named Roadways," Helena said. "They gave me a quote of six hundred dollars to drive a dog down to Kentucky, but they couldn't give me an appointment for two weeks. The next service I called apparently had gone out of business."

"Anyone else?"

Silence.

"I forgot," Harold admitted.

"I don't have time to play games," Lyle said. "I'm a man of action."

Action-—in a bar?

"It isn't a game," I said. "It's called sleuthing."

"How's that going to bring our dogs home and land that O'Meara scum in jail?"

He sounded sincere, genuinely puzzled. I bit back a sarcastic retort and tried to explain.

"Our purpose was to check out all the transport services we could find and try to separate the legitimate ones from the scammers."

"In the meantime our dogs are getting used to other owners," Harold said.

Again, Sue attempted to soothe the turbulent waters. "Your dogs won't forget you, no matter how long they're in other homes. They'll be overjoyed to be reunited with you. Wait and see."

"Does anyone know how to contact the shepherd's owner?" I asked.

No one did.

"Kate Brennan should know," Sue said. "Why?"

"I think Harold will feel better if he can talk to him."

"I'd like to meet him and compare notes," Harold said. "Maybe he noticed something about O'Meara we all missed."

"For those of you who didn't watch the news yesterday, Kate showed pictures of all the missing dogs," Sue told us.

Helena said, "Maybe at this very moment somebody is looking at her new tri collie and wondering if it's Arden. Maybe she's already called Kate."

"Keep dreaming," Lyle said.

Although I was sympathetic with his plight, I found his negativity disheartening. His comment had erased the spark of hope from Helena's countenance.

"If any of you want to know what we can do, I suggest continuing the Rover Project. Find out what services Helena called and contact the rest."

"And give us a report at our next get-together," Harold said.

~ * ~

The hot spell continued. Research in a cool, quiet library was infinitely more relaxing than sitting through a meeting of O'Meara's victims. I could understand their frustration, though. Kate Brennan was moving slowly, but at least she was moving. O'Meara couldn't stay under the radar forever, and fortunately Kate's reports had likely put him out of business.

I bit into a blueberry doughnut—one of the dozen I'd bought for Miss Eidt and Debbie—and surveyed the folders I'd pulled from the vertical file. I'd already searched the internet and found the same information again: Holly's sparse biography and a list of her published books. Nothing about her disappearance or death.

It was impossible to know which book contained the tornado-murder plot without examining all of them.

As for Micah Frost, all I found was the ad for Frost's Outfitters. As a clue, Jane Wickersham had vanished like her cousin. Her address was a new mansion built on the site of a demolished ranch house.

I had spread a trio of promising folders out on the table: *Foxglove Corners Crimes of the Last (Twentieth) Century, Natural Disasters, and Local Authors and Artists.*

After thirty minutes I concluded that Foxglove Corners was indeed a peaceful place to live. Clippings told of accidental shootings and robberies. In 2000, a jewelry store in Lakeville, long since shuttered, had been robbed of a fortune in jewelry, none of which had ever been recovered. I paid special attention to disappearances, noting several that had happened on the ill-famed Brandemere Road. But nowhere could I find a disappearance connected with a tornado.

The tornado Micah Frost had told us about, however, had done serious damage to several local houses, ripping off roofs, chimneys, and porches, and sending cars far from their driveways.

Local Authors and Artists looked promising. Miss Eidt had saved many articles that featured Lucy Hazen but none about Holly Wickersham.

Miss Eidt opened the door, books in hand. "I found something for you, Jennet. I hope one of these is what you're looking for." She laid two dog-eared paperbacks on the table: *Ghost in the Gazebo* and *Peril in the Sky*.

"They were in the Gothic Nook," she said. "I'm afraid they won't hold up very long."

Peril in the Sky had a dark and provocative cover. A mansion silhouetted against a purple and threatening clouds. A tornado sky?

I opened the book and frowned at the yellow pages and tiny print. Reading it would take a toll on my eyesight. A paragraph on the back gave the gist of the plot: *Did Alicia die in the storm or was she murdered? Linda must find out lest she become the killer's next victim.*

"This one, I think," I said. "I'll be careful with it."

"It cost ninety-five cents when it was new. Amazing."

"Holly's cousin accused a man of murder because of a book like this," I said.

"That must be a powerful story."

"I'll let you know."

"And I'll let you go back to work," Miss Eidt said. "I already checked the books out to you."

I flipped through a few more clippings and finally found what I was looking for on the back of a page dedicated to making sodas and other summer drinks. The article was short, confirming what I already knew. Maple Falls resident, Micah Frost, was questioned and released in the suspected murder of Foxglove Corners author Holly Wickersham.

That was all. With only a cousin to push for justice, the case had languished in perpetual cold storage until Brent purchased the house on Loosestrife Lane where Holly's tragedy had unfolded.

Quickly I scanned the contents of the last folder, ate another doughnut, stacked the files neatly and left the office. I looked for Miss Eidt but didn't see her.

I'd done the best I could. If there was nothing more to find, I'd reached the end of the road.

Outside the sky was heavy, laden with the scent of rain. And was it a little darker than it had been when I arrived? Tornado weather?

I wondered what the odds were of a person living through two tornadoes in a lifetime, unless she lived in Tornado Alley. Even if we were only about to have a thunderstorm, I'd better get home and take care of my collies.

Thirty

The storm arrived during the night. It set the room alight with lightning flashes. Thunder crashed overhead, too close for comfort. Crane and Halley slept on, but Misty whimpered softly and padded across the room to sit at my bedside, facing the nightstand.

"Hendrick Hudson and his men are playing a game of nine pins in the sky," I whispered, my standard comment if one of the collies was fearful of thunder.

Misty shoved her head in the space between the bed and the nightstand. This behavior was unusual for her. What was different about tonight's storm?

Perhaps she had been dreaming. I remembered fragments of my own dream. Dark images of pond water whipped to a frenzy and a wild sky pressing down on the earth, stealing the air. I was spinning, like Lucy on the landing. Like clothes in a dryer.

Now fully awake, I tried to breathe, to catch my breath, but it went whirling away like autumn leaves in a dream. My thoughts went whirling along with them.

Should I wake Crane? Ask him to call an ambulance?

No. It was only the after effect of that horrible dream still holding onto me.

I stroked Misty, concentrated on calming myself, and finally took a deep breath. *Bliss.*

Breathing, like walking, isn't something you should have to think about.

In the lull between rolls of thunder, a familiar sound insinuated itself into the customary nocturnal stillness, a sound of water running. Could one of us have left the faucet on in the bathroom?

Possibly I was hearing rain water dripping from the downspout. But suppose one of the faucets was still turned on. I'd better check.

With a sigh I swung my legs out of bed and walked quietly to the bathroom, trailed by Misty, then Halley who had awakened and wanted to know what was going on.

The house wasn't quite so silent now. As if my sense of hearing were amplified, I heard every sound the night produced: the ticking of the clock in the bedroom, Misty panting at my side, the click of collie nails on the hardwood floor, a board creaking. But no sound of water. Inside the house, that is. Outside heavy rain struck the windows with angry force.

I glanced in the bathroom. The faucets over the wash basin and the tub were turned off. The sound I'd heard had to have been in my dream.

Wait! I heard it after I woke up.

It was the downspout then, I told myself. *And I should still hear it.*

But I didn't. Okay. I didn't.

Resigned to having one more mystery in my life, I sank back into bed. Halley flopped down in the doorway to guard us from evil spirits that wandered abroad in the night, but Misty lay beside the bed, resting her head between the bed and the nightstand again.

In time the thunder moved on, and I slept.

~ * ~

The next morning I had seven restless collies to entertain. None of them liked to get wet, but all of them wanted their walks, which weren't going to happen. What was left to do but sulk and sleep and every now and then whine at the window?

It was supposed to rain all day.

I sent Crane on his way with a hearty breakfast and a kiss, then did my day's baking—apple pies—and settled down in the living room with Holly's books. I soon discovered that *Peril in the Sky* wasn't about a tornado as I'd assumed. The peril was the crash of a small plane in the Upper Peninsula of Michigan and a heroine running from a demented husband. The other book had a similar situation in a different locale.

Turning to *The Edelweiss Lure*, which I'd already begun, I immersed myself in a nerve-wracking tale of a heroine driven to distraction by a cuckoo clock that inexplicably continued to stop and start again of its own accord.

Holly's heroine, Rowena, believed the clock could somehow transport a person to another time. She had a boyfriend, Mike Winter, a ski instructor, who thought the clock was simply defective.

Mike Winter/Micah Frost. Was the similarity in names the reason Holly's cousin's suspected that Mike was really Micah?

By chapter seven, Rowena suspected that Mike was hiding a secret agenda behind his charming ways. Gradually she began to be afraid of him. Uneasy with a situation she couldn't understand, she began to distance herself from him.

Petulant whines drifted into the living room from the kitchen. A glance through the bay window told me the rain had stopped, leaving Jonquil Lane a virtual quagmire. We couldn't go walking until the sun dried the mud, but I let the dogs out. They stayed close to the house.

Now that I was up, I made a sandwich and a fresh pot of tea, let the dogs back inside and handed out biscuits to all.

With the collies settled for afternoon naps, I took a cup of tea into the living room and began a new chapter—in which Rowena lost an entire day, a period coinciding with one of the clock's silences. She was convinced the clock had supernatural powers. They appeared to be triggered by one of the clock's songs, *Edelweiss*.

In the meantime her relationship with Mike deteriorated. In fact, it turned deadly on the day Rowena had a suspicious accident when the brakes in her car failed. She suspected Mike of tampering with them. The pace slowed dramatically, and I began to skim. There were no signs of an impending tornado. She *did* contemplate escaping into the past but didn't know how to accomplish it.

I could see why *The Edelweiss Lure* had faded into obscurity. The best part of the book was the beginning, which she had failed to build on. What I couldn't see was why Holly's cousin thought the plot reflected Holly's relationship with Micah Frost or why the police took her claim seriously.

Should I even bother to finish the book? The answer was easy. Not if I didn't care what happened to the characters.

As I set the book aside, the dogs alerted me to activity outside the house. Through the bay window I spied a vintage white Plymouth Belvedere with green fins in the driveway. A redheaded man in a forest green jacket strode up the walkway, carrying a large bag from Pluto's Gourmet Pet Shop. In other words, a happy diversion was on its way. Brent always knew how to brighten a collie's gloomy day—and mine.

I waded through wagging tails and joyous yelps to the door. As soon as I opened it, Candy jumped on Brent, nudging the bag of treats with her long nose.

"Candy, down!" I grabbed her collar. "They're wild. It's been too wet for their exercise."

"Not all of them," he said. "Just Candy."

Misty initiated an endearing play bow, and Sky yawned. Only Candy had forgotten her manners at the prospect of treats from Pluto's.

"I could use some cheering up," Brent said.

"What's wrong?"

"My plans are falling apart."

"That sounds serious."

He gave each of the dogs a venison tartlet and settled in the rocker with a heavy sigh.

"Tell me what's wrong," I said.

"I thought I found my perfect caregivers, but it turns out they don't want to live in Foxglove Corners. They'll accept the job if I open the house for geriatric collies in another location. How the devil can I do that? I don't even want to."

"Didn't they know the address before the interview?" I asked.

"Sure. I told them everything. I'm thinking that wasn't the real reason. All that matters is that they don't want the job."

"You'll find someone," I said. "For the right person, it's a wonderful opportunity."

"There's a little problem with the house, too," he added.

Actually the house had many problems, none of which could be described as little.

"What now?"

"My contractor started the kitchen renovation, then quit. He said his men were uncomfortable working in the house. Now I have cupboards torn apart and have to find someone else to take over the job."

"Uncomfortable in what way?"

"He couldn't give me a reason. Or wouldn't. Anyway, I'm not going to abandon the project. Whatever it takes, my old collies are going to have a home of their own, and it's going to be the one I picked out for them."

"I'll help you," I said.

Thirty-one

"Stay for dinner," I said. "We'll figure something out."

"I need a working kitchen. That's the one room that has to be ready."

They all followed me to the kitchen, Brent and the seven collies. Brent pulled out one of the oak chairs for himself, and the dogs crowded around him, anticipating human refreshments. I opened the refrigerator, contemplating what to cook.

"Do you know of any other contractors?" I asked.

"Not off hand. I can find one, but after this setback, he has to be reliable. I offered them a hefty bonus, but they wouldn't consider staying."

"I wish you knew what troubled the men," I said. "Would they have gone upstairs?"

"To the landing, you mean? They shouldn't have."

"If one of them had an experience like Lucy's..."

He interrupted me. "He'd have to be like Lucy, though, wouldn't he? Able to pick up...uh...feelings from the walls?" He added, "Lucy doesn't want to set foot in my house again, but she will if I ask her."

"That leaves you with me."

I could have wept for Brent's beleaguered vision—a spacious house with an acre of land for elderly, tired dogs to explore at their own pace, a cool pond of their own, and the shade of a massive weeping willow tree on a sweltering summer day. I couldn't let the dream die.

Neither could he. This untoward discouragement wouldn't last.

I set three steaks on the lower shelf and assembled makings for a salad. That done, I cut a slice of pie for Brent and poured two glasses of iced tea.

"Let's have a brainstorming session," I said. "First, here's what we know that's off about the house and yard. I saw the face of a collie in the pond before you had it cleaned. I heard a scratching sound inside the house but never found the source. I don't believe in Annica's giant rat. There's Lucy's reaction to the landing, and one day I heard a siren. Neither you nor Annica were aware of it. Last, your workers' complaints."

Brent scooped the orange slice out of his tea. "When you put it all together, it sounds pretty bad. What did I get myself into?"

"That's easy. A haunted house. I suspect what's happening is tied to Holly Wickersham in some way."

It occurred to me that Brent didn't know about our trip to Maple Falls to talk to Micah Frost, so I told him about it.

"He was questioned in Holly's disappearance but never charged," I said. "He isn't even sure she's dead."

"Speaking of dead, that's a dead end then. What can we do?"

"You can start looking for another contractor right away. At least find someone who can put the cupboards back the way they were and clean up the mess. I want to be able to have coffee and doughnuts in peace the next time I'm at the house."

"You'll go back then?"

"Of course. I'm not going to leave a mystery unsolved, and this time I'm bringing Misty."

Hearing her name, Misty materialized at my side. I stroked her head. "My beautiful psychic collie. We're going ghost hunting."

She nudged the bag of treats, which was empty but still held interest for her. I let her pull it off the table.

"It's for the dogs who don't have a good home like you do," Brent told her.

"Misty was with me when I saw the phantom in the pond," I said. "If he sees her again, maybe he'll make another appearance."

~ * ~

When they heard Crane's Jeep on Jonquil Lane, all seven of the collies made a dash for the door as usual, even Sky, although she lagged behind.

"How do they know he's out there?" Brent asked.

"Super sharp hearing and intuition. Also, Crane usually comes home around the same time."

Crane came in, raindrops glistening in his fair hair. He gave the collies individual greetings and me a kiss. Then he locked his gun in its special cabinet.

"I see you come after the dogs, Jennet," Brent observed.

"I heard that, Fowler." Crane joined us at the oak table and favored Brent with one of his special glares.

Candy sat and stared at him. Had everyone forgotten the dogs' walk? To remind him, she tapped his leg smartly with her paw.

Crane fixed his eagle-eyed gaze on Brent. "You don't look happy, Fowler. What did I miss?"

"My contractor quit," Brent said. "His crew didn't like the bad vibes in my house."

"You're talking about the house on Loosestrife Lane?"

"Yeah. My haven for old, hard-to-place collies."

"Your haunted house," Crane said. "Good luck finding another contractor."

I poured Crane a glass of tea and added ice and an orange slice.

"I don't see any dinner on the stove," he said.

"That's because you're grilling steaks tonight. But I baked this morning. We have apple pies."

He drained the glass. "Thanks, honey. That's just what I wanted. Did you hear the news about O'Meara?"

I sat forward. "Did they find him?"

"Someone did. That man from Tennessee whose dog he stole. He started a fight with O'Meara in a bar, and it ended up in gunfire."

"That's Lyle," I said. "Don't stop there. Did he kill O'Meara?

"He's still alive, but it's touch and go."

"Serves O'Meara right," Brent said.

"And Lyle? Did they arrest him?"

"Not yet. He took off. Maybe all the way to Tennessee. His wife claims he went out and didn't come home."

"If O'Meara dies, how will people ever get their dogs back?"

Crane shrugged. "They'll have to go after the partner."

"Darn Lyle," I said. "Why did he have to take the law in his own hands? He's made everything so much worse."

Thirty-two

Once she knew I was going ghost hunting with Misty, Annica wanted to be part of the team. In truth, I'd hoped to recruit her. Even with Misty I didn't feel brave enough to challenge the house on Loosestrife Lane on my own. We agreed to meet tomorrow on Annica's day off.

Brent wouldn't be with us. He'd reclaimed his enthusiasm and made appointments with two prospective caretakers. August was rapidly approaching. He hoped to move his collies into the house before the fundraiser for the animal shelter.

I took a sip of my lime cooler. Heavenly. "The basement," I said. "We never thoroughly explored it."

"We didn't explore it at all," Annica reminded me. "We concentrated on the attic. That's where all good secrets hide out. Basements are cold and damp."

"And I want to take Misty to the pond," I said.

"Are you still looking for the phantom dog?"

"Yes, especially since I learned that Holly Wickersham had a collie."

I imagined Holly trying to outrace the tornado. Grasping her dog's leash in a death grip, Holly would have been determined to hold on to her, come what may. But they'd be trapped. The two of them sharing a watery grave.

Whoa! Where did the image of water originate?

Most likely in my intent to lead Misty to the pond.

Annica said, "I wish Lucy would go with us."

"We could ask her. She doesn't have to set foot on that landing."

"Which one of us will do it?"

"I will," I said. "I'll stop at Dark Gables on the way home."

Having Lucy accompany us would be an enormous bonus. Perhaps another part of the house would reveal a secret, and it wouldn't have a traumatic effect on her.

"I want to find out what caused that scratching noise," Annica said. "Even though I have yet to hear it."

"I was thinking. Could it have been part of the past that somehow lives on, like the disturbance on the landing?"

"If we haven't found evidence of rats or some other creature, then, maybe yes."

And the siren I'd heard. Perhaps that sound also originated in Holly's time, a warning she'd heard that had maintained its wail across the years.

What had Brent's contractor and his workers experienced that had driven them away from the house and a lucrative job? That they didn't even want to talk about?

We would never know.

"I'm glad you're taking Misty along," Annica said. "I think we're finally on the right track."

~ * ~

I was surprised when Lucy readily agreed to join our expedition.

"My curiosity won out in the end," she confessed. "I was afraid when it happened. Now I want to know more." As she laid her hand on Sky's head, the gold charms on her bracelet jangled. "I was hoping you'd invite me to accompany you again."

"I was hoping you'd accept."

I turned my teacup around, watching the patterns form. Would one of them give Lucy a preview of what waited for us in Brent's house?

"I want to help Brent," Lucy said. "He was so disappointed when his contractor quit, and no one seems interested in the caretaker job. He had a good and generous idea, but it looks like the fates are conspiring against him."

"It can all change in the blink of an eye. We can make it happen."

I made my wish, this time for Brent's house to be up and running soon, and gave Lucy my cup.

After a single glance, she said, "Uh oh."

"What?

"I see an initial 'V'."

Oh, no.

That symbol could only refer to Veronica the Viper, the glamorous female deputy sheriff who had set her sights on Crane.

My husband, I thought. *Don't you forget that.*

Veronica had conspired to cross Crane's path as often as possible. She even resorted to lying about the time she'd spent with him. Wounded in the line of duty, Veronica had decided to leave the force, but her fellow officers had talked her into giving law enforcement another chance. That meant she was bound to run into Crane.

"V is heading toward your home," Lucy said. "There's good news, too, though. I see an overflowing basket."

Overflowing with flowers, I thought. That symbol represented all good things. As for Veronica the Viper, I didn't need another complication in my life.

"Here's a successful undertaking," Lucy said.

"A solution to the mystery, I hope."

"But a large boulder stands in the way." She pointed to a large tannish tealeaf. "You'll have an obstacle to surmount."

When did an obstacle not stand between me and any goal I wanted to achieve. "I'll take the basket," I said.

"That's all I see today." Lucy set my cup on the wicker coffee table next to the dessert plate. "That was a good cup."

"Except for Veronica."

I reached for another vanilla wafer. "I really don't want to deal with her, but I guess I'll have to take the bad along with the good."

~ * ~

The house brooded, waited in silence for a human to breach its defenses. It rose against a dull gray sky filled with floating dark clouds. A light wind carried a medley of floral scents across the grass along with a sound of water.

"It's supposed to rain," Lucy said, looping the ribbon of a black umbrella over her wrist.

"This is perfect haunted house weather," I said.

I took Misty's leash and led her out of the back seat. She was excited, tail wagging, eyes bright in anticipation of a new adventure with me.

"She remembers being here before," Annica said.

"She remembers the pond. Let's check it out first."

I recalled my first sight of the fishpond. Befouled water, weeds interspersed with dead plants in the rock garden, missing boulders, flamingoes lying on their sides. What a change a little tender loving care had wrought.

We stood at the rock border, gazing into the clear surface. Would the phantom collie rise from the depths?

Be still. Wait... Maybe.

Tiny living things, bits of shining gold, rippled through the water, the finishing touch to Brent's pond restoration.

"Look!" I said. "Brent bought his goldfish."

"I hope they'll be safe," Annica murmured.

"Why wouldn't they be?"

"Feral cats," she said.

I hadn't thought about that grim complication.

"I hope Brent didn't create a buffet for felines," she added.

"When the dogs move in, if there are any cats in the area, they'll keep their distance," I said. "I hope."

The wind rose. Low hanging willow strands swept across the pond's surface, but the water lay still like a giant's mirror set down in the grass. Misty swiped the water with her paw and withdrew it. She shook herself.

"This has to be the most peaceful place on the planet," Annica said. "I'd like to bring a lawn chair out here and sit and read or just dream."

Splash!

"Did you hear that?" I asked.

"What?"

I knelt on the ground and trailed my hand through the water.

"That splashing."

"I do now. Take your hand out of the water, Jennet. You'll scare the fish."

She hadn't heard what I had. Something untoward was going to happen today. I felt certain of it.

Thirty-three

When I opened the door, Misty pulled on her leash, eager to investigate all the new scents suddenly available for her sniffing pleasure. I freed her from her restraint, and she lost no time in rushing across the room and burying her nose in a pile of discarded rags.

Only a dog can find wondrous scents in an empty house.

"Ugh," Lucy said. "You'd think the workers could have taken their dirty clothes with them." She sidestepped a red shirt torn and stained with a mystery substance.

"Brent will have to build a bonfire," Annica said.

I called Misty, who looked up from the jumble of rags. "I want you to turn your sixth sense on, girl. Find something. We're counting on you. Go!"

"Do you honestly believe she understood all those words?" Annica asked.

"Yes."

Misty bolted into the kitchen, and we followed her.

"Let's see how bad it is in here," Lucy said.

It was, as Brent had claimed, torn apart, looking half its size with wood and cabinet parts strewn everywhere. The coffeemaker had vanished, and I didn't see a box of doughnuts. Still, Misty had ample scents to follow.

"Leaving this kind of mess is unconscionable," Lucy said. "I hope Brent didn't pay a deposit."

"I think he did. Maybe they gave him a refund. Well—"

Fortunately the flashlights were where we'd left them on the table. The kitchen had two exits. One door led to the back porch and the outside, the other to the basement. I opened the second door and turned on the light. Shadows fell across the staircase that curved down to unseen darkness below. Luckily a bannister provided a handhold.

Misty paused at the head of the staircase as if to contemplate her chances of descending a new set of steps safely, then she moved with ease down the stairs.

"Be careful," I told my companions, as I switched on the flashlight. The lighting in the basement was inadequate, perhaps three or four sixty-watt bulbs. Brent would need more brightness in this cavernous space.

"I don't like basements," Annica said. "This one is especially spooky."

"It's just darker than most."

"How many people spend time in a basement?" Lucy asked.

This one was fairly ordinary. It contained a washer and dryer, an old furnace, and a large pantry with its own door, obviously homemade. Empty quart and pint jars shared space with an old pressure cooker and boxes marked with such labels as 'extra utensils' and 'Christmas dishes.' A stove and refrigerator suggested that some past homemaker had enjoyed cooking in the house's lowest level, perhaps for large gatherings.

Annica pulled open the refrigerator door. It gave an ungodly squeak.

"Empty," she said.

The western wall had been designated as a storage area for gardening tools, brooms, snow shovels, and a dusty set of luggage.

Were the suitcases Holly's property?

"Let's open them," I said.

The luggage was definitely a relic of another age. Each one bore a tag: *Holly Wickersham, 7 Loosestrife Lane, Foxglove Corners, Mich.* The pieces probably had different names.

"Train case," I murmured. "Hat box... How vintage."

"Who wears hats anymore?" Annica asked.

"English women," Lucy said. "But you could carry anything in that box. It doesn't have to be a hat."

I opened the largest suitcase and examined all the inner pockets. It was empty. Holly had obviously been meticulous about clearing out and cleaning her luggage. The hat box looked as if it had never been used. Maybe it hadn't.

"This proves that Holly didn't plan to leave on a trip the day she vanished," I said.

Not if she was caught in a tornado, I told myself.

I couldn't stop connecting the tornado with Holly's disappearance, even without evidence to back it up. But wait! Wasn't Lucy's experience on the landing evidence? For me it was.

I scanned the rest of the basement, looking in all the corners. My next and last discovery was a long-sleeved pink blouse, silk, I'd guess, and very elegant. It had fallen behind the dryer.

Did Holly realize the blouse was missing? Did she ever wonder what had happened to it?

"I think we've seen everything there is to see down here," Annica said. "I'm cold. I hate basements. Or did I say that already?"

"It'll be more comfortable upstairs."

I was cold, too, but the icy waves I felt had nothing to do with the chill, unmoving air. It originated in the unsettling atmosphere that hung over this lowest level of the house. In a sense, the basement was like the landing.

A spate of high-pitched barking drifted down from one of the upper floors. At some point Misty had gone upstairs. And found something?

"Let's see why Misty's barking," I said.

She lay in the kitchen securing a bone with one paw while she indulged in one of her favorite past times.

"Don't let her have that, Jennet," Lucy said. "You don't know how old it is or where it came from."

"Where did you find it, Misty?"

"Why was she barking?" Annica asked.

Both were good questions, but I had no hope of getting answers from Misty. I wondered if the bone had belonged to Holly's collie or to the pet of some tenant who came after her.

"That wasn't what I meant when I told you to find something," I said, taking it from her. I placed it on the counter, and she stared at it wistfully.

"Let's find something else," I said.

~ * ~

"Oh dear." Lucy leaned against the wall. "Suddenly I don't feel well."

"Here, sit down," I said.

All of the kitchen chairs were in use as table extensions, heaped high with various parts. I moved a box of hardware and pushed the chair closer to her.

"Would you like a cup of tea?" Annica asked, then searched the counter for the electric teakettle that had been there on our last visit. "What did those jerks do with Brent's stuff?"

"Just rest, Lucy," I said. "Is it your stomach? Your head?"

"Both."

She didn't look well. She was pale and kept rubbing her throat. Misty had given up watching her bone and lay beside Lucy, whimpering softly.

"It just came on," Lucy said. "A pain in my head. A weakness. For a moment I felt as if I were going to faint."

"You're not, are you?" Annica asked.

Lucy didn't answer but rested her head on her palm.

"Let's get Lucy home," I said, knowing we'd lost our enthusiasm for the day's adventure. Lucy hadn't gone near the landing, although she had intended to accompany us up to the second story. Did the kitchen also hold echoes of Holly's terror or was Lucy suffering from another, natural malady like vertigo?

"Could we wait a little while?" she asked. A brief half smile brought a faint tinge of color back to her face. "Just a few minutes. I'd like to get my sea legs back. I feel so foolish."

"There's no hurry," I said.

Misty laid her paw on Lucy's lap.

No hurry, I thought. *That isn't right. We have to hurry and get out of this house before something happens.*

Annica was still searching for the teakettle and the bag of tea bags she'd left in the kitchen weeks ago.

"Did Brent's workers steal his stuff?" she demanded.

"I don't want any tea, Annica," Lucy said. "That is, I do, but I'll wait till I'm home."

"Try to stand," I said, holding on to her arm.

She did; she took three steps. "But I'm a little unsteady on my feet."

Misty abandoned her role of canine nurse and, reverting to madcap puppy mode, crossed in front of Lucy. She faltered.

"Misty! Sit and stay."

Misty looked puzzled and rightly so. *Sit and stay when we were leaving? When Annica was already at the door?*

"I'll help Lucy to the car," Annica said as I approached Misty, leash in hand. She danced gleefully away from me, training tossed to the winds. Her dark eyes glittered with mischief.

I grabbed her collar and attached it to the leash. "Misty is bad," I told her, "and I'm the alpha dog," I added for my own benefit.

As we went through the door, Misty lunged forward and dragged me toward the pond. I hadn't anticipated her choosing her own direction over the one I'd decided on. Sometimes she was so like Candy.

"I don't want to see the goldfish," I shouted.

Laughter reached me from the lane. It's always amusing to see somebody else's dog cause a commotion.

She came to a sudden stop at the pond's edge and stood frozen, staring down at the surface.

A collie, a dark sable with one pricked ear, stared back at her.

Thirty-four

The apparition didn't last long. I blinked, and it was gone, replaced by graceful ripples and tiny streaks of gold shimmering in the sunlight. Misty swiped her paw through the water and turned to me for an explanation.

Where did the other dog go?

"Are you coming, Jennet?" Annica called.

The phantom had vanished, having timed its appearance well. Only Misty and I had seen him.

A rustle in a stand of loosestrife and giant ferns drew my attention away from the pond. It then moved to two tall, bushy lilac trees that grew beyond the weeping willow. A creature, probably, whose instinct was to hide from an intrusive canine and the human.

Could it be a real dog who had somehow exited the pond in that blink of an eye? Unlikely; still I walked quietly around the lilacs, with Misty who wasn't as quiet. By then nothing was there. Woodland creatures need to be fast in order to survive.

"Jennet!"

Annica had settled Lucy in the passenger seat of the Focus and was advancing toward me through the tall grass.

As I came back to the pond, I looked again. Nothing was there either.

"What's so fascinating?" Annica asked as she reached my side. "Did you see the phantom dog?"

"I did. For a moment."

Misty gave a little yip. *That's what we saw. The ghost.* She stared down into the pond as if waiting for it to reappear.

"It took off," Annica said.

"Yes, in the manner of spirits everywhere."

A cool breeze wound itself around me, a pleasant sensation and a welcome one on the hot morning.

"Could you have seen a goldfish?" she asked.

I smiled at the notion. Annica and I often played a game of devil's advocate, taking turns as the advocate.

"I know the difference between a fish and a dog."

"This is the weirdest place, but I think I want to come back without Lucy," Annica said. "It's unhealthy for her. You and I appear to be immune."

"At present, for now anyway."

I took a final look at the pond, silent and still, and we walked back to the car.

"I hoped Lucy would sense something helpful today," I said. "I never wanted her to be sick."

"Well, no. She seems all right now."

"Because she's out of the house. I don't know how Brent can move his dogs and a caretaker in while everything is so unsettled."

~ * ~

"We shouldn't have left," Lucy said as I turned on the road that would take us to Dark Gables. "I feel all right now, just a little weak. But at the time..." She paused, frowning. "At the time I felt so sick. It came on suddenly."

"We can always go back another day," Annica said.

"You don't know what would have happened to you if you'd stayed," I added. "Look on those symptoms as a warning."

The house had sickened her. Suppose its intent was to kill her? How would it accomplish that?

Don't overreact, I told myself. *A house can't kill a person.*

My inner voice disagreed. *Sure it can. With poisonous fumes. With fire. With water. With wind.*

But why would the house wish Lucy harm? Because eventually she could divine its secrets?

"I won't let a house get the better of me," Lucy said. "After all, it's only wood."

I thought it best to change the subject. "If you'd come with me to the pond, you'd have seen the resident phantom."

Immediately she brightened. "You saw Holly's dog again. How exciting!"

"If that's who he is."

We amused ourselves with speculation. Assuming the dog in the pond was a true ghost, what part had he played in the old mystery? Why did he appear in the fishpond? The connection seemed obvious. The pond itself had been part of the mystery.

I pushed away a sudden image of the dog drowning in the pond.

"On the other hand, he could be a real dog, a stray."

"Maybe that dog I threw the crullers to came back," I said.

"Did anyone notice a doggy door?" Annica asked.

No one had. The turn to Spruce Road loomed ahead. We would make Lucy comfortable, make her that cup of tea she craved, and go on with our day. I planned to call Helena and wanted to know if O'Meara was still among the living and if Lyle remained a fugitive.

But my thoughts remained with the house on Loosestrife Lane. All I knew for certain was that Holly Wickersham hadn't packed her suitcases and taken a trip from which she never returned. The mystery was in the house and the surrounding yard and the long-ago tornado.

~ * ~

Helena had the answers to my questions. O'Meara was out of danger and had been released from the hospital. He denied running a crooked pet transport service and swore he knew nothing about the missing dogs. He cast blame on his boss, a man of mystery whose name he'd never known.

As for Lyle, nobody had been home for several days. Neighbors thought he and his wife were somewhere in Tennessee.

"And Arden is still missing," Helena added. "She's my dog, and I never even saw her."

I'd invited her over, and, as the morning was warm and balmy, we sat on the porch with the collies, drinking lemonade and eating ginger cookies, an unexpected gift from Camille.

"I keep hoping that whoever has her will recognize her from the picture on TV and get in touch with me," she said. "But Arden is so beautiful that whoever has her now won't want to return her, especially if he paid for her."

"O'Meara caused this mess. They should force him to clean it up."

That was unlikely to happen as long as he denied any association with Sea-to-Sea Transport, as long as the elusive partner or boss stayed out of sight, and no one came forward with proof of O'Meara's wrong doing. For all anyone knew, the other man could be a fabrication.

"I don't approve of what Lyle did," Helena said, "but someone had to do something. Too bad it didn't work."

"I'm out of ideas."

"So is Kate, I'm afraid. She's investigating a tax man who left his customers high and dry, taking their confidential information with him."

"But surely she'll be back with an update," I said.

Candy dashed off the porch, followed by Misty. The others came to attention, slowly or quickly according to their personalities. A white vintage Plymouth with long green fins was coming up the lane, slowing down, turning into our driveway.

"You have company," Helena said.

"It's Brent Fowler."

"I'd better go."

"No, stay. You know him," I said, recalling that she boarded her horse at his barn. He hadn't been part of our efforts to bring down Sea-to-Sea transport, though.

Candy and Misty dashed to the car and circled around it, barking wildly. As soon as Brent stepped onto the ground, they jumped on him, pretending not to hear my shouted "Down!" They'd do this even if he hadn't carried a bag from Pluto's Gourmet Pet shop in his hand.

They ran to me, then darted back to the car to escort Brent to the porch. He acknowledged the more sedate members of the pack with hasty pats and sank into the wicker rocker, transferring the Pluto's bag of treats to my lap.

"Hot out today. Hello, Helena. Any news yet about your dog?"

I poured him a glass of lemonade while Helena brought him up to date on the latest developments.

"What's new with you?" she asked.

"I think I found my caretaker," he said. "Yes, I'm sure I have."

Thirty-five

Brent had said that on previous occasions with the same optimistic tone. I hoped this time would be a charm, but I detected a slight reservation in his voice.

"What's the drawback?" I asked.

"Near as I can tell, there isn't any. Alberta Coulder is a widow who loves animals and old houses. I took her to the barn to meet the collies. It went well. Next I'll show her the house. She'd like to move out of her apartment, but she can't afford to buy a house of her own. It's perfect."

"But there's a drawback."

"Not with Alberta. The problem is I still can't find a contractor as good as the last one."

"But he abandoned your job. That wasn't good."

"He was supposed to be the best," he said. "I can't open the house with a kitchen all torn up."

"And a mystery unsolved," I added quietly.

"Do you mean the whereabouts of Holly Wickersham? We may never know what happened to her."

"That and..." I hesitated. Lucy hadn't sworn us to secrecy, but she wanted to downplay her latest experience. "The disturbance in the

180

house. Lucy was with us yesterday, and she got sick. As soon as she left the house, she was okay. Well, a little weak. She didn't go near the landing."

Helena had been listening to us intently. "I'd *love* to see this house."

Brent's natural good humor resurfaced. "If my rest home for older collies falls through, I can always sell tickets: *Tour Fowler's Mansion—See a ghost. Five dollars.*

"No one actually saw an apparition there," I pointed out. "We've heard strange sounds. Lucy Hazen sensed a disaster from the past on the landing."

"That doesn't sound so bad," Helena said.

I didn't mention the phantom in the pond. I considered him my personal ghost. But I filled her in on the house's strange properties, including the scratching sound that Annica thought was made by a gigantic rat.

"May I have a tour sometime?" Helena asked. "A kind of rehearsal for the real one?"

Brent laughed. "Why not? Everyone's familiar with the house except my collies. I have seven waiting to move out of the barn."

Brent's stable was more comfortable—luxurious even—than some people's houses, and at least one of his men was devoted to the collies. But the house on Loosestrife Lane would be so much better with Alberta at the helm. I pictured her as a loving, motherly woman, like Lila Woodville at the animal shelter.

"You can go with us, Helena," I said.

"And next time I'll be there," Brent promised.

"Lucy is determined to go back to the house," I reminded him.

Brent frowned. "I don't think she should. This is her second serious episode."

"You know we mystery mavens don't like to leave a puzzle unsolved."

"I've been told I'm a little psychic," Helena said. "So was my mother."

That was a welcome surprise. With Lucy, Misty, and Helena, how could we lose?

"All the better," I said. "Can we get together tomorrow around noon?"

The day and the time worked for everybody.

"Tomorrow then," I said. "I'll call Lucy." I glanced at Brent. "We need her, she wants to be there, and you'll be on hand to protect her from the bad vibes."

"How can I do that?" he wanted to know. "I wouldn't recognize a vibe if I fell over it."

"Be prepared for anything," I said. "All right. Here's what has to happen. You find a reputable contractor. Offer him a bonus if he finishes by your deadline. Our ghost catching team drives the restless spirits out of the house. Alberta and the collies move in."

"It sounds so simple," Brent said. "It's what I want."

"We'll make it happen."

I had no idea what fired my confidence, but I truly felt that we were all due for a happy ending.

~ * ~

I invited Brent and Helena to stay for dinner. Later, while we were relaxing over coffee and cake in the living room, Crane said, "I'll stop by the house tomorrow. I've never seen it."

"The sheriff will lock the ghosts up," Brent said.

"I'm not that powerful," Crane countered.

The prospect of Crane's visit cheered me immensely. Whenever he joined in one of my adventures, good things usually happened. In any case, he would provide an extra level of protection if the house turned surly.

"Jennet," Helena said, "it's time for the news. Shall we see if *Kate in Your Corner* is on tonight?"

"Good idea." Crane turned the television on as the weather report was ending. Hot, hotter, hottest... Afternoon thunderstorms.

"Maybe we should postpone tomorrow," Helena said.

"Not at all," I said. "A little thunder will be good for atmosphere."

Kate's report was next. In a deep pink suit with a chunky white necklace, she looked brighter and happier than we'd seen her to date. She must have good news.

"There's been a development in a story we've been following," she announced. "Five of the missing Sea-to-Sea Transport dogs have been recovered. Motorists traveling on White Pine Trail in Grenville spotted the dogs making their way down this rural country road in an orderly line. Two good Samaritans stopped and coxed them into their cars..."

Helena sat forward eagerly on the sofa. "At last."

"Shhh." Brent turned the volume up.

"The animals are currently being evaluated at Starfield Veterinary Hospital. At this time, Duncan O'Meara, suspected scam artist and dognapper, can't be located to throw light on the situation."

"In an orderly line?" I pictured small children walking in line to the cafeteria. Wouldn't unleashed dogs be more likely to run in a pack?

Pictures of the dogs, previously shown, filled the screen. The last was a tricolor collie.

"It's Arden!" Helena rose from the sofa. "When can I get her?"

"Listen," Brent said.

Kate continued. "The dogs will be turned over to their owners with proper identification."

"Where's Grenville?" Helena asked.

"It's a little town northeast of Maple Creek. I'll go with you if you like."

As the clock struck seven, Helena consulted her watch. "Oh, no. It's too late now."

"We'll go in the morning."

I remembered then that we'd made other plans for the next day. "Early tomorrow morning," I said.

She nodded. "As soon as they open. I'll have to bow out of the haunted house tour. I'm not going to pick Arden up, then leave her alone."

"She comes first."

"I assumed she was sold to somebody else," Helena said. "What was she doing walking down a country road with four other dogs?"

"Maybe the people at the vet's will know," I said. "Or Kate."

Kate finished her report with a promise of an update as soon as she gathered further information.

Part of the Sea-to-Sea mystery had been solved, but many aspects were still unknown. What had become of the other stolen dogs? Would O'Meara ever be found? Now that he had presumably recovered from his injury, would Lyle come out of hiding? He might still face charges.

Well, I had done what I could, which wasn't much. Now I would leave the tying of loose ends to Kate and concentrate on the many mysteries at the house on Loosestrife Lane.

Thirty-six

As soon as we set out for Grenville the next morning, Helena began to worry.

"What will I do if they don't give Arden to me?" she asked. "I've been thinking. Anybody could claim her."

"But you're her owner. You must have proof."

She patted her purse. "I have her registration and the receipt the breeder sent me. I have her picture on my cell phone and messages dealing with her purchase, too. Oh, and I have her rabies tag."

"Well, then. What more do you need?"

"She won't know me. I'll be a stranger."

Mmm. What Helena said was true. I thought about it for a moment, then knew what to say. "Sea-to-Sea was transporting other dogs to new owners. I'm sure most of you are in the same boat. The people at the animal hospital won't expect her to know you."

"I won't be happy until I have her under my roof." She rested her hand on the new collar and leash in her lap.

"It'll be all right," I said. "Don't borrow trouble."

"It's just that I've been through so much. We waited so long."

"It'll all be over soon," I assured her.

Except, of course, not all of the missing dogs had been found. O'Meara and his elusive partner might have started a new transport service using a different name. And Lyle... I hoped he was back in Michigan and could avoid arrest for attempted homicide.

What a tangle! Kate's investigation was far from over.

The drive was pleasant, through Maple Creek, a small, picturesque town, and on through farmland and pinewood countryside. I left the air conditioning off and powered down the windows so that fresh air could circulate through the car.

The Starfield Veterinarian Hospital was charming, once a private two-story residence with banks of purple coneflowers blooming in the front yard. Rows of dark pink impatiens interspersed with silver mounds grew along the foundation, and a pair of stone spaniels flanked the entrance.

"Here goes." Helena looped the leash over her wrist, and we walked up to the hospital. Beyond the heavy door we found ourselves in a vestibule with leashes of all sizes hanging on a pegboard shaped like a generic canine.

"Who comes to the vet without a leash?" Helena asked.

"You never know what people will do."

Helena took her place in line behind a young girl holding a lethargic black puppy in her arms while I sat and surveyed the other patients. They were mostly small to medium sized. Not one of them looked as if they were enjoying the experience.

At the counter, Helena produced her proof of ownership, and Gwen, a bubbly, brown-haired vet tech, escorted us to an empty room.

"We only have two Sea-to-Sea dogs that haven't been claimed," she said. "Which dog have you come for?"

"A tricolor collie," Helena said. "Her name is Arden."

"Ah, our pretty black Lassie. She's a popular little girl. I'll bring her right out."

As soon as she left, an ear piercing scream echoed through the hospital. I hoped with all my heart that the screamer was expressing fear and wasn't in agony.

"No wonder dogs hate coming to a place like this," Helena said.

I nodded. "The air is thick with trauma."

And whatever happened had taken place behind closed doors.

"Here's your girl." Gwen paused in the doorway, her hand brushing lightly along the rib cage of a small black collie. Arden held her ears flat against her head. Her eyes were wary, and her tail seemed to have disappeared.

"Come, beautiful girl," Helena said.

Arden gave a pathetic little whimper. She didn't move.

"She's so pretty," Helena murmured. "So thin…"

She seemed disappointed that Arden hadn't jumped into her arms. Gwen gave the leash to Helena.

"She takes a few minutes to warm up to people, but she has a loving disposition," Gwen said.

"That's what her breeder said."

"Is one of your Sea-to-Sea dogs an Irish setter?" I asked.

"Yes. His owner claimed him this morning."

Helena cast me a meaningful look. Lyle was out of hiding, then, and out of trouble, I hoped.

Gwen left the office and returned with Helena's bill. "Your dog is in the best of health, just a little underweight."

"I hope they fed her, wherever she was." Helena dropped her hand to Arden's head. "You're coming home with me where the living is easy."

Arden wagged her tail, and I felt the sting of tears in my eyes. Happy tears. The warm-up had already begun. I loved nothing more than a long-awaited reunion.

~ * ~

I said goodbye to Helena, drove home to pick up Misty, then proceeded to Dark Gables where Lucy was waiting for us, ready for the day's adventure.

"Brent is going to meet us there." Lucy set a box from the Hometown Bakery on the back seat. Let's hope the storm holds off."

"Let it come," I said. "We have everybody we need. Except Helena, but she's staying home with Arden."

"I'm anxious to know the extent of Helena's psychic powers," Lucy said.

"We'll have to wait till the next time."

"I was counting on wrapping up the mystery today."

"Mmm. Unlikely."

With Lucy, Misty, and the bakery box safely stowed, I set out for the house on Loosestrife Lane. The sky was overcast. On Brent's property, willow strands whipped back and forth over the pond in a growing wind. It tore pink petals from the loosestrife and tossed them onto the grass.

The house waited for us, silent and brooding and wrapped in shadows. It didn't look particularly welcoming. On the other hand neither did it seem forbidding—from the outside, that is. Inside I turned on the oversized fixture, and light flooded the living room.

"That's better," Lucy murmured.

As soon as I freed Misty from her leash, she took off up the stairs, a sleek white comet on a mission.

"There's a strong sense of peace here," Lucy said. "That's good."

"How do you feel otherwise? I asked, remembering her sick spell.

"Fine. Eager to strip the layers from the mystery, one by one."

She set the doughnuts on the kitchen counter. Nothing had changed in this room. I thought Brent might have sent someone from the barn to tidy it. Obviously that hadn't happened, but the coffee maker had reappeared. Beside it sat a gleaming new electric teakettle and a box of Red Rose teabags, probably furnished by Brent with Lucy in mind. Four clean mugs were drying on a large white towel.

"What now?" Lucy asked.

"We wait. Brent should be here soon."

"We might as well sample the doughnuts while we're waiting," Lucy said.

"My thoughts exactly."

I slipped the string off the box and lifted the top. Ah, all jelly doughnuts.

Misty began to bark angrily as if she'd discovered an intruder in her domain and was sounding the alarm. The barking came from the second story, but it sounded closer.

Lucy paused in the act of filling the teakettle. "What's gotten into that dog?"

"Let's go," I said, forgetting Lucy's problem with the landing.

She must have forgotten it as well. She followed me up the stairs, bypassing the haunted area without incident.

Misty stood outside the furnished room barking at... What? I came up beside her and peered inside. Nothing was there; nothing appeared to have been disturbed since our last visit to the house. Misty seemed focused on the window and the trees visible through the window with their blowing leaves.

I stepped inside and scanned the room, confirming my initial impression. Everything was the same. There was nothing to send an excitable collie into a barking frenzy.

Except for the annoying scratching sound that suddenly broke the heavy silence.

Thirty-seven

"Annica's giant rat strikes again," Lucy said.

"I doubt it."

"What is it then?"

"I don't know, but I'm glad you can hear it, too."

"Have you heard any other inexplicable sounds in the house?" Lucy asked.

"Once I heard a siren outside. I was in the kitchen with Brent and Annica, and they didn't hear anything. It stopped abruptly."

"As sirens do when they reach their destination," Lucy said. "It could have just been a normal everyday siren. Or could it have been an echo of a tornado siren—from the past?"

A tornado siren? Of course. If Holly was in the house, she would have heard it and gone immediately into panic mode. While Holly's emotions were trapped in the walls of the house, the sounds she had heard also lived on. I didn't understand how this could be, but because we were dealing with the unknown, I simply accepted it.

"I have an idea about the scratching," Lucy said. "The other day I closed the porch door without realizing that Sky was sleeping on the other side. She didn't bark but scratched desperately at the door. That sound reminds me of this one."

Desperate scratching. A dog locked in a room by mistake. Or out of it. Another holdover from the past?

"That's a thousand times better than a scratching rat," I said.

Piece by piece, Holly's story was coming together. Where did Micah Frost fit into the picture? If he did. In any event, I thought I could say goodbye to the elusive rodent and was happy to do so.

"That could be it, Lucy," I said. "You're a marvel."

"It's just an idea."

Misty hadn't followed us into the bedroom. She stood in the doorway, growling softly, her eyes fixed on me. The scratching sound had gradually died away. No, that was wrong. It had *moved* away. I still heard it coming from the general direction of the kitchen. But why wasn't Misty following it?

"I wonder if Tristan was trapped in the basement," I said.

"I can close my eyes and almost see Holly and Tristan," Lucy said. "I think they were together to the end."

"The end? Do your feelings tell you that Holly died in the tornado?"

"Sadly, yes. But there's more to their story."

Misty gave a yelp, spun around, and dashed down the staircase as another sound invaded the house—a door slamming and heavy footsteps on a hardwood floor.

"I'm here," Brent called. "Where is everybody?"

His booming voice brought the echoes to life.

"Enter the homeowner," Lucy said as we started downstairs.

Once again Lucy was able to glide past the landing with no dire consequences. We met Brent at the foot of the staircase.

Misty had forgotten her manners. She was leaping at the large white bag Brent held about a foot above her nose, communicating her desire for food with high pitched yips.

"I brought burgers," he said. "Who's hungry besides Misty?"

"Do you have one for her?" I asked.

"Sure thing. With just meat and a slice of cheddar."

He handed the bag to me. It was wet. For the first time I noticed the sheen of rainwater on his green jacket and in his hair and the light pattering of raindrops on the window.

"Is the ghost at home today?" he asked.

"We haven't seen her," Lucy said, "but we heard the scratching. It's stopped now."

"Well, let's forget about it and eat. I'm celebrating. The new contractor starts work tomorrow. This is the last meal we'll have in a torn-up kitchen."

"Is coffee all right for everyone?" Lucy asked, hovering over the coffee maker.

It was. Brent unwrapped the burgers. He'd also brought large orders of French fries and garden salads. I shouldn't be hungry yet but found that I was. His enthusiasm for the burgers was infectious.

"It's all coming together," he said. "The house will have a new look. I'll move my caretaker and the dogs in as soon as possible. I'll stock the pantry and buy dog food and treats. We'll have a grand old house warming."

Lucy looked up in alarm. "But we're not ready yet."

"It'll be okay. I don't want to wait any longer."

I sympathized with him. His project couldn't remain in limbo forever. On the other hand, I couldn't help but feel that plans for a grand opening were premature.

~ * ~

Another sweep of the attic netted a surprise. On opening the old trunk, I found a Christmas stationery box that contained one of those 'Anything' notebooks with a blue unicorn on the cover and, inside, entries from Holly's journal dating from the year of her disappearance.

Finally, a real clue. I couldn't wait to go home and read it.

"I expect a report as soon as you finish," Brent said.

"Me too," Annica added. "Before you do anything else."

"You'll both hear from me later. I'm so glad I opened that box."

Brent closed the lid with a resolute bang. "That's it for today then."

A bolt of thunder rolled across the sky. Annica started and Misty whimpered as heavy rain began a merciless pounding on the roof. I felt as if it had the power to break through the shingles and saturate us.

"Looks like the storm's back with a vengeance," Brent said. "We'd getter go back downstairs."

Misty whined again.

"It's all right, girl," I said. "She doesn't usually fuss during storms. Let's wait inside till it eases up."

Clutching the 'Anything' book, I led the way out of the attic, walking carefully across the uneven floor, down the stairs, and across the landing. I grasped the bannister, glad the workmen had stabilized it before they fled the house. The stairway had darkened considerably. On the landing, the rainbow colors of the stained glass window momentarily regained their brilliance as lightning struck at the window.

In my peripheral vision, I saw a shape. Something brushed against me. An unexpected weight pushed me off balance, and I felt myself falling forward down the stairs.

~ * ~

The dog was in my arms. I held her so close to my chest that she might have been a part of me. She was heavy, but I couldn't relax my grip. I had lost Holly's 'Anything' book. Somewhere. That didn't matter. If I lost the dog, I would die.

The dog I held was Misty. She cried as we went whirling through the void with the leaves and the furniture and the trees, buffeted by a mighty wind.

A train. We had to reach the station or the train would leave without us.

All aboard!

The voice drowned in the wind.

It wasn't a train. I had heard that sound before in a nightmare-turned-to-life on the day the tornado touched down in Oakpoint. The day the massive poplar tree in my backyard crashed into my house. The day...

Misty didn't want to stay in my arms. She tried to free herself. She fought desperately to regain the ground and control of her legs. I held fast to her, but the monster winds were too strong for me. They ripped her from my arms.

I had lost her.

I tried to call her name, but I had no voice.

My world broke apart with a weak cry from an unknown throat.

Thirty-eight

It was like a dream. You, the dreamer, are the main participant, and at the same time, you remain yourself, observing the proceedings. Difficult to comprehend, yes, unless you're experiencing it.

I was Holly torn away from her dog, Tristan, and I was Jennet separated by the all-powerful winds from her collie, Misty. I was Jennet cast adrift in the void. I forced my eyes open, afraid of what I was going to see.

The air was filled with moving objects. An entire tree sailed past me, trailing its massive root system, dripping particles of dirt. In its wake, a white lawn bench flew perilously close to my body. Leaves, ripped from their branches, whipped against my face in passing. I felt wet and chilled as if I'd been dunked into water and pulled out again.

In the distance I could barely make out a patch of white, a shooting star in the shape of a collie. Could I possibly reach her?

Strong hands closed around my wrists, tugging me downward to an unfamiliar earth, a desolate plane stripped of vegetation.

Was this my world? Or had the mighty winds set me down in the magical land of Oz where I didn't belong?

Oh, how I wish again I was in Michigan, down on the farm...

The dream began to slip away from me. The darkness, the debris whirling through the air, the white collie—all vanished. I lay on the hard earth, unmoving and hurting.

"Holly, wake up. Holly—"

I knew that voice. Micah. He had come to rescue me.

I tried to sit up. Pain exploded in the back of my head.

"Tristan," I murmured.

"I didn't see him. Lie still for a moment, Holly. It was a tornado. It's gone now."

"Where are we?" I asked. "Is the house gone?"

"I don't know."

I tried to remember. Bits and pieces danced giddily in my mind, just close enough for me to grasp them. "I was inside writing," I said. "I heard the siren—didn't think I could get out in time. I couldn't find my dog. I promised Tristan we'd be together forever."

A memory flickered in my mind. A bride standing proudly beside her groom, saying 'Forever.' Was that my memory? I was never married.

Micah pushed aside a piece of wood that in another life had been an intricately carved mahogany table leg.

"I'll see if I can find him, but later."

I closed my eyes again. "It's so quiet. It's like the world ended. Maybe that's what happened."

"It was a tornado," Micah repeated. "It passed. Hopefully it didn't take anyone with it."

*I felt a strange emptiness as the Holly spirit left my body—*and I was Jennet again. Brent lifted me and carried me to a red striped ivory sofa I'd last seen in the attic of his house on Loosestrife Lane.

~ * ~

"She's waking up," said a familiar voice. Not Micah's.

"Oh, thank God. Oh, Jennet." Another voice, a woman's voice. I recognized it, then heard a plaintive little whimper.

"That damned dog." That was the first voice. The man.

"It wasn't Misty's fault. Jennet would never blame her, not in a million years. That accursed landing tripped her."

How could a landing do that?

I reached into space. My hand landed on warm fur, and my world came back to me slowly. But it came. My white collie, Misty, stood at the sofa's side, ears flattened, tail wagging. It wasn't Micah hovering over me but Brent and Lucy and Annica. My dear friends.

Misty placed her paw on the cushion, and collie kisses brought the rest of my world back to me.

"Welcome back, Jennet," Lucy said softly, touching my forehead lightly.

"Yeah, welcome back." That was Annica. "Don't you dare leave us."

"Crane," I whispered.

"The sheriff's going to kill me," Brent said. "He gave me orders to keep you safe. I promised I would, but hell…"

Fully restored to consciousness, I said, "I'm all right, Brent, except my head is pounding. Do you have some aspirin in your purse, Lucy, or any pain killer?"

"Sorry," Lucy said. "No."

"You're not taking any pills," Brent said. "We're going straight to Emergency."

I tried to sit up at that pronouncement. "No. I just lost my footing—"

"You fell," Lucy said. "All the way to the ground floor. Misty made you lose your balance. You fell on her."

I didn't remember that. I never ever wanted to hurt one of my collies. "Oh, my poor baby. I might have crushed her."

"She wasn't hurt. Just surprised."

I tried to sit all the way up, but my body rebelled. I felt as if it had been slammed against a concrete wall. Not that I'd ever had that experience.

"You lock up, Annica," Brent said. "I'll carry Jennet out to the car. Lucy, you come with me."

"Wait!" I said.

"No arguments, Jennet." He lifted me. "And we're off and running."

Under her breath, Annica said, "This house is haunted. It's vengeful. There's no doubt of it now."

There never was, I thought.

As Brent carried me to the door, I noticed the 'Anything' book lying at the foot of the stairs where it had fallen out of my hands. Holly's journal. The answers.

"Annica," I said. "Get the book."

~ * ~

Hours passed before Crane took me home. Hours of questions and watching each second pass on the clock. Lying on what must be the most uncomfortable bed in the hospital. Drive-by visits from medical personnel. Being pushed down cold corridors to rooms with strange equipment.

I was thirsty. I longed for a tall glass of fruit juice with ice cubes in it, but all they offered me was water.

I didn't even attempt to keep the whine out of my voice. In my room, in a brief peaceful interlude, I said, "I want to go home. I just took a tumble—"

"You will," Crane said. "Be patient."

"Should you take Misty to the vet?"

"Misty's okay. It's you I'm worried about."

"They said my tests were good."

"It's your knack for inviting trouble," he added. "You shouldn't have been anywhere near that house. I don't know what its attraction is."

My beloved husband had slipped with ease into his stern deputy sheriff's lecture mode. I wondered what he had said to Brent.

My head started to ache again.

"You're right, Crane," I murmured. "Right about everything."

I set my mind on a walk down Jonquil Lane where golden daffodils bloomed in the spring and our green Victorian farmhouse in its surround of summer flowers waited for me at the end of this terrible day.

Where the dogs were.

Thirty-nine

At home with a clean bill of health and a myriad bruises, I sat in front of the bay window with my beautiful collies grouped around me. Halley and Misty insisted on lying closer than their sisters. The message from all seven was clear: *We thought you were never coming home.*

I sipped herbal tea, rested, and remembered. In my unconscious state, I'd had a dream that was more than a dream. Perhaps like Lucy I'd had a fragmentary vision of a world long past. I had been Holly Wickersham. I remembered the tornado, Micah, losing my collie, Tristan, and being carried to a distinctive green-striped sofa that existed in the real waking world.

Facts previously guessed at were now clear to me. Holly loved Micah. He seemed solicitous of her. In the dream, that is. The tornado had flung her far from Loosestrife Lane to an area ravaged by the killer winds. Here Micah had found her. Along the way she had lost Tristan.

One more detail surfaced. As I was propelled through the air, I'd felt as if someone had dunked me/Holly in cold water. In the pond, perhaps. Was there anything I'd forgotten?

I went over the memories again. Micah... The tornado... No; that was all. I sat back and drew my conclusions.

Micah didn't kill Holly, at least not at that time. Tristan, the collie, may have perished in the tornado. Holly survived.

But darn and double darn! She still vanished. I wasn't any closer to discovering her fate. And that wasn't likely to change. I could hardly throw myself down the stairs of Brent's house hoping the dream would continue and give me the 'what happened afterward.' I had to keep looking for answers, to look elsewhere.

Then I remembered Holly's 'Anything' book, her journal. I could have been reading it at the moment, but Annica had it. If she'd remembered. At least I hoped she'd taken it out of the house. I reached for my phone to call her, then remembered she was still working at Clovers.

In the mid-afternoon, Lucy came over with a box from the Hometown Bakery. My friends knew how to cheer me. This morning Camille had brought a loaf of banana bread, a favorite of mine, created with her own recipe.

Lucy set the box on the dining room table. The collies went into their traditional welcome frenzy, eventually settling, which allowed Lucy and me to hear ourselves talking.

"What did you bring?" I asked.

"Chocolate meringue tarts. I'll make the tea. We need to see what the leaves know."

I rose. "I can do it. I'm not an invalid."

But every joint, every muscle rebelled as I made my painful way to the kitchen, trailed by Candy and Misty.

Lucy sat at the oak table while I filled the teakettle with water and brought my plainest teacups down from the cupboard. I preferred floral patterned bone china, but Lucy required a white background for her tea leaf formations. I cut the string on the bakery box and exclaimed over the chocolate tarts, another favorite of mine.

"They look *so* good," I said, sitting opposite her. "I've been waiting to talk to you, Lucy. Yesterday when I fell I had a dream. Well, it was more than a dream."

"What was it?"

How could I do it justice? "It was an out-of-body experience. No, wait. That isn't quite right. I fell into the body of Holly Wickersham. I was her. Does that make sense?"

"I think so. You stepped into Holly's life for a moment."

"It couldn't have been only a dream. It was too real, and I remember every detail, as if it actually happened to me. Maybe it did."

I told her about the strange experience while the teakettle's whistle cut into the silence, and Star howled in response from the living room.

"That's like what happened to me, without the bells and whistles," Lucy said. "I was flying through the air along with furniture and branches and a dog. I felt so terribly ill, and there was no Micah to come to my assistance. I never saw Holly and never left my own body.

"My problem is that I came to before anything could happen. Apparently Micah had just found Holly some distance from the house. The dog wasn't with her. He was carrying her to safety when I woke up."

"Brent carried you to the sofa," Lucy said. "That was such a terrible time. We didn't know if you were still alive, if you'd broken your arm or leg. One minute you were standing on the landing. The next you were falling. It happened so fast. Like a tornado."

"Yes. Exactly like that."

"Your experience reinforces the terror I felt on the landing," Lucy said. "In your dream, Holly was in an upstairs room writing. It was summer. The dog was probably outside—"

If that were the case, the scratching sound couldn't be Tristan trying to free himself from behind a closed door.

I thought of something else. How did my out-of-this-world experience mesh with what Micah had told me about Holly and the tornado? Which version should I believe?

My own, I thought.

Lucy continued. "Holly heard the siren and possibly saw the funnel cloud through the landing window. The original might have been plain glass. She would have had a clear view."

And the landing absorbed her terror and kept it fresh for someone at a future time with Lucy's abilities.

"Holly panicked," I said. "She didn't have time to escape to the basement. She was thrown out of her house. But I didn't notice any sign of damage."

"That happened ages ago," Lucy said. "The owner at the time would have made repairs."

"I was ready to believe Holly had died in the tornado. Now, with my dream or vision or whatever you'd call it, I'm not so sure. That means we still have a mystery to solve."

"Holly isn't at peace," Lucy said. "She left something undone. And she wants us to help her."

~ * ~

The somber mood of our visit changed as Lucy interpreted the formations in my teacup. My fortune was a mixture of good and bad. The bad was the initial 'V' representing Veronica the Viper. She was still on the scene and, if the tea leaves told the truth, dangerously close to my home. Crane hadn't mentioned her. I didn't think he would.

"I don't know why you're concerned about Veronica," Lucy said. "It's obvious. Crane is devoted to you."

"She's the one who's in my cup."

"Maybe she's going to do you a good turn."

"I don't believe that."

"You still have a good fortune. You'll get your wish. You're going to take a trip. I still see the overflowing basket that was in your last cup. But I see clouds."

"Storm clouds?"

"Stormy skies perhaps. Trouble down the line. You have an enemy." She pointed to a long light leaf.

"I always have an enemy somewhere," I said. "Do I defeat him?"

"The leaves don't say."

"Well, then, I'll hope for the best. Let's each have another tart."

~ * ~

I had two more visitors that day. Annica brought four fried chicken dinners from Clovers, and Holly's 'Anything' Book. Brent came with her, carrying an apple pie and a shopping bag from Pluto's.

I took the book from Annica's hand eagerly. "Did you read it?" I asked.

"Well, sure. It answers some of our questions. I found out that Holly had another boyfriend, but you'll want to read it yourself. How are you feeling?"

"Better."

"I'm beginning to think my house has a curse on it," Brent announced as he doled out treats to my ravenous pack.

"Just beginning to?" I asked.

"It's like someone doesn't want to see my Collie House succeed."

"Did another contractor quit?" I asked.

"No, the guys are hard at work, but my caretaker backed out of the deal. You'll never guess what happened?"

"She saw a ghost?"

"Not even close. Miss Coulder accepted a marriage proposal. She's moving to Florida."

"For heaven's sake."

"You'll still have time to find someone else while the contractor works on the house," Annica said.

"I was getting discouraged. Then I looked over my collies, the senior fringe. They're counting on me. I can't let them down."

"So it's sail on, sail on, and on," I said.

I didn't remind Brent that his collies were quite likely happy in his barn, that they had no way of knowing about the house on Loosestrife Lane and the green acreage and the cool pond with the largest weeping willow tree in Foxglove Corners to lie under.

I longed to be back on Brent's property, to bring out a lawn chair and watch the gold fish in the pond. To read or rest or simply dream.

Even though I was afraid.

<h1 style="text-align:center">Forty</h1>

"Since we invited ourselves to dinner, we thought we'd bring the food," Brent said scooping up a handful of cashews. "I didn't think you'd feel up to cooking after your fall."

He was right about that. I'd brought two steaks out to defrost, the easiest meal I could think of for Crane and me, but Clovers' fare was infinitely better.

"Mary Jeanne just came back from visiting her cousin in Louisiana," Annica said. "She brought back a fantastic recipe for fried chicken. I had to hurry and make up our dinners before we sold out."

Brent hovered over the table. "It sure smells good."

"She made her cousin's prize-winning coconut cake, too, but we *did* sell out of that."

I surveyed the table with a hostess' critical eye. The food was plain but eminently appetizing, as was a surprise side, the pizza Crane had brought home, thinking, like Brent, that I wouldn't want to make dinner. Annica had taken over my kitchen to toss a salad and bake cornbread muffins. I was being treated like an invalid, and our simple dinner took on the spirit of a celebration.

"Fried chicken and pizza," Brent said. "That's my kind of diet."

I lit the candles in the antique candleholders that had belonged to Crane's Civil War era ancestress, Rebecca Ferguson. As I transferred the contents of the Clovers boxes onto plates, I glanced at the 'Anything' book. It lay on the credenza, tantalizing me with its unread pages. But I couldn't be rude. I'd have to wait until my friends departed, before I could read the entries. Annica refused to say anything more about the book, claiming she didn't want to spoil the suspense, but the fact that Holly had another boyfriend opened a wealth of new possibilities.

Darn it all! I was the one who had found it. Oh well, it would make excellent before-bed reading.

"We don't want to miss the news tonight," Brent said. "Did you hear what happened to Kate Brennan?"

"No, what?"

"She was in an accident last night. A hit-and-run."

"Oh, no. Is she hurt?"

"I heard she was in stable condition," he said. "David Ardmore is taking over her segment."

"And the investigation, too? Because some of the dogs are still missing, and no one ever found O'Meara's partner."

"No one knows where O'Meara is," Brent added.

Annica brought in the beverages, and we took our places, Crane at the head of the table.

"We'll find out tonight," Brent said. "Remember, Lyle and Marguerite are still missing one of their dogs, Lady."

"I wonder..." I helped myself to a cornbread muffin and passed the basket. "No, that's too far-fetched."

"What is it, honey?" Crane asked.

"I just wondered if the two incidents were related. If by some chance Kate was targeted because of the investigation."

"Mmm," Annica said. "I'll bet that's what happened. O'Meara ran her down."

"Unfortunately hit-and-runs are a dime a dozen," Crane pointed out. "Just like road rage. People don't want to get in trouble. If there were no witnesses, they just take off."

"There's a thousand dollar reward for information about the accident," Brent added. "It's expected to go up. Kate's fans are sending in donations."

"The people who were affected by Sea-to-Sea should get together again," I said, thinking of the dogs like Lady who were still unaccounted for. "I'll call Helena and see if she'll host another meeting."

Finally Brent and Annica departed on a wave of bonhomie. I blew out the candles, cleaned the kitchen for the quick morning breakfast I always cooked for Crane, and saw that a good portion of the evening remained. I opened Holly's 'Anything' book and began to read.

At first the entries were a disappointment. Holly recorded her writing progress which slowed down dramatically as summer came. Instead of working, she lay in the backyard of her shady new Victorian rental or strolled on Sagramore Beach.

In Holly's time, the trees must have been younger and the landscape tamed. Her favorite place to sit was in front of the fish pond with the water fresh, the rock garden flowers flourishing, and the flamingoes newly painted a silvery peach color.

She was writing in a different genre, a western saga, and it wasn't going well.

The first reference to a man, Mark, came in July. They met at a peach festival.

Her new boyfriend?

After that, Mark's name appeared on every page. "I think he may be the One," she wrote. "Although it's early. Time will tell."

After that initial meeting, they were often together, mostly dining out in upscale restaurants; she recorded that Micah was jealous. She didn't tell him about Mark, only that she was busy writing.

I skimmed through pages detailing dates—summer concerts, romantic picnics, movies—then came across this telling entry: 'I'm taking the dog and driving up to Mackinac City to meet Mark this weekend,' she wrote.

It was August 15, the day the tornado struck.

~ * ~

Going up and down the stairs was a painful chore. By then, I should have felt better, not worse. Oddly enough, when I had distractions, like company for dinner, I didn't think about how much it hurt to put one foot after another. My discomfort was especially worse in the moments after I got out of bed.

The next morning I paused at the top of the staircase frozen by the rush of memories that assailed me. A shape at my side, barely discernible in my peripheral vision. The sickening sensation of a stair melting to nothingness under my feet. A fall into darkness. Into the body of Holly Wickersham.

Something was wrong with this version of the incident, and suddenly I knew what it was. Misty hadn't caused me to lose my balance. She wasn't the shape. There was another dog on the stairs. I knew this even without having seen her on the landing.

Oh, but Misty was there. Lucy, Annica, and Brent had told me that I'd fallen on top of her. Now that I was remembering more details, I had heard Misty screech, a high pitched cry I'd never heard before.

What exactly had happened?

What if *two* shapes had brushed against me just before I fell? Misty and the other dog, Holly's collie, Tristan, who haunted the pool. Or was there just one shape, the phantom collie?

It wasn't the house that was dangerous; it was the revenants who lurked in the shadows of time, waiting to cause a catastrophe. But why they'd wish to harm me was a mystery.

I could have sustained more than cuts and bruises in my fall. I could have lost my life.

But was a fall so unusual? People fell all the time. Once a Foxglove Corners woman had fallen down a flight of basement stairs, and a deluded friend had blamed a collie, my own Gemmy, for leaving a dog toy underfoot.

Almost never did a phantom cause a fall. As far as I knew.

Crane's voice cut through my meanderings. "Ready for pancakes, Jennet?"

Crane was the cook this morning. His inquiry stirred the collies to action. They all began to bark at once.

"He said *Jennet, not dogs,*" I had to say that even if no one was there to hear it.

I followed the delicious breakfast smell of bacon into the kitchen where Crane ladled pancakes onto my plate. "It's lucky you're not going to school this morning," he said. "The kids would tease you."

"Do I look that bad?"

"Not bad. Just manhandled."

"The story would be: I fell, having been pushed by a ghost."

"They'd never believe that. By the way, is that what *you* believe?"

"I don't know."

"Whatever happened, I hope you're going to boycott Brent's place from now on. That fall may be the tip of the iceberg."

I cut my pancakes in sections and reached for the syrup.

How could I answer him? I planned to return as soon as I could walk without pain.

Forty-one

I resolved that the next time I set foot in Brent's house, Misty would be at my side. Not that she'd been helpful when I'd fallen, but I had faith in her abilities or sixth sense or whatever I chose to call it. She had heard the eerie scratching sound inside the house, had seen the phantom dog's face reflected in the pond, and I believed she was aware of shadow figures from another dimension that walked the halls.

I didn't know how she could protect me from malign forces, but knew I'd feel safer if she were with me. As for Holly, she had more to tell me. I couldn't help her or Brent or the collies who waited to move into their new home until I knew the whole story and neutralized the evil vapors that lived on in the house.

Of course I didn't discuss my plans with Crane. First, at present they were nebulous. Then I told myself that I didn't want him to worry about me. He had enough stress every day as he patrolled the roads and by-roads of Foxglove Corners. Besides, chances were the house had already done its worst and there would be no second incident.

Or so I told myself.

In the meantime, my bruises faded, and I found I could move without pain. Kate Brennan returned to the air with her arm in a sling, but as bright and energetic as ever. She promised an imminent update on the Sea-to-Sea case and the slippery Duncan O'Meara. And June gave way to July.

The days were long and sultry. Brent kept searching for his caretaker with mixed results. As soon as he interviewed a likely prospect, a complication reared its head. In the meantime, little by little, the contractor completed the work on the house with no untoward incidents. Shiny new kitchen appliances replaced the old outdated ones, the walls glowed with fresh paint, and the new windows sparkled.

"It's in move-in condition," Brent said. "If only we could move in."

That week Helena invited the Sea-to-Sea victims to an impromptu gathering at her house. One person was new, a lady with silver curls and a quiet manner, named Abby Rineland who had never received the beagle puppy she had purchased. Marguerite had found her on Facebook and reached out to her.

As the evening was warm, Helena gathered us together in her patio crowded with pots of fragrant colorful annuals and hanging ferns. Arden, looking freshly groomed, greeted each of the guests with flattened ears and a vigorously wagging tail, then lay at Helena's feet, her paws crossed. She was a perfect lady. It hadn't taken her long to adjust to her new home.

"You're one of the lucky ones, Helena," Lyle said, giving Arden a rough pat on the head. "You have your dog."

"Yes, and you have Shamrock."

"But not Lady," Marguerite said. "They must have separated them. Our two were always together, and poor Lady suffered from motion sickness."

Lyle had been lucky in another way. He had escaped the hand of the law because Duncan O'Meara had vanished into the ether without pressing charges, which wasn't strange as O'Meara undoubtedly wanted to keep a low or non-existent profile. No one knew where he was; no one was currently looking for him.

"I know why some of the dogs came back and not others," Lyle said.

Helena passed a plate of cookies around, pausing to let Harold take three. "Do tell."

"That scum had them all together in one place, likely waiting to sell them off. After the crash, he figured the law was on to him, so he let them loose. They stayed together until people noticed them wandering down that road. It's a wonder they weren't run over."

"What about the others, the ones that are still missing?" Sue asked.

"They were in another place," he said. "Maybe together, maybe not. He could have sold them already, for all we know."

Marguerite added, "Lady has been gone a whole month. We'll never get her back."

"Don't say that," Harold said. "I'm not going to stop looking until I have my dog under my own roof and that lowlife, O'Meara, is behind bars."

"He hasn't been going to his favorite bars," Lyle said. "At least not when I'm there. I've been checking."

Sue muffled a laugh. "I hope you leave your gun at home."

"He does," Marguerite said. "I see to that. I never signed up to be a fugitive."

Sue said, "Maybe O'Meara left the state."

Helena sat the plate of cookies on a wicker side table. "Everyone, help yourself. There's more in the kitchen."

Including my contribution of two dozen pineapple drop cookies. I hoped Helena would have enough to serve, given Harold's fondness for sweets. His three cookies had already disappeared.

"I've been checking the internet everyday looking for a new pet transport service," Sue said. "Yesterday I found Oceanview Transport Services, but no one answers their phone. I'm going to keep trying."

Sea. Ocean. I considered. "That name sounds similar to Sea-to-Sea. But a smart con artist would choose a completely different name. If he's back in business."

"If he's smart," Harold said. "I don't think he is."

Abby sighed. "I guess we have to see if Kate has anything new to report."

"I'll bet you two to one that O'Meara was the hit-and-run driver," Lyle said. "Kate is getting too close."

"Let's hope she is," Abby murmured.

These get-togethers weren't accomplishing anything practical. How could they? But they did foster a sense of camaraderie in a group that had little else in common. They kept positive energy flowing, and I detected another benefit. Helena and Harold seemed easier with each other. It was almost as if they'd spent time together apart from the meetings.

Also, Abby had expressed an interest in Sue's rescue work and asked if she had to have a collie to join the League.

I stirred in my chair. I'd been sitting too long, and the effects of my fall were making themselves known. Luckily the meeting was winding down.

First recover completely, I thought. *Then carry on.*

~ * ~

Annica had helped Brent furnish the rooms of the house on Loosestrife Lane. Most of them, that is. They'd incurred very little expenditure, using furniture brought down from the attic. Annica had made curtains for the kitchen and stocked the cupboard with both human and canine staples. On a shopping trip to the Green House of Antiques, she had found an old-time collie print in an elaborate frame for the living room.

"It's perfect for the house," she said as we cooled off on another record breaking hot day at Clovers with lime coolers. "There's this sweet little girl playing with a litter of collie puppies while the mother looks on. You can just see the worry in the mother's eyes."

"I'd like that myself."

"You'll see it. Can you go with me while I hang it? I want it to be a surprise for Brent."

"When?" I asked.

"Tomorrow, sometime after noon."

I didn't have to think about it. I wanted to return to the house sooner rather than later. My calendar was free, and I was almost back to normal.

"I'll pick you up around one," I said.

"Promise me you won't fall down any steps."

"There's no reason to go upstairs."

Annica had reported that the attic was practically empty. Only Holly's possessions remained, along with furnishings too shabby to grace the newly restored house.

"I'm bringing Misty," I said.

"Bring whoever you like. Brent thinks he may have found his caretakers. After they move in with the dogs, we can't roam around at will."

"We've had the house to ourselves for a nice long spell," I said.

And it was still a place of mystery. All the new paint in the world, all the restoration and rearrangements, couldn't rid Brent's house of its dark ambience.

Could anything?

Forty-two

Steamy morning. Afternoon storms.

I thought about the day's forecast as I came down the stairs the next day. I could have hoped for better weather, but we'd be there and back before the storms. I hoped.

I fastened Misty's leash to her collar and reached for the umbrella. Candy, who had followed me downstairs, treading in my shadow, retreated with a short bark and growl rolled into one.

None of the dogs liked my umbrella, dating from the day I'd inadvertently opened it in the house. I had no intention of doing so today. "It's bad luck," my mother used to say. Who believed that? Still, out of habit, one paid heed to old superstitions like knocking on wood and walking around a ladder rather than under it.

Candy sensed an adventure and wanted to be a part of it. Impossible, of course, and she knew that. Crane was the only one who could handle her when the urge to break away on her own overrode training and manners.

"Misty is going to be working today," I announced for the benefit of all. I imagined a happy scenario in which she pranced through the house like an ice princess, uncovering all of its secrets. And we lived happily ever after.

Right. We weren't going to wander through any rooms, nor the attic or basement. Annica would hang the picture, I'd supervise, and perhaps on the way back, we'd stop at the Green House of Antiques where Annica said as of yesterday three similar prints were displayed on the wall. Admittedly I was running out of wall space, but if I saw a picture I liked, I'd find room. Somewhere.

As I led Misty toward the door, the others watched me quietly. They knew this wasn't going to be a walk bestowed on a favored one.

"I'll be back soon," I told them and, at the last minute, grabbed my raincoat. And we were ready.

~ *~

Some days the house on Loosestrife Lane looked innocuous and even inviting in its surround of green lawn, now freshly mowed, neatly pruned shrubbery, and the massive weeping willow tree that shaded the pond. Other times it seemed to glower, warning away all comers who paused to admire its beauty.

Today was a glowering day. The house waited silently under low clouds. Waiting to pounce?

But I was being fanciful. Soon I'd see collies patrolling the grounds, bestowing new life on an old structure. I'd knock on the door instead of unlocking it, and Brent's kind caregiver would make me welcome.

Annica lifted the print out of the backseat. She had wrapped it in heavy brown paper to protect it from the elements. I carried a package containing a picture hanging kit and a hammer.

"This frame is gorgeous, but it's so heavy," she said as Misty gave it an interested sniff. "I can't wait till Brent sees the picture."

We walked up to the porch, Annica holding the print while I tried to keep Misty at my heel. As soon as her paws had touched the ground, she had turned into a whirling dervish.

"She's wild today," Annica observed.

"For some reason. Misty, heel!"

Surprisingly, she obeyed me. I unlocked the door, and she pushed inside ahead of us, long nose first. I unfastened her leash and set it on a chair.

Annica shivered. "It feels clammy."

"No more so than usual. It needs fresh air."

But we weren't going to stay long enough to warrant opening windows. Annica leaned the print against the wall and tore off the protective paper, letting it fall to the floor. "There, Jennet. Look."

I beheld one of those nostalgic turn-of-the-century scenes set in a flower garden with a stately white house in the distance. A little girl, clad in pink with a white pinafore, held a fluffy golden collie puppy in her arms. The puppy's littermates were gathered around her under the watchful eyes of the mother.

"I call it, *Don't Drop Him*, Annica said.

I smiled. "Children and collies used to be a popular subject for artists. Not anymore."

"Sometimes they added ponies."

She took the picture hanging kit out of the bag and studied it. "All these nails. How are you supposed to know which one to use?"

"You need a long, strong nail. The picture is heavy. You don't want it to fall off the wall. Did you bring a level?"

"A what?"

"A gadget that tells you if you're hanging it straight."

"Uh, no." She took a pencil out of her skirt pocket. "We should be able to see if it's straight. I want it above the sofa, in the middle. It'll be the focal point of the room."

I helped her move the sofa. She marked the wall with a small 'x' and lifted the print.

"Maybe I should have let Brent hang it," she said, handing it to me.

"It'll be more of a surprise if he walks in and sees it."

"Here goes." She picked up the hammer. "This has to be right the first time. I don't want to crack the plaster."

She pounded the nail into the wall. Instantly the house filled with the most ungodly shriek I'd ever heard. She jumped back as if the wall had bitten her, and my heart skipped a beat. The hammer fell to the floor; the nail remained imbedded in the wall.

I heard a heart-rending howl. Misty?

Annica made no move to retrieve the hammer. "For the love of God, what was that?"

I battled an inappropriate urge to laugh. To keep laughing until my body compelled me to stop. "You wounded the wall."

"Don't make jokes, Jennet. Wood can't feel."

"And the house isn't haunted," I said.

It seemed I could still hear the echo of that cry. What had we done? Yes, we. Annica and I were a team.

Suddenly Annica froze. "What's that sound? Do you hear scratching?"

I listened. Nothing would surprise me, but what we were hearing was pattering on the windows. "It's raining," I said.

"Oh, yes, of course. Rain." Gingerly she touched the nail. Embedded firmly in the wall, surrounded by a quarter-sized pool of cracked paint, it didn't move.

"You did well," I said.

"Let's hang the picture and get out of here," Annica said. "Help me, Jennet."

I took one end of the print, and together we lifted the thin cord attached to the back over the nail. Annica moved the frame slightly to the left and gave it a small tug.

"It's as straight as I can make it," she said.

"The picture looks good there."

The many shades of green in the scene blended perfectly with the stripes in the sofa. The print added a final finishing touch to the room.

"I think something else hung above the sofa at one time," Annica said. "A mirror or a painting."

"In which case the wall shouldn't have cried out when you drove the nail into it."

"Good grief, Jennet, you have a morbid turn of mind. What we heard was the wall settling."

"Walls don't settle. Floors do that."

"*Houses* do that."

She picked up the wrapping paper and gathered the picture hanging kit and the hammer. "Let's get out of here," she repeated.

"Where's that dog?" I murmured. "Misty?"

But she was at the foot of the stairs, dragging her leash, as ready as we were to leave Brent's house.

Annica said, "I wish Brent had never bought this place. I've lost all my enthusiasm for it. It's evil."

"It does have some strange properties."

"It's too much for us, Jennet."

"Well, you're finished decorating, aren't you?"

"I thought I'd look for some more collie prints, but I'll let Brent do that. Maybe he'll want pictures of his collies instead."

"We'll have to tell him about the sound the wall made," I said.

She nodded. "And we both heard it. I hope he believes us."

Forty-three

It was pouring outside. I paused on the threshold, one hand on the umbrella, the other on Misty's leash. She pawed the floor impatiently. She might be eager to get wet, but I had to summon all my courage to plunge into the maelstrom.

"Should we wait for it to let up a bit?" I asked.

Annica glanced back at the print and frowned. It seemed to have moved a little. We'd have to straighten it, or Brent could do that. I didn't mention it to her.

"It may get worse," she said. "I vote we make a dash for it."

The Ford Focus waited for us, parked on the lane, a port in the storm. I took the keys out of my pocket. How far to the car? If we ran?

I struggled to maintain my control of Misty who was acting wild again, not like herself at all. Annica reached for the umbrella, and we stepped into the temporary shelter of the wraparound. "Stay close to me. One, two, three—Go!"

She dashed into a wall of water. A sudden wind turned the umbrella inside out. I struggled to hold on to it and the leash. To my dismay, Misty veered to the right, in the direction of the fishpond.

A bolt of lightning split the sky, for a fleeting moment illuminating the pond. The water churned under wind-whipped willow strands.

Then the world sank back into darkness. The only reality was the driving rain.

I concentrated all my strength on pulling Misty away from her chosen path.

"Jennet!"

Annica's voice seemed far away. High and desperate. Had I heard it? Or imagined it?

"Jennet! Over here. Hurry!"

Misty gave the leash a mighty tug, and a streak of pain burst in my arm, the one I had fallen on.

Drop the leash!

I hesitated too long. With an incredible surge of power, Misty dived into the pond, taking me with her.

I couldn't breathe. I was going to drown.

Drown in a backyard pond?

My body felt as heavy as if it were weighted with a boulder. Whirling water closed in on me, choking me. I swallowed a mouthful of vile warmish liquid. Frantically I reached for the surface. It had to be there. Just above me. If I could grab one of the large jagged-edged stones that ringed the pond—if I could hold on—I could pull myself to safety.

Help!

That was a thought, not a cry.

Annica would have seen what had happened. She'd be here. Any minute now.

Would she be in time?

Misty had wrenched the leash out of my hands. I couldn't see it, couldn't see her. My long wet hair and the pounding water blinded me. The world turned dark.

~ * ~

No human can outrun a tornado. It had wrenched the leash out of my hands, taken hold of Tristan and thrown him into the pond. Too fast. It had happened too fast. And I couldn't see him.

The water in the pond reached the boiling point. It leaped up, turned dark and ravenous. The leash floated on the surface and promptly disappeared, snatched away by the wind.

I couldn't leave my dog in the pond to drown.

I turned to look at the sky, dark and eerie. To my horror, the monstrous funnel cloud bore down on me.

It was too late.

A crash splintered the air as the cupola and the small porch beneath it broke apart, raining wood and brick and pieces of glass. Debris flew through the air. A piece of glass cut into my forehead above my left eye. Warm liquid trickled down my face.

My dog!

How deep was that pond? Why didn't I know?

I stepped over the rock border and sank down into the pond's churning depths.

~ * ~

"Hey, Jennet. Give me your hand."

A voice in the darkness and rain.

"The tornado?" I said.

"There's no tornado. Just rain."

Like a jet-propelled ball of fur, Misty leaped out of the pond water into the rain and jumped on me.

Annica shouted. "Run!" She grabbed my hand, and Misty sprang forward.

I barely heard her. But I ran, plowing through the wind and rain. Misty beat us to the Focus and pawed at the door. I pulled it open and collapsed on the seat, which was already drenched.

I held her leash in my hand. How had that happened? Hadn't the wind snatched it away?

I sat for a moment, letting my heartbeat resume its normal rate, letting water drip from my hair. Puzzled I touched my cheek. It was wet with rainwater, not blood, and it didn't hurt. My hair was its usual shoulder length. For a moment, it had seemed to hang down my back.

"Thank God," Annica said as she dropped into the passenger's seat. "I thought you were right behind me. Then I didn't see you. What made you go toward the pond?"

"Misty dragged me."

"Well, why didn't you let go of the leash?"

That was a good question, one without a good answer.

Annica was shivering. "Let's get home and change into some dry clothes. Can you turn the heater on?"

"We can't go anywhere yet," I said. "I can't see to drive. I can't see anything."

"Who else is going to be out on the road in this storm? You can drive slowly."

"I still have to be able to see what's in front of me."

Deer leaping across the road, a dog—

"I guess so." She quieted, then asked, "Back there... What did you mean about a tornado?"

Here in the safety of the car, with Misty standing up on the back seat shaking herself, I remembered. "I stepped into Holly's body again."

"No!"

"Yes. That is, I think so. My hair was long."

It was still wet, dripping down my neck. But it came down to my shoulders. No further. I touched it to make sure.

I turned on the heater and the windshield wipers, for all the good they did.

"In Holly's world, there was a tornado," I said. "She was trying to save her dog who'd jumped into the pond."

"Like Misty?"

"I didn't see that part, but it was her collie, Tristan. The phantom in the pond."

"What else happened?" she asked.

"There was a horrible crash. The cupola and the porch came down. I was caught in the explosion."

Again, I touched my cheek, still thinking I might feel a trickle of blood. It was wet but still only water.

"Well, that didn't happen. The house looks fine now."

"That part must have been rebuilt after the tornado," I said.

But how did this version of the past mesh with my other vision— of being rescued by Micah Frost who carried me into Brent's house and laid me on the sofa?

Annica held her hands in front of the heater's fan, shaking them. "Is that what happened to Holly?"

"Maybe, but you'd think if she drowned in the pond, somebody would have discovered her body. Her disappearance wouldn't have remained a mystery all these years."

"And where is it now?"

"Obviously not at the bottom of the pond. Brent had the pond drained and cleaned. The water is fresh. There are fish... That reminds me. Where are the goldfish?"

"That," Annica said, "is the least of our worries."

Forty-four

Finally I was able to drive away from Loosestrife Lane, slowly and carefully.

After a while, Annica said, "What you say makes sense," Annica said. "Except for the body. What happened to it?"

I reached over to turn the heater off. We were still wet, but the initial cold had passed. As I drove through ever-lessening rain, I relived my time in the pond, which had seemed longer than it could have been. I shivered just thinking about it.

From now on, stay out of the water.

"If Holly died in the pond, someone must have removed her body," I said.

"Someone like who?"

"Possibly Micah Frost or the other boyfriend."

I thought about what I had said. "In that case, though, they'd have told the authorities. Holly would have been listed among the fatalities of the tornado. Her death wouldn't become a decades-long mystery."

"That could be. But let's go back a little. Why would anyone move Holly's body and not say anything about it?"

I couldn't think of a reason. "Well, that's another aspect of the mystery. Remember this is all speculation."

"And where would they put it?" she asked. "Isn't stealing a body illegal?

"We're getting in over our heads," I said.

I slowed, as I turned onto a narrow road, its gravel slippery with water. The rain had tapered off to a drizzle, and I could see the sparkling wildflowers and myriad shades of green shining in the fresh wash. Everything renewed.

"When a tornado touches down, there's always a lot of confusion," I added.

I remembered my own experience in Oakpoint. My slow realization that the danger had passed, but a tree had crashed into my roof, leaving my house vulnerable to the elements. I recalled my arms around Halley who was trembling in the aftermath of the tornado, recalled thinking that in an instant my life had changed.

"If Holly died in the pond, I moved out of her body just in time," I said. "But I don't think she did. Tristan, her collie, died though."

The phantom in the pond. Holly couldn't save him.

A curious question remained. If my scenario were true, where was the dog's skeleton? Annica didn't ask. Anything could have happened to it, especially if the grounds had been unvisited for a long time.

We drove on in silence. Without a shred of hard evidence, I felt we were close to solving the mystery of Holly Wickersham's disappearance. Call it a premonition. Lucy would understand.

"I want us to get together soon to start assembling pieces of the puzzle," I said. "We're running out of time."

"You and me?"

"All of us who've experienced oddities at Brent's house. We can have dinner. Something simple like pizza."

"I'll bring dessert from Clovers, and we'll compare notes," Annica said. "Five heads are better than one."

"And Misty will be there," I said. "I wish she could talk."

~ * ~

Dinner couldn't have been simpler or more appealing: Two large pizzas, my salad, and strawberry meringue pie from Clovers. Even if we didn't end up with any breakthroughs, it was a pleasure to sit together and concentrate only on the mystery.

"All I want is a house that's quiet and doesn't push people down the stairs," Brent said. "Is that asking too much?"

"Not at all," I said. "I hope you'll have it."

"When the unhappy spirit is at rest, so will the house be," Lucy said. "I give you the case of the ghost in the wildflower field."

She referred to the ghost in white who had materialized to help herself to the flowers Brent and Annica had planted on the site of the burnt-to-the-ground pink Victorian. "You haven't seen her lately, have you, Annica?"

"No," she said. "Not since Jennet figured out who she was. Does that mean she's at rest?"

"I assume so. Let's do the same for Holly Wickersham."

"I don't think Holly was murdered," I said.

"Why not?" Brent asked. "We have the perfect villain—a jealous boyfriend."

"As a motive, it's weak. Who kills his girlfriend because she finds another man? Or because he resents her success?"

"What if they had a lover's quarrel?" Annica asked. "It could have been an accident. He struck her, she fell and hit her head on one of the stones around the pond. He panicked and hid her body."

"Annica may have a new career as a fiction writer one day," Lucy said.

"What about the man Holly was driving up to Mackinac Island to meet?" Annica asked.

"We don't have any information about him, only his first name," I said. "Besides, the tornado struck on the day she planned to leave, so she probably didn't go."

"Or she *did* go—and got caught in the tornado somewhere on the road between here and there."

"In that case, she could have been thrown out of her car into the woods," Brent said. "We'll never find her. But I hold with the idea that she was murdered."

Annica cut a dainty piece of her pizza, carefully removing the mushrooms of which she was always suspicious. "Finding a modern day killer is hard enough. When we're dealing with a cold case, hard becomes impossible."

"Not necessarily," Crane said. "It's been done."

"What difference does it make, after all?"

"I'm surprised you'd ask that, Annica," Lucy said. "We have a haunted house and a soul that isn't at rest."

"Don't forget my dream," Brent added. "A house where old collies can have a new home and happy caretakers who won't be spooked by spirits and—things. Now that I've found the perfect couple, I'm eager to move the collies in."

"Those people may never experience what we have," Lucy pointed out.

"I can't count on that."

"I don't see Micah Frost as Holly's killer," I said, "and I couldn't locate Jane Wickersham. I've read all Holly's books and her journals. There's nothing more in the attic. All we have to go on is...uh...what we have. Which isn't much."

I was missing something, but what? The explanation for the doughnut thief was most likely a vagrant who'd taken advantage of a door carelessly left ajar. Jane Wickersham had either moved out of the state or passed away. As for the eerie sounds in the house, like the unexplained scratching, there could be a logical explanation for it. The house was old. Didn't all old houses squeak and sigh and groan every now and then? Maybe the answer was simpler. Brent's house had mice that were good at hiding themselves.

I chose to slide over the cry the wall had uttered when Annica had pounded the nail into it. Logic held no explanation for that phenomenon.

There comes a time in every mystery when there is no other place to look, no other road to follow.

I glanced at Crane. He was breaking off a piece of pizza crust for Candy. I couldn't see her. She must have sneaked under the table. In any event, he looked nicely distracted.

"I went back to the house yesterday," I said. "I took Misty with me. We stood at the pond for a long time. I fixed my thoughts on that last vision I had. Nothing happened. Then I stood on the landing. Again, nothing. My memory was like a screen gone dark."

"Perhaps the story ends there," Lucy murmured. "At the pond."

"You should have called me," Annica said.

"Wrong." Crane looked up. "Neither of you should have gone. Haven't you had enough warnings?"

"It appears there's nothing else to know," Lucy said. "I could go back myself—"

"No," Brent countered. "You're too vulnerable, Lucy. Not until we're settled in, and I'm sure it's over. Then we'll have our housewarming."

"Nothing else to know," I repeated Lucy's words. "But what if there is and we give up too soon? I hate not knowing what happened to Holly."

"Let it be a literary mystery," Annica said. "I'll bet we're the only ones who care about it. Does anyone have any brilliant ideas?"

"I do." Brent picked up the server lying in the empty box. "Let's open up the other pizza."

And that was it.

~ * ~

That night I lay awake, thinking. Crane slept at my side. Halley and Misty guarded the doorway as usual. All was peaceful and calm, except for my runaway thoughts.

If I were never to have another glimpse into Holly's life, if indeed she had died on the day the tornado touched down in Foxglove Corners, I had to make sure to wring every ounce of significance out of the last look I had.

Reaching in vain for her collie, feeling the churning water closing around me/Holly, hearing the mighty crash as the cupola and the small porch beneath it broke apart, its pieces swept up by the killer wind along with all the other debris that blew in the air of Foxglove Corners that day.

A sharp-edged piece, possibly glass, had flown into Holly's face.

And the winds tossed her skyward as if she were a part of the cupola, flung her up and up—

And down again.

Forty-five

The cupola. That was the answer.

It had been destroyed in the tornado. At some point, repairs were made and a new cupola erected complete with a porch underneath which had always seemed purely ornamental without a door leading from the house. In time, the few people who lived in the neighborhood and the occasional passerby would have forgotten that it had been replaced.

Misty had shown an inordinate interest in that part of the property, sniffing, wanting to dig a hole in the bed of dandelions and impatiens that flourished at the foundation of the porch.

She was trying to tell me something.

Suppose the tornado had thrown Holly away from the pond, toward the house. Suppose as the cupola disintegrated, she had been caught in the maelstrom and it buried her in the wreckage? By the time the debris was cleared away, perhaps Holly's body would have been lying in a huge depression in the earth well hidden from sight? And never discovered.

It could have happened that way. Repairs completed, all traces of the original removed, and no one aware of the body buried deep in the ground.

By then Holly would be dead, her passing and her grave a mystery never to be solved, her fleeting hold on fame forgotten, all the terror of those last moments trapped in the walls of the house.

It *did* happen that way. Without a shred of evidence, I was certain I was right. Well, fairly certain. I needed proof if I were to convince anyone else.

I almost reached for my phone to call my friends back. In doing so, I glanced at the time. It was almost midnight. I'd have to wait until tomorrow.

Should I wake Crane? He wouldn't thank me. But this was important. I touched his shoulder lightly, then reconsidered and withdrew my hand. I would tell him tomorrow. He'd be more receptive to what he would no doubt call one of my wild ideas when he was full of pancakes and bacon.

I had someone else to convince. Someone who could help me prove my theory or shoot it down. Would Brent be amenable to having a part of his house torn down to search for a decades-old skeleton?

Maybe. He could afford it. He was congenial and fond of me and committed to giving the house everything it needed. Still, there were limits, even to Brent's good nature.

I couldn't guess what he might say, but I was going to find out.

~ * ~

"Have you gone completely crazy?" Brent demanded. "I can't have heard you right. You want me to do *what*?"

I set the last piece of strawberry meringue pie in front of him and poured him a cup of fresh hot coffee.

Crane's frosty eyes twinkled. "Jennet knows how to persuade a man, Fowler. She and I have a bet going," he added. "I'd like to win, so think carefully before you decide."

"Tell me again why you want me to take my house apart?" Brent said.

"Not the whole house. The cupola and the porch beneath it. That's where we'll find Holly's body or, rather, her bones."

"How do you know this?"

"Do you believe what I experienced at the pond yesterday?"

"I believe *you* believe it."

In a bid for time, he cut into his pie and took a long swallow of coffee, grimacing as he complained. "That's scalding. Are you trying to take me out?"

"Let it set for a while. Summarize what happened for me."

"Let's see. Holly heard the tornado siren. She ran out of the house and saw her dog in the pond. She went in after him. Did I miss anything?"

"No. What do you think happened afterward?"

"Holly might have died on the spot, drowned, or hit her head on the concrete and lost consciousness."

I nodded. "Anything can happen when a tornado touches down," I said. "And that one did, with the house right in its path. Last year I read about a family whose dog ended up all the way in the next town. After the earth settles, rescuers find the victims scattered far and wide."

"That makes a nice story," he said. "But I still think Holly's boyfriend or that other guy did her in. Her death didn't have anything to do with the tornado."

My version of the past tragedy was infinitely more credible. How to convince him?

"Well, I believe what I experienced. Did I mention Misty's attachment to that part of the house? Misty, my psychic collie?"

Hearing her name, Misty padded over to me and leaned her head against my leg.

Brent sighed. "Have you talked to Lucy about this?"

"Not yet. The idea just came to me last night."

"If I do what you're asking, it would mean another delay in opening the house," he said. "I've waited long enough."

Ah, he was beginning to bend, a hardy plant swaying in a strong wind.

"It shouldn't affect the rest of the house," I said. "Think of it as rebuilding a damaged porch. In the end, you'll have a brand new addition to the house."

"It's a lot of trouble and expense," he said. "Maybe for nothing."

"Do you really want to move people and collies into a house that sits on a grave?" I asked. "Don't you want all the disturbances to subside?"

He nodded slowly. "That's true."

His dessert dish was empty. Unfortunately, so was the pie plate. I should have baked another pie.

"Drink your coffee," I said. "It should be cool enough by now. Think it over."

"How about this?" Brent said. "Couldn't I have some of my men dig down deep all around the porch?"

"If we're going to investigate, we should be thorough."

He drained the cup. Quickly I refilled it. "I want to know what Lucy thinks about this."

"So do I. I'll call her."

He fell silent. Finally he said, "Damn, Jennet. Now that you've put the idea in my head, I'll always wonder. I can't have the ghost of Holly Wickersham rising out of the ground and walking through the house. How sure are you that that's what happened?" he asked.

"Ninety-nine percent," I answered promptly.

"You've always been right before."

Except for Crane's discreet cough and Misty's heavy breathing, the kitchen was silent.

Brent said, "Okay, I'll do it."

Success! "You won't be sorry," I assured him.

I hoped I wouldn't be either.

"It would be giving the house a fresh start," I said. "A clean slate."

"It looks like Jennet wins the bet," Crane said. "I didn't think you'd cave, Fowler. I hoped you wouldn't."

"What did you guys bet?" Brent asked.

I glanced at Crane, suppressing a triumphant smile. "If I lost, I'd have to give up all potentially hazardous activities. But I won. The show goes on."

~ * ~

Brent claimed he'd have to find the right company to accomplish the demolition safely. "It won't be easy. What we're about to do is dangerous."

As it turned out, one of the men who had worked on the house was the former owner of a demolition company in the south. He had reduced scores of buildings to powder. He referred to the job as a piece of cake. The contract was signed and the date set for the following Friday. I waited impatiently to see if I was right.

I knew I was right. That is, I was ninety-nine percent certain.

~ * ~

Then next day Lucy and I visited the house on Loosestrife Lane and the pond that drowsed in the shade beneath waving strands of weeping willow.

"The goldfish are back," I said.

"Brent bought a dozen more. He's mad that something must have eaten the others."

"The dogs will keep predators away," I said. "How peaceful the pond looks now."

But I would never forget the events that had played out when Misty had dragged me into the wild water.

"The sense of peace here is heavy," Lucy said.

We strolled over to look up at the cupola. Misty raked her paw through the dirt, uprooting a healthy dandelion.

I was right; I knew it.

"But also there's a feeling of restlessness," Lucy added. "Of waiting. I never stood in this exact place before. It was always the landing."

I nodded. That landing. Holly seeing the funnel cloud through the window. Possibly seeing her Tristan in its path as well.

"Holly was foolish to leave the house instead of seeking shelter in the basement," Lucy said.

"She wouldn't have gone without her dog."

I rested my hand on Misty's head and was rewarded by a wag of her tail. "I'd never leave one of mine to the mercies of a tornado—if I could help it."

"Man and dog are meant to stand together," Lucy said. "Make that woman and dog."

"If Holly had stayed in the house, the story would have had a different ending. The house survived the tornado, after all."

"No doubt."

Holly Wickersham might have written enough books to fill a whole shelf. Modern readers would know her name. She and Micah, or the new man, might have gotten married and had children. She would have lived.

I could have wept for the life that didn't happen because of a choice.

Forty-six

On the day scheduled for demolition, soft light bathed the house on Loosestrife Lane in a golden haze. It sat quietly in its green surround, resigned to losing a part of itself. I thought the cupola had never looked more beautiful. For a moment I was sorry it had to come down.

"Sunshine is a good omen," Lucy murmured. "God bless our enterprise."

"It's so hot, but I feel cold," I said, wishing I'd brought a cardigan.

"That's the cold of the grave."

Brent had ordered us away from the site, well behind the picket fence. A small crowd had gathered to witness the event. Annica had requested time away from her shift at Clovers, and Crane arrived in his official capacity. Having somehow found out about the demolition, although not its purpose, a reporter from the *Banner* named Will Latham was on hand.

He zeroed in on me. "What are they hoping to find today?"

I had an answer prepared. "The skeleton of a woman who vanished without a trace several years ago."

"And they think she's under the porch because...?"

That question was trickier. "Because of some clues in the house's attic. They were found when the house changed hands recently."

As an English teacher, I knew the advantages of using the passive voice.

"Do they know who this unlucky person was?" asked Latham.

"Holly Wickersham, a local mystery writer."

"Never heard of her."

"She died young," I told him.

Without a word of thanks for the information or any comment whatever, Latham jumped the fence and advanced on the demolition team, only to be sent back by Brent.

Crane slipped his arm around my waist. "Do you have a story ready for the public?" he asked. "And the police if they're curious?"

"I'll tell them about finding Holly's journal," I said. "They can't suspect me of killing her. I'm too young."

Lucy stood close enough to us to hear our exchange. "Everybody loves a good mystery," she said. "Then they forget about it when the next tantalizing tale comes along."

"In spite of our attempts to keep the story quiet, it's being treated like a seventh day wonder," I said.

"Well, this is Foxglove Corners," Annica pointed out. "A drowsy little town where nothing of note ever happens."

"I wouldn't say that," Crane said.

"All right. A drowsy little town where strange things happen."

"Better."

Brent moved away from the demolition team and gave me a jaunty thumbs up.

"They're almost ready." Crane took my hand and led me still further away from the fence into a patch of sunlight. "Lucy, Annica, follow us."

The blast held the power of a thousand thunderbolts. The cupola and porch crumbled together, raining pieces of wood and plaster and glass and shingles into the air. My ears rang with the assault. I breathed in flying grit while the echo of the implosion hung heavily over the earth.

I leaned into Crane's chest and said a quick prayer that the rest of the house still stood.

Opening my eyes, I saw that it did.

The time of reckoning had arrived.

~ * ~

"They found something!"

Brent's shout rang out through the settling dust. The crowd swarmed closer to the fence, several people talking at once.

Found what?

What's happening?

Did they find a body?

As Brent advanced toward me, Latham seized his opportunity to jump over the fence again. Brent didn't notice him. Lucky for the reporter.

"You were right, Jennet," Brent said. "Holly was lying under the porch all this time. Not very far down, either."

Then why hadn't her body been unearthed during the rebuilding of the original structures? I guess we'd never know.

"From what I could tell, she was about your height," Brent said. "Tatters of grayish material clung to the bones. There's not much left of it, but a medallion on a chain survived. Its picture was the silhouette of a collie."

"Holly," I said softly.

Lucy added, "May you rest in peace."

"How can she?" Annica asked. "You guys just disturbed her grave."

"She'll go to a better one," Lucy said. "But think, Annica, her spirit was never in the ground. It's all around us. Perhaps she's in the crowd or at the fishpond."

I nodded and couldn't help glancing at the pond. "I think she'll approve of what we did. What's next?"

"She'll have to be reburied," Crane said. "Considering what we know about the first cupola and the porch being destroyed in the tornado, there'll be no question of foul play. I don't think so anyway."

My mind leaped ahead to providing a proper resting place for Holly. "Maybe we can arrange for her to be buried in that cemetery at the end of Huron Court."

"I'll commission a gravestone," Brent said. "Meanwhile, I'd like to get rid of these gawkers." He raised his voice. "Everybody, go on home now! Show's over!"

A few people left. Some drifted away but re-formed in small groups to talk and speculate. I didn't see Latham. He was probably already filing his story.

Brent turned to me. "There's something else you should know, Jennet. Holly didn't die alone. There's another skeleton lying near her. Unless I miss my guess, it's a canine skeleton."

"Tristan."

"I'd say so."

The phantom collie hadn't died in the fishpond, then. Holly had managed to pull him out only to be caught in the tornado's deadly pitch and slammed into the torn earth. With her dog in her arms.

Lucy laid her hand on my arm. "Man and dog will stand together."

"Make that woman and dog," I said.

~ * ~

To my surprise, Miss Eidt was one of the onlookers. In her pastel blue suit with a triple strand of pearls and a straw hat to keep off the blazing sun, she looked out of place. She carried the library's camera and a large tote bag decorated with lilacs.

"I thought I'd take pictures for the file," she said. "I had no idea what they were looking for."

"It all came together suddenly," I said.

"I'm a bit confused," she said. "How did you know that anyone was buried here, let alone Holly Wickersham?"

"A hunch," I said.

Seeing her skepticism, I added, "A strong hunch. I put together her story from several sources. Having access to her books was invaluable. I learned that several houses were damaged during the tornado from your vertical file. Lucy had a few strange experiences in the house. So did I."

"I understand," Miss Eidt said. "Holly Wickersham was a hometown writer who didn't receive her proper recognition while she was alive. I'm going to rectify that."

"How?"

"I'll have Debbie scour old bookstores and estate sales for her paperbacks and display them in a special carousel right by my desk. Mark my words. People will be asking for them. We should be able to find her picture on a dust jacket to copy and enlarge, and I'll collect news clippings about today's event and paste them into a book."

"There's a picture of Holly with her friend, Micah Frost, on a beach," I said. "Maybe they were at Sagramore Lake, for all we know. You can have a copy of that—or better still, the original."

Miss Eidt's face fairly glowed with enthusiasm. "It'll be a wonderful memorial to a forgotten writer. When I'm through, Holly Wickersham will be a household name. In Foxglove Corners, anyway."

"I'll bring back the paperbacks I took from the library, and when the police release her journal, I'll see that you have it. There might be more of Holly's possessions in the attic that would give us a clear picture of her."

Not make-up or clothing but something meaningful like the picture of her and Micah. Everyone agreed that her collie medallion should be reinterred with her.

"I can't wait to get started," Miss Eidt said. "Stop by as soon as you can to see what I've done."

Every writer hopes her works will live on after she dies. Thanks to Miss Eidt, this was going to happen for Holly. I thought she would be pleased and finally at peace; and the house on Loosestrife Lane would be also at peace.

I hoped.

Forty-seven

The next day Brent brought us the evening edition of the *Banner*. The demolition story, complete with photographs, covered the front page. A sidebar contained a brief biography of Holly, taken from one of her dust jackets.

"We made the front page," he said. "I'm inviting everyone to have dinner at the Hunt Club Inn tomorrow. We'll drink a toast to Holly Wickersham and celebrate a job well done."

I set the paper on the coffee table. We now had four of them. "Everyone meaning?"

"You and Crane, Lucy and Annica. Miss Eidt, if she'll come."

I recalled the last time we had been together at the Inn. We were a larger group gathered to celebrate Lucy's movie, *Devilwish*. Helena Millay was the thirteenth guest that night. She'd been so excited about the arrival of her new collie, Arden.

Everyone knew how that had turned out.

"It sounds lovely," I said, "but we can't do it tomorrow. Did you forget the fundraiser for the animal shelter? I'll be too tired to go out after washing dogs all day."

"I guess I lost track of the days. Okay, I'll make the reservation for next Saturday."

"Are you going to move the collies to their new home or wait until the new construction is finished?" Crane asked.

"Wait, of course. That's the story of my life."

As he looked suddenly despondent, I said, "What's the matter?"

"I lost another caretaker, a couple actually. A husband-and-wife team."

"Oh no."

"My latest offer was declined this morning. It turns out that Mrs. Anderson was spooked when she read about the bones they found."

"But that's in the past now," I said. "The skeletons are gone and that part of the house is being rebuilt. I trust the workers will dig down deep to make sure there are no other skeletons on your property."

"That doesn't make any difference to her. She says she couldn't sleep in that house for thinking other bodies may be under the foundation. She's afraid they're going to rise up through the floors and get her."

Crane clapped him on the arm. "You just can't win, Fowler."

"Mr. Anderson thinks it's nonsense, but he won't force her to live in a house she's afraid of."

"I'm sorry," Crane added. "You'll have to keep looking. Sooner or later you'll find the right person."

"I'm back to square one," he said.

Hoping to refocus his attention, I said, "Are you bringing your dogs to be bathed tomorrow?"

"Just Chance and Tempest. They pick up more mud and burrs than all the others put together."

"I guess I'll see you there then. It's supposed to be warm and sunny. I hope we'll have a good turnout. The shelter needs all the help it can get to stay in business."

~ * ~

Red, white, and blue balloons swayed in the gentlest of breezes on Sagramore Lake Road the next morning. My heart lifted at the carnival atmosphere that permeated the normally quiet street. Large portable tubs and tables had been set up on the five front yards south of Jennifer's house which served as the fundraiser's headquarters.

The sounds of barking, yipping, and screeches of canine protest filled the air.

I made my way toward the lake and Jennifer's house. Across the street, Lila and Letty Woodville stood behind a card table dispensing iced water, iced tea, and lemonade. It seemed only yesterday that Molly and Jennifer were little girls selling lemonade and homemade cookies. Now here they were young ladies who had organized this impressive fundraiser to help the animal shelter.

In Jennifer's front yard, eight identical tubs were arranged on the lawn, together with boxes holding shampoo, detangler, rags, and a large selection of grooming implements. A separate box contained colorful bandanas.

Jennifer was washing a reluctant Irish setter who was crying and trying in vain to escape from the tub. How pathetic elegant, long-haired dogs looked when they were wet. She dabbed at the dollop of suds that had landed on her nose.

"Hey, Jennet," she called. "Didn't you bring your dogs?"

"I wanted to, but I came to work."

Fortunately I'd slept well and felt fairly energetic, if a little warm. I glanced at the equipment set out in front of the house.

"It looks like you're ready to open a pet supplies shop," I said.

"Yeah, Mr. Fowler ran all this stuff over to us early this morning. He went back for two of his dogs. Then he's joining the Wash Team."

"Brent? I'm surprised."

I knew how generous he was with his funds and time, but I always pictured him as the delegating kind.

"The Woodville sisters wanted to pitch in and work along with us, but we put them in charge of refreshments," Jennifer said. She lowered her voice. "We think they're too old to wash a bunch of dogs."

"Don't let them hear you say that. Are all the dogs taken?"

"Right now. You can have the next one."

"Then I'll go say hello to Lila and Letty and get a drink before I start," I said.

I crossed the street. At the moment, the Woodvilles didn't have any customers. Unlike the rest of us, they hadn't donned casual clothes. Lila wore a mint green gingham house dress and a matching hairband, but not her trademark voluminous apron. In a short denim jumper and white shirt, Letty came a little closer to fitting in. They both greeted me with happy smiles.

"Will you have iced tea or lemonade?" Lila asked. "I made the lemonade myself."

"Lemonade," I said. "It's my favorite."

She poured the beverage into a large paper cup. "You're an angel to help out the shelter. I know how busy you are. I read about your latest adventure," she added.

Eager to veer away from demolition and bones, I said, "Anything for the shelter. If you can stay in your home a little longer, we'll come up with other ways to help."

"Oh, but the house on Park Street doesn't belong to us," Lila said.

"I always thought it did."

"No, Major March let us live there rent free, and he sent us a generous monthly stipend to maintain the shelter. Now the house is part of his estate."

"It'll be sold," Letty added. "But we kept our old family house and the farm. We'll just move back there and take whatever dogs we have. So every little bit will help."

"That's what we did before Major March came into our lives," Lila said. "We rescued dogs. We could only take care of a few, though. With his help, we've had as many as twenty-five at one time." She sounded cheerful enough, but her smile seemed forced. "We're getting too old to take care of that many dogs anyway. So maybe losing the house is a blessing in disguise."

"It's a shame Major March didn't remember the shelter in his will," I said.

"Like many of us, he must have thought he'd live forever," Letty said. "But he died suddenly in that plane crash and left us to carry on as best we can."

I finished my drink, threw the paper cup in the receptacle provided, and crossed the street again. Like the library, the animal shelter was a fixture in Foxglove Corners, two old white Victorians enjoying a new life in a new century. Wherever the sisters' farm was located, it wouldn't be so easy to visit with treats for the shelter dogs and relax over tea and Lila's wonderful coffee cake.

And Caroline Meilland. Her portrait commissioned by Major March, hung in the vestibule, a gentle reminder of the slain animal activist who had so loved all the creatures with whom we share the earth. Would her legacy be lost along the way?

In front of Jennifer's house again, I found a tub and everything I needed to get to work. Molly turned over a pretty black and white cocker spaniel to me. "Hi, Jennet, here's Waffles, your first client. Her mom left her with us. I set you up next to Jennifer. The water's warm, and you have soap and towels. If you have any trouble, Jennifer can help you."

"Hello, Waffles. You're going to have a nice bath."

She wagged her tail as I removed her leash and collar and lifted her into the tub. "I won't have any problems. I'm an expert at grooming dogs."

As the reality of her situation dawned on her, Waffles tried to leap from the tub.

"Waffles! Stay!" I said in the voice I used for Candy at her most rambunctious.

The spaniel stayed, but uttered a canine scream of pure terror that must have been audible all down Sagramore Lake Road. No one else's dog was making such an ear-splitting commotion.

"Are you trying to kill that dog?"

I looked up to see Brent standing on the sidewalk holding tightly to his collies, Tempest and Chance. He had an amused smile on his face, and merriment danced in his eyes.

I'd never seen him looking quite so dressed down. He wore paint-stained jeans and his green shirt must have been one of his favorites, appearing to have endured many launderings. With sleeves rolled up to his brawny elbows, he was quite definitely ready to make a hands-on contribution.

"You'd think so," I said. "Waffles, behave. It's just water. Water is good."

The breeze blew a strand of hair in my face, and I felt as if some of the bubbles had landed in my eyes.

"Let's have a race," Brent said. "See who can wash the most dogs with the least amount of trouble."

"Unfair. You're grooming your own collies."

"The dirtiest on the street," he said.

In my brief moment of distraction, Waffles had her paws on the rim of the tub, poised to jump down and make a run for it. I pushed her gently back into the water.

"You're on," I said.

Forty-eight

As I tied a red bandana around Waffle's neck, the sounds of an altercation shattered the carnival atmosphere that had prevailed on Sagramore Lake Road. Until now.

Four houses down, two women were shouting at each other. Their voices grew louder with each angry exchange. The steady conversational hum around us died, and even the more vocal of the dogs grew silent. All eyes turned to the antagonists who faced each other on either side of a tub in which a white and tan pointer stood passively, its coat dripping with soapy water.

A young girl with long platinum blonde hair wrapped her arms protectively around the dog in the tub. "Go away! Leave me alone!"

"Cat fight in Dogtown," Brent said.

"Shh. Listen."

"That's my dog, and I'm taking her. You stole her right out of my yard."

The speaker, also blonde, but older, reached over the tub for the dog, drenching her black sundress in the process. "Come here, Tilda," the woman said. "I'm taking you home."

"Over my dead body!" the blonde girl cried. "Get your hands off my dog!"

The tall woman lifted the pointer out of the tub. Holding the wet dog close to her chest, she took off running in our direction.

The girl screamed. "Stop her! She stole my dog!"

I started at a popping sound. Thinking *gunshot!* I almost threw myself on the ground with the retriever.

"Don't panic," Brent said. "A balloon bit the dust."

Jennifer, who had just finished drying her dog, pulled her cell phone out of her pocket. "Uh-oh. Should I call the police?"

Brent said, "Call them. I'll stop her."

He moved to intercept the woman and dog, but not quickly enough. The woman hoisted the dog into the back seat of the car she'd left at the curb with the motor running, got behind the wheel, and sped down to the lake. Fortunately no people were in the street or she would have run over them.

My mind registered a late model car styled like a Taurus and a bland color. Beige, perhaps. But I could only make out the first two letters of the license plate: M and I.

Jennifer dried her hands on a towel and let it fall to the ground. "Okay, I called. I'd better find out what that was all about. Molly, keep an eye on things here."

"I'll go with you," I said.

"Wait up." Brent passed his dogs' leashes to Molly and sprinted after us.

The blonde girl was sobbing over her empty tub, her cell phone in hand. All activity around her had ceased. The stillness on the street reminded me of a scene from *The Day the Earth Stood Still.* Bits of red and blue balloon lay shining on the grass, the last vestiges of the festive air.

Brent broke the spell. "The cops are on their way, Miss. Did that woman just run off with your dog?"

At the same time, Jennifer said, "Is the dog's owner here? The one who brought her?"

"I'm her owner," the girl said. She looked shell shocked and pathetic, holding tightly to a leash with no dog attached to it. "I'm Lorna Courtland. That woman got out of her car and walked right up to me. She started saying Sissy belonged to her."

I frowned, appalled at the woman's boldness. "That's a new approach to dognapping."

"We had flyers up all over town," Jennifer said. "She must have come here planning to snatch one of the dogs. Don't worry, Lorna. She won't get far."

They were comforting words, but she would. With her good head start, the woman in black could be out of Foxglove Corners before the police arrived. As if on cue, a siren wailed in the distance.

"Now we can get to the bottom of this," Brent said.

Lorna dried her eyes on a damp towel, smearing her blue eye shadow. "I walked over here from my house. I don't drive. How'll I get Sissy back?"

In his best lord-of-the-manner tone, Brent said, "We'll help you."

~ * ~

Tall and imposing, Lieutenant Mac Dalby consulted his notebook. "Miss Courtland, where did you get your dog?"

"Why does that matter?" she asked.

"I'm trying to fill in the blanks. Did you buy her from a breeder? An ad in the paper?"

Lana swiped a tissue across her eyes again. "Sissy was a present from my boyfriend. She means the world to me."

"Where did *he* get the dog?"

"From a pound up north. He didn't want to leave her there to be put to sleep."

"When was this?"

Lorna paused. "Last month sometime."

"So, conceivably, your Sissy could have been this woman's pet."

"You're wrong. If that was true, what was she doing in one of those high-kill places a hundred miles from here?"

A woman standing near Lorna, holding onto the leashes of two exuberant ginger colored puppies, said, "She was so nasty. If she had a legitimate claim, couldn't she have presented it civilly?"

"She just snatched Sissy and ran," Lorna said. "You can't let her get away with it."

Mac chose his words carefully. "We'll do our best to find her and get her side of the story."

That wasn't the response Lorna wanted to hear. "There's only one side. Mine." She turned to Brent. "You said you'd help me. Can we start now?"

Brent glanced at me. Most likely he was wondering if he had spoken too soon. "We have to find Sissy and the lady first, Miss Courtland."

"How are we going to do that?"

"It's a little late to follow her. Maybe the lieutenant can put out an APB—or something. Wet pointer. Light brown Ford."

"Hold on, Fowler." Mac turned to Lorna. "Can I have your boyfriend's name and contact information?"

"Sure," she said. "It's Duncan. Duncan O'Meara. He'll tell you."

"O'Meara." Mac repeated the name, and Brent and I exchanged looks. Mac's expression was unreadable.

Was it possible Lorna didn't know about her boyfriend's checkered past? In particular, about his dealings with dogs? She didn't seem to. She was young, perhaps impressionable. And O'Meara, even though I'd never met him, might well be a charmer. An Irishman with a handsome face and a gift of gab?

Brent stepped back and lowered his voice. "She has to know what he's been up to. His name has been in the papers and on television."

"And on *Kate in Your Corner*," I added.

"...and your boyfriend's address?" Mac waited, pencil in hand.

"I'm not sure," Lorna said. "He just moved into a new apartment."

She knew. I was certain of it. Perhaps not everything, not about Sea-to-Sea Transport, perhaps, but she must know where O'Meara lived.

"He just moved," Lorna repeated.

"Is this place in Foxglove Corners?"

"It's south of Maple Creek," she said. "I really don't have his address yet."

Mac snapped his notebook shut. "We'll be in touch." He nodded to us. "Fowler, Jennet. Carry on with whatever you're doing."

Lorna turned to Jennifer. "I'm so sorry."

"It wasn't your fault," Jennifer said. "The day isn't ruined, and no harm's been done, except to Sissy."

"Can I leave everything here?" She pointed to her supplies scattered around a heap of soiled towels and the tub, still full of water. "I just want to go home."

Apparently she'd forgotten about Brent's offer to help her. He didn't remind her. I watched her walk slowly toward the lake, my heart breaking for her. Or for the woman in the black sundress. At this point I wasn't sure. Whoever truly owned the dog.

"That no good O'Meara is still in the dog business," I said. "Only now instead of stealing them in transport, he's taking them out of people's yards."

Brent stared at the departing form of the blonde girl. She reached the lake and turned left, disappearing from our sight. "That little girl looks too young to be mixed up with a crook."

"An apartment south of Maple Creek," I said. "That may lead Mac straight to O'Meara."

"I don't know about that. South of Maple Creek is pure country. State land. There's a log cabin or two, an old farmhouse. Off hand, I can't think of any apartment buildings in the area."

"What a coincidence, this happening at the fundraiser," I said. "But like Jennifer said, it hasn't ruined the day."

Washers still bent over their tubs, squeezing shampoo out of bottles, rinsing sudsy coats, or aiming blow dryers at their clients. People waited in line with their pets for a free station.

"I've bathed and groomed six dogs already, including Chance and Tempest," Brent said. "Where do you stand?"

In the excitement I'd forgotten about our, that is—his—bet.

"Three," I said. "You may win this one."

Forty-nine

"What happened over there?" Lila asked as I accepted a second cup of lemonade. "Why is the policeman here?"

"One of the dogs was stolen right out of the washtub," Brent said.

Seeing that he wasn't going to elaborate, I said, "Two women are claiming ownership of the same dog, and it looks like Duncan O'Meara is in the middle of the conflict."

"Oh, my," Letty said. "We saw a pretty girl run by. She was crying. We couldn't imagine what was wrong."

"Did you see a speeding beige car?" I asked. "The driver is the person who took the dog."

"I did," Lila said. "But I didn't know it was going to be important."

"What a lot of drama for a small town fundraiser!" Letty said.

Like almost everyone else in Foxglove Corners, the Woodville sisters knew about O'Meara and his fake transport service, if only from watching *Kate in Your Corner*.

"The girl, Lorna Courtland, says she's O'Meara's girlfriend," I said.

"And the police are hot on his trail," Letty added.

"I hope so."

Lila took Brent's empty cup, refilled it with lemonade, then added a scoop of crushed ice.

"Thanks," he said. "O'Meara's leading them on a merry chase."

Lila laid her hand on Brent's arm. "We want to thank you for your donations, Mr. Fowler," she said. "Everyone has been wonderful, but you've gone above and beyond."

"We all want the shelter to stay in Foxglove Corners," he said.

"Yes, well, so do we."

"Will it make a difference?"

"Every little bit helps," Letty told him.

Back at our work stations, Brent began to fill his tub with warm water while Molly stood by with an Australian shepherd puppy, a blue merle like my Sky. Unlike Sky, the shepherd was a bundle of quicksilver. Brent would have his hands full.

Although the drama of Lorna and the pointer hadn't lasted long, the brief interruption had chipped away at my energy and motivation. The sun grew progressively warmer. I was happy I'd worn a sleeveless blouse but feared my arms were burning. I moved closer to the house and the shade of a towering blue spruce.

"We ought to plan another fundraiser right away," Brent said.

That was a good idea but... "The animal shelter won't stay on Park Street," I said. "I just learned that the house belonged to Major March. It's part of his estate and will be sold."

Brent turned off the hose. "But that's the Woodville sisters' home. Where will they go?"

"They have a farmhouse and acreage. I'm not sure where it's located."

"What will they do with the dogs?"

I shrugged. "Take the ones they can't place with them, I suppose."

"That isn't good," he said.

"All the fundraisers in the world can't match the money Major March contributed to keeping the shelter up and running," I pointed out.

Bent fell silent. He lowered the shepherd into the tub from which the pup promptly tried to escape.

"I wonder if—"

At the same time, I said, "Do you think—?

The idea must have come to us at the same time. Anyone watching might have seen lightbulbs turn on over our respective heads.

"Lila and Letty would make perfect caretakers," I said. "They've been rescuing strays for years, even before they came to Foxglove Corners."

"But my collies aren't strays. They lost their homes, nine times out of ten because they grew old. The house is going to be a refuge for geriatric collies, not strays."

"Still," I said. "Something might be worked out. You haven't had any luck with your other prospects. If Lila and Letty accept your offer, they'll stay in Foxglove Corners. And they're not the kind to be spooked by a ghost or two."

"It could work."

Caroline's portrait, Lila's coffee cakes, Letty with her down-to-earth practicality—they'd all have a new home on Loosestrife Lane.

"I'll think about it," Brent said. "I'll talk to them."

"There's no time like the present."

He squirted shampoo over the coat of the struggling shepherd. The dog shook himself, giving Brent's shirt another dousing.

"I'll have a word with them as soon as I'm through with Laddie here."

I had a feeling the deed was as good as done. Brent would welcome dogs of another breed. His aging collie pack would have the happy, peaceful future they deserved. Still, one unhappy dog was caught between two homes, and O'Meara remained at large.

Well, we can't have everything.

I ran my hands over my arms. Yes, I was getting sunburned. How many more dogs were waiting for a bath? All of a sudden I wanted to go home to my own collies. Brent was winning the bet and I didn't even care.

~ * ~

The next day, I entered Clovers to find Annica and Brent in the window booth I always gravitated toward. It was as if they were waiting for me. They were drinking lime coolers. Seeing the drink topped with a scoop of frothy green whipped cream, I wanted one more than anything.

"Join us," Annica said. The sun struck dancing lights in her red-gold hair and her seashell earrings had a shine. "Brent has good news."

I eased into a seat beside him. "I think I know what it is."

"Lila and Letty agreed to sign on as caretakers for my collies," Brent announced. "They're happy. I'm happy. They're coming to dinner at the Hunt Club Inn on Saturday. We have a lot to celebrate."

"What about their policy of taking in stray dogs no matter what their breed?" I asked.

"We compromised. If a stray is in need, it'll be welcome. But collies will rule."

"When will this happen?"

"As soon as they can move. They're bringing five dogs with them. No collies."

"Once again, all's well that ends well," Annica said.

"Well, not quite. I haven't heard that Lieutenant Dalby arrested O'Meara yet. Is that man destined to be a fixture in Foxglove Corners?"

"He's the last blight on our fair summer. Look..." Annica drained her drink. "I finished my shift. How about if we take a little trip to Maple Creek?"

"Who?" Brent asked.

"Jennet and me. You can come along if you like."

"Why?" I asked. Although I thought I knew.

"I've been thinking. That girl said O'Meara moved into an apartment south of Maple Creek. The last time I passed that way, there weren't any apartments there. So she lied."

I consulted my mental to-do list. Except for walking dogs and making dinner, it was blank.

"It's a nice day for a drive," I said. "I'm free. I think Lorna lied, too. Who knows? She looked young and innocent, but she might even be O'Meara's partner in crime."

Brent rose. "Shall we go then?"

Yes. One more adventure!

"As soon as I have a lime cooler," I said.

Fifty

A little later we piled into Brent's vintage Plymouth Belvedere and drove out of Clovers' parking lot.

Annica settled in the back. "I feel like I'm in a space ship," she said. "Destination Mars. You're so lucky to have this car, Brent."

"I feel lucky."

"What's that saying?" I asked. "From your lips to God's ears."

The area south of Maple Creek was heavily forested, and a soft haze lay lightly on the road. The land was ripe for a developer's touch, but I hoped it would remain wild and pristine exactly as I saw it today.

Occasionally we came to a horse farm enclosed by a three-board plank fence with a farmhouse in the distance or a rustic cabin, but mostly we passed 'pure country' as Brent would say. This would be the perfect hideout for a miscreant-—if the miscreant's girlfriend hadn't given away the location.

"Are you sure that girl said south?" Brent asked.

"Positive." But I had to stop and think. "Yes, she'd said O'Meara just moved into an apartment south of Maple Creek."

"I don't see any apartments," Brent said. "No construction at all."

"Maybe the apartment was closer to Maple Creek, like on the outskirts," Annica said. "Could we have passed it?"

"No, I've been looking. Unless it's well-hidden like Lucy's Dark Gables."

"Then we'll never find it," Brent said. "I wonder if Mac drove out this way."

"I'm sure he did. He'd check out every road and by-road in a hundred mile radius. If we see anything suspicious, we'll call him," I added. "No way are we taking the law in our own hands."

"Chicken," Annica said, but she laughed. "I don't have to answer to anybody."

She had her own ideas. "Lorna probably said the first thing that came into her head. She didn't want to give O'Meara to a cop."

"I can't see that young girl with an older man, especially a crooked one," I said.

"She may be older than she looks."

I considered that but didn't think so.

We passed two Deer X-ing signs about a mile apart and a glimpse of blue-green lake water. A reddish animal dashed across the road in our path, a small dog or a fox. It was hard to tell. Fortunately, we didn't encounter leaping deer.

"This is hopeless," Annica said after miles of unbroken wilderness. "We might as well be looking for a needle in a haystack."

Privately I agreed with her. "Well, I'm enjoying the scenery. I never just get in a car and drive for pleasure."

"Listen," Brent said.

Somewhere ahead of us and off to the right, multiple dogs were barking, an onslaught of noise pouring in through the windows with the fresh country air.

"I'll bet we're about to hit the jackpot," Brent said.

We approached a narrow road with no sign to indicate its name. The barking grew louder, almost frantic in tone. Brent turned right and maneuvered the Plymouth over a rugged trail of dirt and potholes with glowering woods on either side and no buildings until we spied a log cabin almost hidden by the leafy trees and conifers that crowded in front of it.

Brent turned in a cleared space that served as a driveway and pulled up close enough so that we could see a large rectangular dog run enclosed by a high chain link fence. Perhaps a dozen dogs of all breeds and sizes vied with one another for viewing space. They were all barking. None of them sounded friendly.

"Bonanza!" Brent said. "We found it. O'Meara's holding place."

Annica opened the door and slid down to the ground. "Let's investigate."

"Get back here!" Brent shouted. "Annica!"

"Remember we're going to call Mac." I took my phone out of my shoulder bag.

She leaned over the fence and waved her hand front of a golden retriever who pranced up to the fence, wagging his tail.

"Wasn't a golden retriever one of the Sea-to-Sea dogs?" she asked.

"Annica!" Brent roared. "Somebody's coming. Get in."

I heard the motor, too. Close and coming closer. Every trespasser's nightmare.

Annica dashed back to the car, Brent made a fast U-turn, and we headed back to the road, passing a mud-splattered van along the way. A massive dark dog sat in the passenger's seat. He looked like Camille's Belgian shepherd.

I caught a fleeting glimpse of the driver's face. He was dark and handsome. Every young girl's dream. He might be tall, but, of course, I couldn't tell as he was sitting behind the wheel. But I had a strong feeling that he was Irish. And he looked furious.

O'Meara.

He made a U-turn of his own. Close on our tail, he followed us out to the road.

"Hang on, girls." Brent stepped down hard on the accelerator. The Plymouth shot ahead over the rugged road, shaking in protest. "It's about to get rough."

Annica's voice trembled. "What's he going to do?"

"Follow us," Brent said.

"Did you bring your gun?" she asked.

Before he could answer, O'Meara rammed the van into the driver's side of the vintage Plymouth. Annica screamed. The front door flew open. I was catapulted through the air onto the hard, unforgiving ground.

The world around me dissolved into a screen of solid black.

~ * ~

My head hurt. And my knee. And...everything capable of feeling pain. Something scraped my arm. A sharp fang? A knife... No, a thorn or thistle.

I opened my eyes to color. Yellow. Pink. I'd landed next to a patch of wildflowers.

I rubbed my eyes. Brent's prized vintage Plymouth lay on its side, battered and clearly disabled. One of the bright green fins lay in a bed of high grasses. I didn't see my friends.

Brent stumbled down the sloping terrain at the road's edge and knelt on one knee in front of me. His face bore several cuts, and blood stained his shirt. "Are you hurt, Jennet?"

Was I? Oh, yes, but not lethally. I raised my arm, then ran my hand over my knee. At least I didn't think so.

"I feel like I was thrown out of a car," I said.

"Lie still for a while."

"Where's Annica?"

"On the other side of the road. She's shaken but otherwise okay. Those seat belts I installed didn't hold. We were lucky. What the hell did O'Meara hope to accomplish by crashing into us?"

"He tried to kill us so we wouldn't lead the police to him. Lucky for us, he's an amateur."

"For an amateur, he did a damn good job," Brent said.

"Where is he?"

"He drove away. You got through to Mac, I hope."

"He's on his way," I said.

"He won't be here any time soon. We were on the road for a good hour."

"Just so he gets here."

He would turn the siren on all the way. Other drivers would let him pass. It wouldn't take him an hour to find us.

Brent rose. "I'll go flag him down."

Brent swiped at his forehead and frowned at the blood on his hand. Something warned me to look up and beyond his straightening form.

A dark shadow descended the slope. Then the man. O'Meara. He carried a gun.

"Brent!" I cried. "Duck!"

A shot rang out. Brent fell forward. Again the world went black.

~ * ~

"Don't panic," Brent said. "A balloon bit the dust."

The pieces had rained down on me. Blue and red glittering on the velvety green lawn.

My nemesis, Veronica the Viper, who had a crush on Crane, hovered over me. "I'm arresting you for littering and theft. You took Foxglove Corners' prime catch out of circulation."

I wasn't in the woods lying in a patch of wildflowers but back at the fundraiser.

A girl with long blonde hair and smudged blue eye shadow said, "He just moved to an apartment south of Maple Creek."

But there was no signpost on the dirt road that led to the log cabin.

I moved my hand. It landed in fur warm from the sun. Misty? No, she wasn't with me. I was stroking a wild creature. The fox?

A siren began its shrill wail in the distance, high, earsplitting. Ominous.

A tornado warning? A sound from the past inaudible to Brent and Annica? Nothing to worry about.

I shrugged and bit into my sandwich.

Fifty-one

I knew the hand that brushed my bangs back and lingered on my head. I knew the voice with its trace of a southern accent. I opened my eyes. "Crane?"

"I'm here." His hand moved down to cover mine. It felt warm and strong. The warmth spread throughout my body. "You're going to be all right, honey."

"Is Brent—alive?" I asked.

Was that my voice? Since when did I sound so hoarse?

"He's on his way to the hospital," Crane said. "He'll be all right."

How could he say that? I'd heard the shot, seen Brent fall. But Crane wouldn't lie to me. I wanted desperately to believe him.

"And Annica. Where's Annica?"

"She's giving her statement to Mac. It could have been so much worse for all of you. The Belvedere is the only casualty. It's totaled."

"Did O'Meara get away?" I asked.

"He tried, but Mac saw his van coming toward him on the road and cut him off. O'Meara's in custody. He was driving drunk."

"Among other crimes," I said. "Someone has to liberate the dogs. They're in a large run behind his cabin. I hope he still has the missing ones. Can we go home now?"

"As soon as you and Annica get checked out at the hospital."

Why had I bothered to ask? I could have anticipated his answer.

"I'm just hurting. Like when I fell down the stairs at Brent's house," I said.

Crane sighed but didn't say anything.

But as soon as I stood, the world began spinning around. I leaned heavily on Crane. It was an effort to walk. That knee... People need their knees.

"Maybe the hospital is a good idea," I said.

~ * ~

And just like that, it was over. In the blink of an eye, or so it seemed. I was examined and released, told to ice the knee and take pain-killing medication. Duncan O'Meara remained in custody. I heard he hadn't been able to raise money for his bail.

Lorna distanced herself from him, claiming they'd only recently met and she never heard of Sea-to-Sea. O'Meara denied that he had a partner. Possibly it was true.

The woman in the black sundress who had taken the setter out of Lorna's tub was only retrieving her property. She chose to stay out of the limelight.

Kate Brennan wrapped up the case with a happy segment of *Kate in Your Corner* on which all of the still missing dogs were reunited with their true owners. I limped across the living room to turn off the television. Kate had been helpful, but, really, I had done most of the work.

Best of all, once Brent's cuts and scrapes were treated, he was released from the hospital. The bullet had grazed his shoulder, knocking him to the ground where he sprained his wrist. Along with a bruised face and miscellaneous lesions, Annica had lost her seashell earring in the crash.

Brent was already attempting to locate another vintage Belvedere.

"I'm looking for a white one, and I'm going to paint the fins green. For luck."

"The luck of the Irish?" I asked.

"The luck of Brent Fowler, Huntsman," he said.

Finally I could say 'All's well that ends well' and mean it.

With nothing more pressing to do with my evening, I looked through my closet and my jewelry box, planning what to wear to dinner at the Hunt Club Inn.

~ * ~

Wildflowers in mason jars decorated our long table, giving the Inn an uncharacteristic feminine touch. I was seated facing away from the stuffed fox's head which allowed me to forget the sorrowful expression in his eyes. For the evening.

As it turned out, we were all wearing black. Lucy, of course, almost always donned one of her black dresses with a prodigious amount of gold jewelry that jingled when she moved. I'd pinned an elaborate glittering rhinestone brooch to my bodice, thinking a curious onlooker would think it was made of diamonds. As for the Woodville sisters, it dawned on me that I had never seen them dressed up. Even Annica joined in with a black sheath that drew attention to her curves.

"Damn," Brent said. "You all look like you're in mourning. This is a happy occasion. Jennet and Company drove the ghosts out of the house. The collies and I thank you."

"I think we look great," Annica said.

"I didn't say you didn't."

"I don't think of Holly Wickersham as a ghost," I said. "She was killed before her time by an act of God. We're here to honor her."

Holly was to be quietly re-interred in the cemetery where Violet Randall of the pink Victorian lay in a well-tended grave.

"I'm going to take care of our strays," Letty said. "They're more likely to find their forever homes than old collies. We're bringing five of them."

"I've always wanted to have one of those magnificent collies," Lila added. "Ever since you brought Winter to us. Do you remember Winter, Jennet?"

I could never forget my first rescue, a blue merle abandoned on a snowy country road.

"We're so excited about living in a house with a history," Letty said. "We were always a bit envious of our neighbor, Henry McCullough, who saw the phantom Christmas tree."

"I don't think you'll have any supernatural experiences," I said. "But if you do, if the house is still haunted, you'll know why. When are you moving in?"

"Next week." Letty set her menu down. Although a pseudo vegetarian, she'd ordered prime rib along with the rest of us.

"So soon?"

"Most of the furniture will go with the house on Park Street," Lila said. "We left our own things on the farm."

Annica said, "We've been filling the rooms with antiques from the attic, and wait till you see the collie picture I found for the living room."

Our waiter served the salads and everyone busied themselves adding their favorite dressings. My thoughts drifted off. If the sisters were going to be at the house next week, I had only one day to make a last solitary visit.

~ * ~

I wanted to see the fishpond again, and I wanted to go to Loosestrife Lane alone. Well, not strictly speaking alone. I planned to take Misty with me. The remains of Holly Wickersham had been buried with the canine skeleton. I trusted that Holly was at peace but couldn't help but wonder if her collie, Tristan, still haunted the pond.

Brent stood. "A toast to Holly Wickersham. Long may her books be...uh...read. And a blessing on my house and my lovely caretakers."

We all drank. Dear Brent. It was the most elegant speech he'd ever made.

~ * ~

A light wind stirred the strands of the weeping willow. They blew over the fish pond, and the water rippled in answer. Holding tightly to Misty's leash, I stood at the pond's edge, enthralled by its beauty. Blown from the nearby plants, pink loosestrife blossoms floated on the surface, and I saw the occasional flash of goldfish. This was such a peaceful place, so like the pond in the backyard of my childhood.

I supposed Tristan had gone.

Brent had promised he'd keep the pond, have it professionally cleaned and regularly stocked with goldfish. We could come and sit in front of it in lawn chairs anytime we liked. The dogs would chase predators away, and the fish would thrive.

Misty stepped over the rock border and lowered her head. I held my breath as a dark sable collie stared back at her, one ear tipped, one pricked, and a look of infinite peace in his eyes. Misty stuck her mouth in the water, and the phantom vanished. All I could see were goldfish and loosestrife blooms and another reflection, Misty's mirror image.

It was enough.

Meet Dorothy Bodoin

Dorothy Bodoin lives in Royal Oak, Michigan with her blue merle collie, Layla. A graduate of Oakland University with Bachelor's and Master's degrees in English literature. Dorothy worked as a secretary for Chrysler Missile Corporation, two years of which were spent in Italy. For several more years she taught English in a Michigan high school. She is the author of the Foxglove Corners Cozy Mystery series, six novels of romantic suspense, and one Gothic romance.

Other Works From The Pen Of Dorothy Bodoin

Treasure at Trail's End (Gothic romance) - The House at Trail's End seemed to beckon to Mara Marsden, promising the happy future she longed for. But could she discover its secret without forfeiting her life?

Ghost across the Water (romantic suspense) - Water falling from an invisible force and a ghostly man who appears across Spearmint Lake draw Joanna Larne into a haunting twenty-year-old mystery.

Darkness at Foxglove Corners - Foxglove Corners offers tornado survivor Jennet Greenway country peace and romance, but the secret of the yellow Victorian house across the lane holds a threat to her new life. (#1)

Winter's Tale - On her first winter in Foxglove Corners Jennet Greenway battles dognappers, investigates the murder of the town's beloved veterinarian, and tries to outwit a dangerous enemy. (#3)

A Shortcut through the Shadows - Jennet Greenway's search for the missing owner of her rescue collie, Winter, sets her on a collision course with an unknown killer. (#4)

Cry for the Fox - In Foxglove Corners, the fox runs from the hunters, the animal activists target the Hunt Club, and a killer stalks human prey on the fox trail. (#2)

The Witches of Foxglove Corners - With a haunting in the library, a demented prankster who invades her home, and a murder in Foxglove Corners, Halloween turns deadly for Jennet Greenway. (#5)

The Snow Dogs of Lost Lake - A ghostly white collie and a lost locket lead Jennet Greenway to a body in the woods and a dangerous new mystery. (#6)

The Collie Connection - As Jennet Greenway's wedding to Crane Ferguson approaches, her happiness is shattered when a Good Samaritan deed leaves her without her beloved black collie, Halley, and ultimately in grave danger. (#7)

A Time of Storms - When a stranger threatens her collie and she hears a cry for help in a vacant house, Jennet Ferguson suspects that her first summer as a wife may be tumultuous. (#8)

The Dog from the Sky - Jennet's life takes a dangerous turn when she rescues an abused collie. Soon afterward, a girl vanishes without a trace. Ironically she had also rescued an abused collie. Is there a connection between the two incidents? (#9)

Spirit of the Season - Mystery mixes with holiday cheer as a phantom ice skater returns to the lake where she died, and a collie is accused of plotting her owner's fatal accident. (#10)

Another Part of the Forest - Danger rides the air when a kidnapper whisks his victims away in a hot air balloon, and a false friend puts a curses on a collie breeder's first litter. (#11)

Where Have All the Dogs Gone? - An animal activist frees the shelter dogs in and around Foxglove Corners to save them from being destroyed. Running wild in the countryside, they face an equally distressing fate and post a risk to those who come in contact with them. (#12)

The Secret Room of Eidt House - A rabid dog that should have died months ago from the dread disease runs free in the woods of Foxglove Corners, and the library's long-kept secret unleashes a series of other strange events. (#13)

Follow a Shadow - A shadowy intruder haunts Jennet's woods by night, and a woman who can't accept the death of her collie asks Jennet to help her find Rainbow Bridge where she believes her dog waits for her. (#14)

The Snow Queen's Collie - A white collie puppy appears on the porch of the Ferguson farmhouse during a Christmas Eve snowstorm. In another part of Foxglove Corners a collie breeder's show prospect disappears. Meanwhile, the painting Jennet's sister gave her for Christmas begins to exhibit strange qualities. (#15)

The Door in the Fog - A wounded dog disappears in the fog. A blue door on the side of a barn vanishes. Strange wildflowers and a sound of weeping haunt a meadow. The woods keep their secret, and a curse refuses to die. (#16)

Dreams and Bones - At Brent Fowler's newly purchased Spirit Lamp Inn, a renovation turns up human bones buried in the inn's backyard, rekindling interest in the case of a young woman who disappeared from the inn several decades ago. As Jennet tries to solve this mystery, she doesn't realize it may be her last. (#17)

A Ghost of Gunfire - Months after gunfire erupted in her classroom at Marston High School, leaving one student dead and one seriously wounded, Jennet begins to hear a sound of gunshots inaudible to anyone else. Meanwhile, she resolves to find the demented person who is tying dogs to trees and leaving them to die. (#18)

The Silver Sleigh - Rosalyn Everett was missing and presumed dead. Her collies had been rescued, and her house was abandoned. But a blue merle collie haunts her woods and a figure in bridal white traverses the property. (#19)

The Stone Collie - Jennet's discovery of a collie puppy chained in the yard of a vacant house sets her on a search for a man whose activities may threaten Foxglove Corners' security. Meanwhile, horror story novelist Lucy Hazen is mystified when scenes from her work-in-progress are duplicated in real life. (#20)

The Mists of Huron Court - The house was beautiful, a vintage pink Victorian in a picturesque but lonely country setting, and the girl playing ball with her dog in the yard was friendly, suggesting that she and Jennet walk their dogs together some time. Jennet thinks she has made a new friend until she returns to the house and finds a tumbling down ruin where the Victorian once stood and no sign that the girl and dog have ever been there. ((#21)

Down a Dark Path - What hold does the pink Victorian on Huron Court have on Brent Fowler who is determined to re-create the home of long-dead Violet Randall? When he disappears, could he have been cast adrift in time? (#22))

Shadow of the Ghost Dog - An invisible dog grieves inside the house chosen as a setting for the movie based on Lucy Hazen's book *Devilwish*, and a landscaper unearths a human skeleton in the backyard while planting shrubs. (#23))

The Dark Beyond the Bridge - The discovery of a secret ghost town in a densely rural area of Michigan's lower peninsula leads to mystery and danger for Jennet Ferguson and her friends. (#24)

The Deadly Fields of Autumn - An antique television set that airs an obscure Western at random times and a woman who disappears with her newly-adopted rescue dog draw Jennet into a puzzling mystery. (#25)

The Lost Collies of Silverhedge - Collie breeder Madselin Rivard was dead, leaving her prized, valuable collies uncared for in their kennel. Jennet and her friends rescue five of them, but eight remain unaccounted for. (#26)

All the Pretty Little Collies - Danger stalks the collies of Foxglove Corners when an unknown villain begins tossing poisoned meat into their yards, and a girl with a winning blue merle collie is warned via threatening messages to withdraw her dog from competition or risk the consequences. (#27)

Letter to Our Readers

Enjoy this book?

You can make a difference

As an independent publisher, Wings ePress, Inc. does not have the financial clout of the large New York Publishers. We can't afford large magazine spreads or subway posters to tell people about our quality books.

But, we do have something much more effective and powerful than ads. We have a large base of loyal readers.

Honest Reviews help bring the attention of new readers to our books.

If you enjoyed this book, we would appreciate it if you would spend a few minutes posting a review on the site where you purchased this book or on the Wings ePress, Inc. webpages at: https://wingsepress.com/

Visit Our Website

For The Full Inventory
Of Quality Books:

Wings ePress.Inc
https://wingsepress.com/

Quality trade paperbacks and downloads
in multiple formats,
in genres ranging from light romantic comedy
to general fiction and horror.
Wings has something for every reader's taste.
Visit the website, then bookmark it.
We add new titles each month!

Wings ePress Inc.
3000 N. Rock Road
Newton, KS 67114

9 781613 095966